The Sky's Edge

A Novel by

Clare Anne McGrory

I would like to acknowledge the First Nations people who were the first storytellers in the lands on which I currently live and work. I will always honour and respect their continuous connection to Country, waters, skies and communities, and I pay my respects to Elders past and present.

I also give thanks to all Australian men and women who have served and grown our modern nation over the years, particularly in our defence force, in our health services, and in their supportive families.

Book cover designed by the author Dr Clare Anne McGrory making use of Freepik image creation software available from www.freepik.com and Canva design software available from www.canva.com.

Dedication

I began putting this tale down on paper during a period of great change in my own life. My supportive family encouraged me all the way, and were the driving force behind ensuring that I never left this labour of love to fall by the wayside among the chaos of those years. My aunt Rose patiently read over early copies, my daughter Evelyn helped me to find a fitting name for this novel that would creatively capture the message it conveys, and my son Sean was always encouraging and optimistic as the work started to come together. I am also truly grateful to Sandra Herner for her professional editing assistance. With their help, this book grew into the polished form which I am so proud to share with all who will read it.

PART I

January

CHAPTER ONE

Saturday night promised to be as boring as usual. Australian Federal Police Superintendent Brian Andersen slugged through yet another uneventful overnight shift. Among other things that were mostly paperwork, he was supervising the team responsible for the monitoring of calls to the private research centre called CAS – The **C**entre for **A**eronautical **S**cience. Although privately run, CAS enjoyed funding from several Australian government linked projects, and Australian university partnerships. Brian and his team had been monitoring CAS for years because some employees of the centre had been pointed out as potential suspects in a fraud case, and fraud was an area that Brian specialised in. Brian knew many more exciting ways a thirty-something man could spend a Saturday night, but those who eventually achieve great things must also deal with many dull and boring things along the way. At least Brian preferred to believe that on nights as monotonous as this one.

Brian decided upon a leg stretch and walk around the duty station. Getting used to a new managerial role, he wanted to maintain an air of respect from the team in his command, but to keep a fairly personal level of contact and bond with them as well. Some who were engaged in chats with those seated nearby would quickly wrap up and get their heads down when he walked past now. It still felt a little bit strange to him. One of the team, Josh, who had been intently listening in to a conversation partially removed his headphones and called out to Brian as he was approaching. Brian made his way over towards him. Josh, a fairly new recruit in his twenties, came highly qualified with university education behind him. Brian had recently undergone some further training himself, earning some diplomas to help work his way up the ranks in the police force. He always admired those like Josh who had stuck with study long enough to have finished a full degree.

'Superintendent, can I have your advice on something that seems unusual here?' asked Josh.

'Certainly,' replied Brian, *maybe something interesting might happen tonight after all* he thought to himself. 'What is it?'

'Well,' began the young officer. 'There's been unusual late-night call activity on the lines we are tapping.'

'How so?'

'For a start, it involves a private security contractor for an Asian airline. He has just called a lab worker in CAS while trying unsuccessfully to get a hold of another employee from there at this hour of the night.'

'Really?' Brian responded 'We don't usually see much activity going on at all there in the early hours of the morning. So, what do you have?'

'The Asian private security contractor claims that a CAS employee has given some advice to Australian airlines which has caused them to change their travel plans just now,' said the young officer eagerly. 'But when he tried to contact the CAS employee on his home phone number, apparently he had taken his phone of the hook.'

'He's probably back off to sleep by now, I should think,' said Brian. 'I have never been aware of CAS advising commercial airlines in any capacity before, and it's certainly not the job of anyone there to be on-call overnight for something like this.'

'I know,' said Josh. 'It's not their job, but the Asian private contractor was calling CAS back, and even went so far as insisting that he should speak to the person who issued the advice. He said that two Australian planes, and another plane, had all changed their flight paths at the last minute based on that. His company has a plane flying to

Hong Kong in the same airspace and he wants to know what's going on.'

'What's that?' said Brian, gesturing towards the switchboard.

The switchboard light had started flashing again. 'That's a call to the same lab employee that I was just listening to', said Josh as he immediately switched to listen live to the call. The calls were all being recorded by Brian's team. Josh handed Brian a second set of headphones to listen in too, and the voice of a man speaking clear English with a heavy German accent came through:

'Hi, I'm flying to Hong Kong on the flight route that some of you guys have been looking at just now. What's happening, is there some sort of problem?'

The reply came from the same lab worker in CAS.

'Oh, so you're the Hong Kong flight, yeah, I think some people have just moved and re-routed some flights who were travelling on the same path as you. They were coming from Europe and heading towards Asia. There are some strange things going on there just now, but I'm not really sure what. The advice was basically just to get clear of it.'

'That's the first I've been told about any of that,' replied the German pilot of the Hong Kong flight. 'No-one has told us of any issues, and when I checked with our company's security contact in Asia, they told us that they had no information about anything unusual. Are you sure that your concerns are justified?'

'Oh yeah. Just a second.' Then the call was muffled as it sounded like the CAS employee working in the lab was privately speaking to another party on an untapped phone line.

Brian looked at Josh and questioned what he was hearing. 'So now the crew actually on the flight deck of an airliner bound for Hong Kong is making contact with workers here in CAS Australia directly? Isn't this highly irregular?'

'I believe so. It's all rather confusing. I think that particular Hong Kong flight is the one the Asian private security contractor I eavesdropped on was speaking about earlier,' said Josh. 'So that would mean it's registered to an Asian country.'

'And their cockpit crew have knowledge of these communications you just heard? How?' asked Brian puzzled.

'I'm not sure about that either. The world of satellite mobiles and Facebook, I'd guess .... it seems someone must have tipped off the Hong Kong plane's flight crew that some security contractors thought it necessary to make some other arrangements relating to their interests in the same region they're travelling in ... wait though, here's the CAS employee coming back on the line to the plane.' Brian and Josh listened carefully to the CAS employee's words.

'Yeah, a colleague I've just been speaking with here thinks you should really try calling your own company's security advisors again to make sure you're not missing something.'

'OK, I'll call our advisors back,' came the snap reply from the German man to the CAS employee.

The switchboard was quiet again for a while. Brian removed his headphones.

'This interaction is definitely a bit different, isn't it?' the young officer asked Brian quizzically.

'It is unusual - but hopefully it's all over nothing too serious and the professionals on their end will deal with it,' replied Brian.

'Yeah, it's just strange that some security personnel are so concerned about an everyday well-used flight path that they've taken immediate action, whilst others in the same situation seem oblivious to any risks or concerns. Worth continuing to listen in to see if anything does happen ... don't you think so?'

'Well, yes,' said Brian. *Although commercial flying is not really supposed to be like a tale of suspense* Brian thought just as the switchboard lit up again. The younger officer rushed to switch to that line, and Brian put his headphones back on. It was the German man from the cockpit again:

'Our advisors have confirmed that there are no official notifications of any concerns ahead; we are to stick to our flight path. They say you are over-reacting about something on your end.'

'Seriously?' came the voice of the CAS lab worker, sounding surprised. 'Well, it's strange that two other Australian aircraft on that route have modified their plans. They have definitely departed, someone confirmed that to me earlier, but they're telling you everything's fine on your end? Wait until I ask my, ah, colleague again what she thinks.' There was the muffled sound again and then, 'Yeah, she thinks you're crazy to continue on that path, so make of that what you will ...'

'I'm just following orders; it's all standard procedure here. Our company's security contact would know if there was a problem,' came the communication from the pilot, his German accent sounding stronger the more exasperated he became.

'My colleague here wants to know if there's any way you can make the decision to change the flight path yourself at this stage?' asked the CAS employee.

'Are you seriously suggesting that? It's against our regulations, potentially disastrous and illegal, I can't just do that,' said the pilot emphatically. 'That's not something we are allowed to do without permission from local towers.'

'Well, please remember,' said the CAS employee, 'I don't know anything about commercial airline routes, I'm just an employee here in CAS who happened to pick up the phone. I'm only telling you what I've heard.'

There were a few moments of silence from the flight deck of the Hong Kong bound flight at that point. What first started off like a perceived over-reaction was quickly becoming rather worrying to those on both ends of the line as they began to realise that they were somewhat on their own in the area.

'Wait', said the German pilot. 'We've confirmed that there is another plane from London that's not so far from us; we're making contact.' After some moments of silence in the police office, the conversation they were listening into picked up again. 'They've said they're not changing their plans; they have heard no serious concerns about anything in the region,' the pilot said.

'Um, ok, I'm just telling my colleague that, since their security advisors might not have been involved in earlier notifications either,' the CAS worker replied.

There was a silence for a few minutes.

The German man came back on the line again sounding somewhat more concerned. 'Hello, are you there?'

'Hey, yes,' confirmed the CAS employee so bewildered it was almost as if he lacked any understanding of the urgency of the situation that seemed to be unfolding as he responded almost casually.

'The relevant airline has just looked into the aircraft that departed London on that route; it's being re-routed too now,' said the German pilot, his voice tense now.

'Again, can you change your route? She said to ask you one more time just in case you changed your mind.'

'No, we can't do that, I told you that already,' the Hong Kong flight's captain stated firmly. 'Do you know if the concerns are about something they're seeing on the satellites there?'

'I'm not sure if it's all satellites, or if they're getting some reports from reconnaissance flights, and look I'm not even sure if we're supposed to be talking to you directly.' After a brief pause the CAS employee spoke again. 'OK my colleague says she can't believe you're carrying on through there and to tell you this: 'Well, goodnight, Hong Kong'.'

'I'm sure everything will be OK. Thank you and goodnight,' said the German pilot leaving the conversation for the last time.

'That's all really strange, don't you think?' commented Josh.

'It does seem so to me,' answered Brian, 'but then again, I don't know very much about aviation safety, maybe things like this happen all the time. Hopefully they've got it all under control between them.'

'Well, seems like they deal with more dramatic calls than we do here at times ....,' joked the young officer.

'Oh yeah, who knew scientists' lives were so riveting, and he's still working at this hour,' said Brian.

'Well,' said the young officer. 'I just wanted your advice and input on whether I can keep monitoring this group so intensely and whether or not I'm authorised to tap into this CAS employee's cell phone?

'Our warrants allow for that so we are legally covered. You can tap into his cell phone to see times of calls. Depending on who the calls are to, and provided they're not on a blackout list, you can listen to the call if you think it might be important from a policing standpoint.'

'I think it just might be interesting, but if I'm being honest, it doesn't seem directly related to any sort of fraud so far. That being said, it is the early hours of the morning now, so maybe most of his calls are finally done for tonight anyway,' said Josh.

'Well, I guess some scientists work really long hours to check on experiments and to get access to specialised labs and equipment, but what was really strange was that he was taking calls from an aeroplane's flight deck directly. Have you ever heard of anything like that from these guys before? Maybe it is a type of work that some senior CAS employees get involved in that we just haven't come across so far, who knows, but it's really odd. Anyway, keep monitoring and call me if anything else out of the ordinary happens.'

Brian returned to his desk and processed the paperwork required to extend the warrant that allowed these phone call intercepts on CAS employees and clients to continue, even if this had literally been the most exciting conversation they had heard since they started this surveillance.

*****

About an hour had passed and Brian hadn't received any calls from Josh. Brian assumed that must have meant that there had been no more unusual flurries of activity on his switchboard again. Brian decided to make his way back across to the young officer's desk anyway to find out for certain as his curiosity had been piqued by what they heard earlier. As he did so, Brian caught Josh surfing the net on his phone, but rather than immediately try to hide it, Josh said:

'Oh my God, ..., you are not going to believe this.'

'What?' asked Brian.

'I've just seen on the news that in the region that Hong Kong flight was travelling in – a plane has totally disappeared. Oh my God, I can't believe it, where have they gone?' Other employees heard Josh's anxious tone and looked up. A brief pause of silence filled the police monitoring unit room.

Brian leaned over Josh, keeping his voice low. 'So, did we just witness that happen? Was it the flight that made contact with CAS tonight?'

'They say that it was a flight from Europe to Hong Kong,' answered Josh.

'Sounds like it could be it,' said Brian, looking at Josh's startled face. 'Don't speak to anyone else about what you have heard tonight, not even others on the team. I'll have to leave a message for my superior to let him know a summary of what we just intercepted.' He shook his head at the enormity of the situation. 'Just like that, maybe three hundred people or more are there one moment, possibly on the other end of a phone line here, and now they've simply disappeared?'

CHAPTER TWO

Sleep was the last thing on Brian's mind when he left to head home after his night duty at five thirty am. The news on the car radio confirmed what they had read in the office during the night, a plane really had gone missing. Potentially hundreds of people were dead, or they were lost somewhere, which was perhaps an even more unpleasant thought. He pulled into his parking spot after the short drive from his office to his unit block, aware that, as usual, he was the only person in the basement garage at this time. He got out of the car and heavily trundled up the empty staircase into a tower of sleeping people to his apartment: unit 28. Brian's front door opened into a small vestibule hall that housed a trendy slim line buffet where he habitually set down his wallet and keys as soon as he arrived home. He closed the door firmly behind him and locked up before heading further inside.

Brian immediately switched on the television news when he walked into his lounge room, rather than falling into bed as he usually would after such a shift. Some sort of adrenaline rush had kicked in, and it was over-riding his exhaustion. The news was filled with images of distraught relatives waiting at an airport in Hong Kong for a plane that wasn't likely to ever reach them and might never be seen again. The news channels had interviews with aviation experts, but no-one was able to offer any credible theories for what could have gone wrong.

Brian was in fact still trying to process himself what they seemed to have just witnessed having happened in the surveillance room.

Brian recalled a plane that had crashed into the ocean in South America many years ago, and how long that had taken to be recovered, so he wondered if it was the same sort of thing that had gone wrong for the Hong Kong flight. It wasn't clear whether they were over land when they disappeared, or if they had also ended up out at sea, or even just flew off to some undisclosed location somewhere in the hands of a hijacker, in which case they might still be alive even if their plane came down somewhere.

Brian couldn't shake the feeling that he and his young colleague Josh had heard more than some might feel comfortable with last night. Brian wondered: *was high level security always so disorganised sounding, or was this a truly bizarre event that was leaving even top experts taken by surprise and confused over what was going on?* It was all rather disconcerting even for an experienced police officer, if truth be told.

Brian had hardly settled in at home before his phone began ringing in spite of his shift having ended quite some time ago. He answered nonetheless, to find a surprisingly senior person on the line: it was his superior Murphy, his light voice streaming through the phone.

'We need a debrief regarding those communications you intercepted last night,' Murphy began. 'I'm sure you've now seen the news of the aeroplane disaster that happened overnight. It's important given the highly sensitive nature of events that we are all on the same page regarding what might have been heard to have taken place over the telephone networks. I have to make you aware that some of it will be classified by counter-intelligence and not for us to look into. In fact, some of the recordings your team made that night have already been classified. The reason being that the details of some of those involved in the communications within Australia and with some parties overseas will be kept confidential in some instances. We will await full clarification on that before deciding how we might wish to proceed, if at all, with our own avenues of investigation. I hope I have made myself clear in that?'

'Oh yes, Sir, very clear,' Brian affirmed.

How very, very awkward that entire conversation exchange had been last night was what Brian was pre-occupied with thinking. It was potentially embarrassing even, given how much confusion there was over the best course of action, and considering the scale of what was at stake, then what had tragically happened in the end. *Not surprising really that damage control had begun so soon.* Perhaps some would say it was best not to delve too deeply into what was behind some of that communication blockage, but as a police officer it was Brian's deepest instinct to do so.

'This missing plane is not really in our jurisdiction,' Murphy continued. 'It's really just by chance we'd come across it in our CAS fraud investigation. That's why I want to be sure we all know what we are, and are not, expected to investigate.'

'I understand completely, Sir,' Brian re-iterated. 'When do you need me in for the briefing?'

'Today is a rest day for you, but today in the p.m. is when I plan to talk to the group in the first instance, and some people are coming over to meet us.'

'Yes, indeed, Sir,' said Brian who was at once left feeling put out that later this day was when he was now due back in. It was supposed to be a rostered rest day for him, and he had been looking forward to it. At the same time though, he was also eager to find out what they knew about what had happened during the night. 'I should be able to manage. Would three o'clock this afternoon be a reasonable time for me to come back in, Sir?'

'That would be good, Brian,' confirmed Murphy.

When he hung up the phone, Brian noticed how time was getting on. Everyone else in the apartment block would be starting to get up soon. Usually, he would sleep through the odd bit of noise that would begin like clockwork as others in the apartment block started their daytime shifts, if he'd already gotten into a sleep himself that was, but it could be hard to actually do so later on in the early morning such as it was now, with a lot of distractions already beginning.

*****

Brian's apartment block was in inner city Sydney, with a handy parking space underneath in the garage, but he was also lucky enough to be able to walk to the head office every day if he wanted to. Often, he drove back and forth to the office when he worked late shifts. He was more aware than most of the crimes that take place in quiet times in city spots that are perfectly safe and civilised throughout the day.

Brian's unit was on the fourth floor, so he didn't have any stunning views of the city or the harbour areas of Sydney, but he could easily use the stairs instead of waiting for a slow lift every time he was coming and going, which compensated for that in his mind. As with most trendy places built in Sydney in the 90s, he had the shared use of a heated lap pool in the roof where there were nice views if he felt like them anyway, but of course, he never used that, or indeed the communal gym, anywhere near as much as he thought he would when he moved into the place.

Brian lived entirely alone with no pets, and with no wife or kids on the scene. Brian hadn't really planned to live a bachelor lifestyle for so many years, if truth be told, but it was just the way that things had worked out for him so far. Even though he was a reasonably good-looking young man who took care of his fitness, and knew how to hold a conversation, he just seemed to get passed over all the time when it came to love. Maybe he was just too dedicated to work, and that perfectionist approach he took, where only the highest standards would suffice, were bleeding through into his private interpersonal relationships and just too much for most women to handle or feel they have to live up to.

Brian didn't know any of his neighbours really, they didn't say hello when they passed him in the corridor, or even do perfunctory neighbourly things such as to post Christmas cards through the door or mailbox in the holiday season. The neighbours tended to be mainly youngish singles who came and went frequently in his apartment block. Sometimes Brian wondered where on earth these people found to go out to so often, but it made him feel bad about himself and his own lack of active social life to dwell on it too much. Brian was one of the longest-term residents in the place having lived there a whole two years, perhaps because he was thirty-eight now, and hence getting more set in his ways. The thought of weekends dedicated to boxing everything in the house to make a move to someplace else, preceded by endless open unit inspections, just didn't appeal quite as much as ignoring rent increases and any minor annoyances did.

Brian tossed and turned in his bed, the missing plane on his mind, and every little sound outside his unit amplified. Eventually he had to get up and resort to taking a sleeping pill to wind down enough to get some sleep, his alarm set for not all that far into the late morning. He hated doing that though, because it always left him feeling groggy. He felt bad for everyone on that plane and their loved ones, but as a curious detective, he couldn't help but feel some sense of anticipation for the briefing on it and at times analysed it in his mind with a cold detachment. He wondered what it all meant as he climbed back into his bed and let every bone in his body relax as he drifted off into a much-needed sleep.

CHAPTER THREE

Brian had made his way into the office in time for the afternoon's briefing on the missing plane. There been no trace of the doomed aircraft still, nor any contact from anyone on board. It was one of the main topics of conversation among the team, but Brian didn't need to be reminded that he'd been ordered not to openly discuss what he and Josh had heard on the telephones last night, no matter how tempting it was to do so, and it certainly was a temptation.

Following the briefing for the whole team, Brian was invited to a second briefing along with Murphy, and some others who were in senior management. Murphy moved decidedly towards his seat close by to where the big management players were getting ready to address the room; tall, slim and spritely for a man in his fifties, after he sat down, he began sweeping back his wispy grey hair from his brow as he began his usual habit of scanning the room with his piercing blue eyes that had a coldness behind them which was quite intimidating. The young officer Josh who intercepted the calls with Brian was present also; he made such a contrast to the others in the room with his pale blonde hair gelled into a modern trendy hairstyle. He made some small talk to one of the managers beside him about his shock that the plane seemed to have completely vanished, and that there were still no reliable theories, let alone an explanation, for what had occurred. His hushed voice was the only thing disturbing the odd silence as they sat in anticipation. Eventually one of the Senior management who was present stood up and began the meeting. The tall and narrow faced man looking down his nose to his audience as he spoke, went on for at least a quarter of an hour talking about how they had to make it very clear to both Brian and Josh that what they had uniquely heard was not to be discussed with anyone, even within the office or with the rest of their team. Eventually the younger officer was told he could leave the meeting, but to his surprise, Brian was asked to remain for some further discussion with his superior Murphy alone. Shuffling over to a seat next to Brian, he began to further explain the situation when it was only him and Brian left behind in the room:

'I think you are well aware, as are many of us, and that includes the general public, that much of this incident remains somewhat of a mystery, even to highly specialised aviation experts and government advisers with many years of experience. Now, while I have stressed the importance of tact in proceeding with our analysis of the information we have in relation to this, and that we do not wish to tread on the toes of groups like ASIO or ASIS, or indeed specialised counter-terror units within the force, it remains of interest, and within our realm of investigatory powers to better understand how these events fit into the wider monitoring role we perform in relation to such incidents and specialised workers. The challenge in doing this will be that there will be times when access to certain phone recordings or names of those on the end of the line might be restricted or classified. It's important to respect that, whilst at the same time ascertaining if there are wider links or crime presences that we need to be aware of. I believe you are well suited to this rather tricky appointment, and a natural candidate given that you are one of only two staff members at your clearance level who have knowledge of some of the discussions and decisions that were made immediately preceding the loss of contact with that missing Hong Kong plane.'

He paused for a moment as if to collect his thoughts, and then he continued:

'I would like to delegate the lead on the CAS fraud case to someone else for the time being, since, as I said, you are the more natural candidate to lead our investigations surrounding the air mystery instead. If you need to take someone along with you to interviews or to assist you in any way, please use Josh, because I don't want anyone else to have to be brought into the loop at this stage. You will be pleased to know that I have arranged a link-up for you with a specialised counter-terror liaison officer. She has the ability to get in contact with relevant people in other government agencies if required, so that's not something for you to worry about. Excuse me for just a moment, and I shall invite her to come and meet you. She's having a coffee with my secretary, I believe.' With that he went out of his office and returned with a woman who Brian correctly assumed was to be his counter-terror partner on this case.

'Superintendent Brian Andersen, I would like to introduce you to a Specialist Response Group Commander Elsie Whitman.'

'Pleased to meet you.' Brian rose to shake Elsie's hand. Elsie was a fairly tall, slim woman. She looked about mid-twenties, but would have to be a little older, at least in her thirties like Brian to be in the role that she was in. Her hair was quite blonde and sat tightly in a bun neatly at the back of her head. Her pretty blue eyes sat in a face covered by a thick layer of make-up likely used in an attempt to disguise bags under her eyes from lack of sleep following the plane's disappearance.

Elsie returned a firm hand-shake and a warm smile, 'Very pleased to meet you also.' Brian saw Elsie glance up at him and straighten her own pose a bit, as even though she was above average height for a woman and wearing fairly high heels, he still towered over her. Then she quickly surveyed his face, without giving a hint of her assessment. Brian considered himself ordinary looking, with nondescript dark hair and brown eyes, not particularly handsome, but not unattractive either. Or so he hoped.

'Alright then,' said Brian's senior officer getting up to lead the way to the visitor's desk he had set up for Elsie off a corridor parallel to the one where he was situated. 'I'll show Elsie to her workplace here, if you could come with us too, Brian, then I'll leave you two to work out how you will proceed with this together. Elsie is here for as long as her group feels it is necessary, and that will also depend on what comes out of initial investigations you make. I think we can end our meeting here and let you both get on with work.'

'Thank you, Sir,' said Brian as he got up to leave with them. Elsie seemed to him like she would be approachable, which is always a good start in a working partnership.

'Thank you once again for welcoming me for the duration of my stay here,' Elsie said with her warm and friendly smile flicking her gaze between both men. Murphy simply nodded, and with that he led the way to Elsie's workspace. Brian let Elsie walk ahead as they followed Murphy, 'So are you available to have a more in-depth discussion on this in my office right away?' Elsie asked Brian.

'Yes, certainly, I am available now.'

Brian couldn't help but think, that if he'd known an outsider would be joining him on this situation, he'd have expected some colleagues in dark suits, but here was Elsie, just by herself and wearing more of a light grey suit, not threatening or distant seeming at all. It had been a pleasant surprise.

They soon reached Elsie's visitor's desk and Brian's superior Murphy summarily excused himself, he began to walk off, before turning back on his heels and pausing to let them know he'd be in touch to arrange the next debriefing session in the not-too-distant future before briskly carrying on.

'So, have a seat then, Brian,' Elsie gestured to her spare chair. 'I think we should start with what I know, and what our group would like to share with you. I am already aware of what you know - I've been made aware of the conversations you monitored and intercepted on that night. I listened to the recordings.'

Amazing, Brian thought to himself, she's efficient, to the point, and refreshingly honest, even if that does mean subtly intimating that he would only be told what they wanted him to know, while they would have access to everything on his end.

'So, here's what I wanted to fill you in on, and where we think some police work from your team might come in useful. We have learned that just a little earlier last night, before those conversations you overheard from the Hong Kong flight, a Mr Li Wu, Asian private security advisor attempted to make contact with Dr John McFay, who is an Australian employee of CAS. Mr Wu tried to contact Dr McFay on his home phone line, but he got no answer as the phone had been taken off the hook. Now, this seemed strange to us in fact, the reason being, that we had confirmed that some others had been able to awaken Dr John McFay around the same time. We also know that after McFay was roused from his sleep that night, he had contacted some Australian private security contractors to give input on the situation in the air space the Hong Kong plane was in, or about to enter, at that time.'

'Yes, that is suspicious in light of what happened. Can I have the names of the contacts involved in that?'

'Well, Brian, the situation is such that I can give you the names of the contacts in the Asia based private security consultancy that works with the missing plane's airline however, we face some challenges when it comes to naming those who work for the Australian government. They have privacy measures in place to protect them from harassment, poaching and stalking, among other things. In fact, the only reason that I'm even naming Dr John McFay here with you today, is because your team has already overheard mention of him anyway in conversations, which I'm sure you've been told are now classified.'

'That being said, working in reverse, I may be able to find some of those links here,' Brian worked out.

'Yes, and there's where we come into a very delicate area. It might be relevant to know who some of those people are, or even crucial if there are concerns about their judgement and motivations, but there is also a need to protect valuable and reliable assets to this country. Do you know what I mean?'

'Yes, that all makes perfect sense, certainly there might be some need for trade-offs in this.'

'Discretion and refraining from sharing the information outside of this special investigation is so important that it cannot be stressed enough. I think that's already been emphasized more than once, but still, it doesn't hurt to re-iterate it.'

'Sure,' said Brian, feeling he was treated like a mushroom, held in the dark yet expected to feed her agency with information or provide anything else they might like from them, no questions asked. 'OK, so do you have any more background on the Asian private security contractor, Mr Li Wu, and is anything else known about him that might relate to those we have been monitoring?'

'He is a national of Singapore who began his career in law enforcement in Asia. He then spent some time studying in Australia and working here in private security roles before returning to the private sector in Asia in the area of aviation security. He wasn't one of the private aviation advisers contacted by the technically Australian government linked employees such as Dr John McFay last night. You would think that it might have been beneficial for his relationship with Australian-based advisors that he has spent time studying and working here in our country, but maybe not in his case, and the reason why is potentially of interest. The files I have for you give details of where he studied and worked here in Australia.'

'So, who exactly did Dr McFay phone or speak to about the risk posed to that flight region? And isn't that outside of his duties?'

'We understand that they are referred to 'aviation liaison officers'. Dr McFay was thought to have had contact that night with one such person who is an Australian citizen and whose name we cannot give you at this stage. We suspect that they would have been the person who first raised concerns about the flight region. These were things happening here in Australia, so on our end.'

'Well, that makes this pretty challenging, doesn't it?' said Brian feeling rather irritated. Although Brian had been made aware from the very start how this relationship was going to be, it was still very frustrating.

'I understand that this is frustrating for you,' said Elsie as if she were reading Brian's mind. 'But we have limits to work within, too. As I told you already, we also have Dr John McFay himself listed as covered by an Australian official secrecy provision. Truth be told, even I find that rather frustrating because I'm not convinced that Dr McFay is really the most useful cog in the wheel, and sometimes the right to secrecy is just getting used and abused as a cover for incompetence."

'But I might come across some of the others in the course of the investigation?'

'That's correct, Brian.'

'Alright. Well, it could just have been bad luck on Mr Wu's part that he wasn't contacted, and also that he couldn't get hold of Dr McFay when he tried to. But nonetheless, I'll see if we can gather anything that could explain why anyone might have a grudge of some kind against Mr Wu. It's worth checking it out just in case something like that was the real reason behind it. That might be difficult though as I said, especially if I can't even have the names of all of the Australians involved, like the aviation liaison officers, for instance. There would be a better chance of us finding information on all of this if we were given names. We are Australian police after all, and that's the standard type of basic information we work off of.'

'I will help you with whichever names and files I possibly can,' clarified Elsie. 'One other name you should have, is that of a Mr Mark Wilson.'

'So, who is he?' asked Brian.

'He is a Canadian aviation security consultant who was informed in vague terms about a risk of some potential problems that could possibly arise within the coming hours the night the plane vanished, and this information was given to him sometime earlier on prior to the incident actually occurring that night. He was informed of this by Australia's own Dr McFay. McFay himself was in fact actively involved in negotiations for some aircraft on that night, and that was in response to those concerns which he shared his knowledge of with Wilson. Presumably McFay had chosen to alert Wilson because the Australian planes he was dealing with were scheduled to be flying close to some that were registered to overseas companies which he knew came under his friend Wilson's remit. It's all of great interest now though, because all of the planes in question were scheduled to be flying within what has just transpired to be the exact same region as the now missing plane last night.'

'That has to be beyond just a coincidence, I should think,' said Brian.

'Even more strangely than that perhaps, is that McFay has also told accident investigators that Mark Wilson bravely took some matters into his own hands that night. When he had been told about the concerns McFay had, and changes he was advising for Australian aircraft in response to those, the Canadian Wilson had immediately requested an authorisation from his own company that would permit him to make a similar route change for planes under his own control. What Wilson's employer said to him in response was, 'No, stick to the path.' They turned down Wilson's request because they didn't want to authorise the extra expense that the fuel wastage involved in flying several planes on a detour with a longer flight time would incur. That official decision was based on their own existing risk assessment which had not flagged any concerns for that area the existing flight path would take them through.'

'You mean they wouldn't authorise any precautionary measures being taken, all over their cost savings concerns, even when a risk had just been flagged to them? That's shocking.' Brian was genuinely taken aback by that revelation.

'McFay's vague concerns which he informally shared with his friend Wilson, weren't considered a solid enough reason to change the assessment of the safety of that region. Wilson trusted McFay's judgement implicitly though. That's the reason why, or so McFay reckons, that what Wilson did next, was to, after simply telling his company, 'Yeah, heeding that,' just go right ahead and act of his own volition. In actuality, Wilson instructed the relevant local towers to lead the plane or planes which he was responsible for that night, to divert and follow the new path of the other two Australian planes which McFay had dealt with.'

'So, you're telling me that the Canadian Wilson just took his own initiative and made a major decision by himself, even when it was contrary to instructions the companies involved had just given him? Basically, that is what you are saying,' said Brian summing up the situation. 'And in this instance, it paid off potentially in light of what happened to the missing plane.'

'Exactly,' agreed Elsie.

'Mark Wilson sounds like a bit of a risk taker.'

'Or he's risk averse, depending on how you look at it,' said Elsie insightfully.

She then continued with her briefing. 'The CAS employee you were eavesdropping on is a man named Dr Gareth Hughes, as you are perhaps already aware. Another person of particular interest is a Sydney woman, Professor

Alice Wirth, an older female physicist with a lot of expertise on weapons and aviation. She's officially retired, but she still works within the academic environment here in Sydney as an emeritus professor. We believe that she was the friend who Dr Hughes was speaking to on a private line, whilst you were eavesdropping on him on his work phone line. It might also be useful to know more about why she seemed to have been so convinced of an issue with the flight path, that she told Gareth to strongly advise the Hong Kong crew to leave it.'

'I can try to get a better picture of who she is and what motivations she might have. The only thing is that it'll be hard to interview her without giving away the fact that we are currently doing surveillance on CAS.'

'I've got us covered on that. The Asia-based adviser Mr Wu has told international accident investigators, whom my group are liaising with, that he spoke with someone in CAS here in Australia. Since Dr Gareth Hughes was listed as working in the lab there last night, it's natural that we would interview him, so there should be no reason for anyone to suspect there was already an investigation into them going on. I believe you can lead him into giving you the name of Professor Wirth, which will then provide the reason for us speaking with her afterwards. I got a lead on where to find Dr Gareth Hughes, too,' said Elsie. 'Supposedly he's in a monastery not far from here.'

'Really?' asked Brian somewhat surprised. 'What is he doing there?'

'Apparently, it's his current home. He actually spent some time in the monastery earlier in his youth, but he left the order behind after deciding to go and study for his PhD in aeronautical engineering, and then he ended up working in CAS. It would seem that the sense of responsibility he felt over his role the other night might have taken some kind of toll on him, because something has pushed him towards retreating back there from his regular life, and given the magnitude of what transpired last night, that's the most likely cause of it. I thought that you might like to be the one to interview him, since it was his conversation which you overheard, and that is what has brought you into all of this in the first place.'

'Yes, I would like to very much, if he'll agree to speak with me.'

'I spoke to a superior there called Brother Michael and he told me that Gareth would be amenable to visitors, including us police, but would like you to speak to him first upon your arrival.'

'We all know the stereotypes surrounding religious orders; it'll be like getting blood out of a stone I should expect.'

'Well, you have the time to go, and I thought it was worth a try. Just don't go thinking of leaving us for the church as well,' she teased.

'Oh, no. No way,' chuckled Brian rather flattered that their interactions had moved on to be slightly less formal than they had been so far.

'Well, that's a good start then, Brian. We should arrange a next catch-up in a couple of days when we might have some more to talk about.'

'Thank you, Elsie,' said Brian rising to leave. 'And I was just wondering, is Elsie short for Elisabeth?'

'No, it's just Elsie. Someone in our family found out that my great, great, great Grandmother was Danish, and we think that was likely her name. It's a little bit unusual around here, so I sometimes get called Elsa by mistake until people get used to it.'

'Well, I'll be sure to spell it right, with the 'ie' at the end always.'

'Thank you, much appreciated,' Elsie said with a smile.

That warm friendly smile again thought Brian. He found it quite pleasant to be around in fact.

As Brian headed back to his side of the office, his head began to fill with the puzzle of how he could discretely, with no warrants at this stage, find out more about some sort of problem network that involves mainly unnamed people in Australia ... if a problem network even exists that is. Challenging was a pretty good description of the whole thing. Still, not to be discouraged by any of it, he decided a rather old-fashioned police work approach was the way to go. After all, it was clear there wasn't going to be free and generous access to databases and files, especially after what had just happened. Traditional police work was something Brian knew how to do well at least; it was definitely something that he could throw himself into for the foreseeable future.

After some more hours at work had ticked by, Brian recalled how he had promised himself at the start of the day that he would respect his duty rota and come home immediately after the briefings. But it was too tempting to at least have a peek inside the files he had been given related to the plane mystery, and to start to read them a little. He noticed as he began to read, that hc had inadvertently already begun investigating whether there might be any potential leads stemming from the Hong Kong contact, Mr Wu, and his time spent in Australia.

Helpfully, Elsie had provided Brian with a list of contacts Mr Wu had during his time studying and working in Australia. He wondered how on earth she had gotten access to something like that, and so very quickly. An interesting detail was that in his earlier police career in Asia, Mr Wu had worked alongside investigatory police teams in the Asian region that provided their police forces with unprecedented access to databases with information on convicted paedophiles and even their victims, including persons in the UK, and in Australia. *It was only natural that some noses would be put out of joint by that* thought Brian. The Asian team was successful in their bid for information in the end – they had been given full access to highly personal information on citizens both in Australia and abroad; assuming it was all provided accurately that is, which was potentially another investigation in itself entirely.

Brian wondered if the Asian police and their paedophile investigation could have had something to do with bad blood that seemed to have been stirred up. It was clear some friction now existed between Asian ex-police employees who were now working in private Asian security groups both over in Asia and here in Australia, and those people ordinarily working here in Australia, or within other commonwealth nations. It wasn't concrete proof of anything untoward, but it struck Brian as possibly highly relevant to understanding what was behind the communication blockages the night the plane vanished. Clearly, it would be very hard for Brian to investigate though, but *time might tell, or Elsie might,* thought Brian.

Another niggling question in Brian's mind, was if Elsie's team was investigating whether anyone involved in the Australian side of security or advisory that fateful night the plane went missing on, might have had a motive to help terrorists. *Or did they suspect there might have been someone who simply wanted to do something to hurt the world? Maybe they saw the world as something that had been hurting them?*

Brian decided that any further thought on that issue would have to wait until another day, because he was feeling so very weary. It was time call it a day and make his way home; he walked the 25-minute stroll through the city to his apartment block, arriving home even more tired than he was when he left the office. Usually, he was good at putting work from his mind, but when he reached home on this day, he realised that every time he turned on the television,   a reminder of the plane mystery faced him and kept his mind running overly active. Some of the same experts from earlier broadcasts gave interviews on the television again; there wasn't really anything new being said, but now they seemed overall less confident of finding any trace of the plane any time soon.

CHAPTER FOUR

Brian was quietly hoping for a good outcome as he made his way to visit the CAS scientist, Dr Gareth Hughes, who was currently living at a monasterial order property not far from central Sydney. Dr Hughes didn't really sound like he was very sure of what was going on in the phone calls they overheard, but Brian's main goal was to officially get the name of his friend Professor Wirth from his lips so that he could interview her, and to see if he knew the original Australian contact, Dr John McFay, whom Mr Li Wu had wanted to speak to.

Brian and Josh made their way to the monastery in the morning after having had a quick cup of tea and a re-read of the transcript of Dr Hughes' recorded conversations from the night of the plane disappearance. His conversation with Mr Wu was brief, and, by itself, not very disturbing. However, in light of the missing plane, it was now most ominous.

The monastery was perched high up on a hillside with views to the ocean in the distance. Driving through its wide gates into a walled world was like stepping out of Sydney for a moment and into some parallel planet of tranquillity. Brian had called ahead to arrange an appointment with one of the senior monks, Brother Michael, as requested, and was expected by him and Dr Hughes; although no-one would have guessed so, given how quiet the place felt. He parked his car near what appeared to be the main entrance, not that there were any other vehicles in the car park. The car park was complete with a quaint wooden sign pointing 'Entrance this Way'. Brian and Josh followed that up a winding decorative path to a large sandstone building where a double doored entrance led to a reception area.

Perhaps it was linked to all the negative press the brothers had received in recent years, but Brian's mind was drawn to think of all the young boys who had at one time come through this centre, attending school and even boarding here, or seeking shelter and refuge in earlier times. It all felt so peaceful, tucked out of the way of the city centre hustle and bustle, and surrounded by such tall green trees. The perfect place to grow up, to play and to learn, or so one would think. Yet there were just so many who seemed to be unhappy with such places now when they were looking back on it all. Perhaps as adults many saw things in a very different light, and it was only then that some of them could finally face what had been too difficult to process or even experience in a full state of presence as a child. He surmised this judging by the number of lawsuits and allegations churches that ran institutions now found themselves facing. Brian had learned well early on in his career as an investigator however, that looks can be deceiving.

As they approached the main entrance, Brian noticed a man in traditional brown monasterial robes scuttling past after a sideways glance at him, as if afraid to be approached by anyone. Maybe it was an unkind thought, but Brian always found it hard to understand people who chose to spend their life in a monastery, and maybe quite a few of them were not terribly social types. He wondered what drew them to a place like this to shut themselves off from society in many senses. Brian and Josh made no attempt to approach the monk, but instead rang the doorbell at the place marked 'reception', and eventually a woman who looked to be in her fifties with greying hair in a decades old style bob, complete with a thick fringe, opened the door.

'Hello,' she said pleasantly, 'how may I help you?'

'My name is Superintendent Andersen, my partner and I are here to meet with Brother Michael, he is expecting us,' replied Brian.

'Please come in and have a seat, and I'll let him know that you are here.'

Brian and Josh followed her into a little waiting room where they sat for around five minutes glancing at the interesting reading materials. No women's magazines or sports reviews on their coffee tables, but rather books on biblical discovery, self-enlightenment, and modern interpretations of ancient scriptures.

Eventually the woman re-appeared. 'He's ready for you now, so please come with me.'

Brian and Josh got up and followed her through to an atrium, then, in through a small little door to a side office where a monk sat. He appeared to be around forty. He stood up as they entered the room.

'Hello, and welcome to our monastery, Superintendent,' said the monk in a very ordinary fashion. His hair was slightly grown out and parted in the middle, an equal mix of grey and brown that fell tightly around his thin and pale face. The man was unremarkable, other than his brown monasterial robes. His eyes were blue, a pale sort of blue, and he wasn't terribly tall. 'Let me shake your hands,' he added.

Whilst shaking hands, Brian added a polite, 'Pleased to meet you, too,' as the monk gestured for him to take a chair, which he did, as Joshua introduced himself.

'I am here seeking some information, Brother,' Brian began, hoping that he was using the correct form of address. 'Dr Gareth Hughes may be able to assist us with some enquiries we've been making.'

'Hmmm, I see,' said the monk broodily, the whole time looking down at the floor. After a few seconds he looked up again fixing his gaze directly on Brian 'I am glad that your colleague whom I spoke to on the phone told me that you recognise that this is potentially a delicate issue for those involved. Gareth is worried that he will be blamed for some accident which occurred.'

'Yes, brother, I understand how he might feel,' responded Brian. Of course, they all realised that placing blame on someone was exactly the purpose of the investigation, but Brian did try to keep an open mind and not take sides without proper evidence.

The monk said, 'I would also like you to clarify something for me first, too: has Gareth come under suspicion of doing something illegal?'

'I really cannot comment on ongoing enquiries other than to say that it might be beneficial to us to be aware of what some peoples' roles in CAS, where he worked, were. That is the reason I am seeking information.'

'Alright,' said the monk this time glancing up to gaze Brian in the eye for a moment before looking away again, 'I understand that this might, in fact, turn out to be important, and I will bring Gareth in here to speak to you. I'm sure he will want to pass on anything which he believes is relevant.'

'Thank you very much for your time, brother,' said Brian quite sincerely. He was well aware though just how difficult it was to get meaningful information out of such institutions.

Brother Michael got up and left the room leaving Brian and Josh sitting alone.

'Going well so far,' said Josh in an attempt to break the silence.

'Well, that was the easy part,' replied Brian.

The door handle turned, and then the door opened to reveal what Brian and Josh correctly assumed to be Dr Gareth Hughes. Dr Hughes was a well-built man, with long striking red hair tied up neatly into a ponytail on the back of his head. He was not wearing the monasterial robes. Instead, he was dressed casually in pale blue denims and a white polo-neck shirt.

Brian and Josh both stood up as Dr Hughes entered the room.

'Hello, I'm Superintendent Brian Andersen, and this is first class constable Josh Brennan. Thank you for agreeing to speak with us today,' began Brian, shaking Gareth's hand as he spoke. Josh then shook Gareth's hand also.

'That's alright,' said Gareth.

'And we are presuming that you are Dr Gareth Hughes, an employee of CAS, is that correct?' confirmed Brian.

'Yes, that is correct, and please feel free just to call me Gareth.'

'Certainly, Gareth,' said Brian. 'I believe you have a rough idea of why we are here. It concerns some events that took place around the time of the flight to Hong Kong's disappearance.'

'Yes, I'm aware, very much so,' said Gareth, it was clear it was a struggle for him to raise his eyes up to make contact with those of the two officers', even for the fleeting moment he did so, the anxiety and hint of depression creeping into his soul was obvious.

Brian continued, 'A man who worked for the airline, and whose company's plane subsequently went missing, had been trying to make contact with someone in CAS shortly before the incident happened. You were working there late that evening according to records. So, we were wondering if you were aware of that, or did anyone contact you in other words?'

'Yes, someone did contact me,' confirmed Gareth, 'but I'm guessing you already know that.'

Keeping a poker face, Brian simply replied vaguely, 'Anything that you can tell us could potentially be of use in solving this aviation mystery. Do you mind if I record this conversation for our records?'

'No,' answered Gareth, and Brian switched on his recorder.

'I was working late in one of the labs when the phone started ringing,' began Gareth. 'I almost didn't bother picking it up since, first of all, it was the early hours of the morning, and secondly it was unlikely to be for me, because no-one knew I was there. But I did pick it up, and the guy on the other end of the phone line introduced himself as a private airline security contractor. He said that he wanted to speak to Dr John McFay, he said it was urgent. I don't know John well at all, but I got a hold of his direct work line and tried ringing it. There was no answer. Not at all surprising given the time of night. The guy on the other end of the line wasn't going away easily though. I can't recall what name he gave, but it was a Chinese name and he spoke with an Asian accent.'

Josh busily noted everything that Gareth said.

'The Asian man said that some employee of CAS had been involved in re-routing some planes' flight paths, and that he required urgent clarification about a plane travelling in the same vicinity. When I couldn't put him through to Dr John McFay, he asked if there was anyone else I could call at this hour. The only person I had the private contact details for on my mobile was a woman I know, Professor Alice Wirth. She's a physicist who works with CAS on some joint academic projects, and she knows most people in CAS far better than I do. Because he said it was urgent, I called her on my mobile.'

'And what did you say to her?' prompted Brian.

'I explained briefly that a man was on the line from a private aviation security contractor, and that he was looking for John because he believed that he had been involved in some advising on commercial flight routes. Basically, Professor Wirth's advice was, that if John had advised it, then they should follow his lead. I conveyed that to the Asian man, but he said he really had to speak to John personally, and that the advice was just too vague otherwise. I checked with Professor Wirth, and she didn't have John's mobile number either. I told the Asian man that, apologised that I couldn't be of more help, and he hung up the phone. I was still on the phone to Professor Wirth at that point when another call came in on the lab phone. I thought it might be the Asian man again, but it wasn't. This time it was a German sounding man who claimed to be in the cockpit of the plane that was under discussion with the man from Asia. Excuse me,' said Gareth, his voice was beginning to crack a little, and he looked like he was fighting back tears. 'The now missing plane.'

'Just take your time,' said Brian trying to be reassuring.

'I explained to him briefly what I had heard had happened that evening, within CAS, with some planes being re-routed, and summed up Professor Wirth's advice which was that they should get out of that space too. He wasn't convinced, and he didn't take my advice in the end, as far as I am aware. I just keep replaying it over and over in my head. I didn't realise at the time just how serious it all was, and I keep reproaching myself over that, in case there was some way that I could have been more persuasive on the phone if I had taken it more seriously myself. It's just so many people gone,' and with that last statement the tears had begun to well up in Gareth's eyes. He was furiously wiping them away.

'Would helping you to get in contact with a counsellor be of any interest to you?' offered Brian. 'We can certainly put you in touch with someone who's very experienced in dealing with the sorts of emotions you are most likely going through just now.'

'No, thank you, that won't be necessary as I have access to all of the counselling and patience that I need right now here in the monastery.'

'Have you been involved in similar situations to this in CAS before? I mean ones where you are being expected to act as an advisor to private aviation security services?'

'No, I haven't personally. I don't know about anyone else. Although it would seem like it, based on what happened the other night. I guess that no-one recalls the incidents that *didn't* happen, just the ones that did, and that includes me. I can't stop blaming myself over it. I can't go back to CAS, not ever.'

'I'm sorry for what you had to go through, Gareth,' said Brian trying to be comforting. 'Is there anything else you can recall, either from that night, or from any of your time in CAS that you believe could be of any relevance to this?'

'No, there is not,' said Gareth.

When it was clear that all avenues of investigation with Gareth had been exhausted. Brian and Josh took their leave of Gareth and made their way out and back along the path to the car park where Brian's car was still parked alone.

'So, Dr John McFay is likely a person covered by secrecy provisions,' said Brian to Josh when they were a reasonable distance away from the monastery buildings.

'It certainly sounds like he was the original contact who came up with the advice to change flight paths,' said Josh.

'Of course, he might have gotten that advice from yet another contact of his own,' said Brian unsure of whether Elsie intended for him to let Josh know that piece of information. 'But I'm guessing the name of that person would be impossible to find out.'

'I should imagine so,' agreed Josh.

Brian and Josh got into the car and began making their way back towards their workplace. On the drive back to the central Sydney area, talk of the missing plane still dominated the news on the car radio. As yet, no trace of the plane had been found and experts were no closer to agreeing on what might have happened to it. Brian still hadn't quite gotten over the shock of what he witnessed in phone intercepts at the beginning of the week either. It was a very perplexing mystery, to be sure, but what weighed heavily on him were the many lives lost so fast, and in such a short space of time.

A spokesperson for the airline came on the radio:

'We wish to express our deepest sympathies to all who had loved ones on our scheduled flight to Hong Kong. At this time, we do not hold out hope of finding anyone alive and will be downscaling our search,' came the official's voice. 'We will continue to work with government and police partners to find the cause of the disappearance.'

Brian wondered sometimes what exactly Elsie and her team were investigating in relation to it. Even if it was an act of terrorism, then how could they find evidence here in Australia that would relate to it? They probably had to investigate and clear every single person involved in the security advisory businesses that the missing plane's company dealt with, and all because some of them were Australian citizens. It felt rather odd to be an assistant of sorts to their team, while being always in the dark about what the main purpose of things were. Brian couldn't help but feel an incredible growing curiosity within himself. *If Elsie's team wanted more information about some of the people she had and hadn't named, did that mean that they were suspected of helping terrorists?* Brian felt sick to his stomach imagining a respectable Australian citizen doing something so heinous.

CHAPTER FIVE

The next field trip on Brian's investigatory journey took him to a tertiary institution in Sydney, so there was not too far to travel from his base for this round of face-to-face chats. The person he had arranged to meet with was the woman professor that Gareth had been in contact with. Emeritus Professor Alice Wirth was an expert in physics according to the brief biography he had read of her on the internet. She had been most accommodating from the very beginning when he had first contacted her and asked if he could speak to her in person on some vague subject matters. Brian brought Josh with him when he went to the university to meet with her. When the departmental secretary showed them through to her office, she answered her door after one hard knock.

'Just a minute,' she yelled out as she got herself up out of her chair to make a move towards greeting the inquisitive police officers. As she opened the door, she gave a serene sort of smile. She was a rather masculine looking woman - a thought that came to Brian's mind, but which made him feel guilty almost immediately, because it was as if he had fallen into the trap of seeing women in traditionally male dominated roles as less feminine somehow. But indeed, when he studied her more carefully, she really did have a slightly more masculine appearance than was typical. She was quite old now, and in fact only in the university as an emeritus professor, meaning she was post-retirement, *or well post-retirement* thought Brian to himself now that he had seen her in person. Her advanced years meant that she was quite scrawny on what would once have been a large, broad and striking frame for a woman, with a large and unusually broad jaw, though now her cheeks were clasped in around it.

She was most welcoming, 'Pleased to meet you, you must be the officer who spoke to me on the telephone, oh, do come in both of you. And thank you Ellen', she said to the admin worker who had kindly showed them to her office door.

'Thank you for giving us this time Professor Wirth,' said Brian.

'Oh, it's no trouble at all, I'm most happy to do so, and please feel free to call me Alice. We have dropped many of the formalities, even around here, since my day.'

The professor seemed so down-to-earth. She gestured towards chairs for Brian and his colleague, and she took a seat behind her desk; through the window behind her, Brian could see students milling around in the courtyard.

'I'll try to be direct and to the point as much as possible,' began Brian, 'and, as I told you in our phone conversation, this isn't a formal interview. However, I must warn you that I will record what we discuss today, and if necessary, it could potentially be used in the future if it were relevant,' Brian informed her.

'That's perfectly fine by me, I'm not likely to have anything to tell you that the police wouldn't already know though, I'm sure.'

'I wanted to ask you if you know anything about the plane that has recently gone missing.' Brian did observe the slight tenseness all over the professor's body as soon as his question came out. And her stare was slightly hardened and fixated firmly into his eyes. It could be that this had sent her deep into thought. Or focusing on how she might be convincing in a denial of useful knowledge of this.

'Oh, take your time,' said Brian glancing around the room quickly. It was a typical professorial set-up: two book filled walls on either side of the professor's desk, and some displays of post cards and thank you notes pinned in various places, meant to show the lighter side of their work perhaps. Brian's gaze returned to the professor who still sat deep in thought.

'I'm afraid,' said Professor Wirth after what felt like an eternity. 'Like other experts it seems, I have no idea what has possibly happened to that missing plane. It's truly a mystery so far.'

'It's just that we have been informed by a Dr Gareth Hughes that he contacted you on the night that the Hong Kong flight went missing,' said Brian. 'He said he wanted advice on some flight paths of international airlines. And if you don't mind me asking, why would anyone approach you in relation to this in any case?'

'Oh yes, that,' said Professor Wirth. 'Yes, Gareth did contact me that night.' The memories seemed to be returning to the professor all of a sudden.

Brian wondered if it were really possible for someone, even at the professor's age, to forget a conversation like that given what had happened afterwards. It seemed more likely that the professor had hoped to avoid discussing the subject with Brian and Josh altogether. *But could she seriously have believed the police wouldn't have heard about her conversation that night?* wondered Brian. *Maybe she was used to CAS employees being more tight-lipped than Gareth had been? That would make sense since Gareth became involved in the conversations that night almost by accident.*

Slowly she responded, 'Gareth is an investigator on a joint project the university has running with CAS. I'm involved too, so Gareth knows me fairly well, and he has my private home phone number. I should say that was the primary reason that it was me he chose to contact in relation to his urgent query.'

'Would you mind telling us, in your own words, what Gareth said to you that night and what you understood to be the issue.'

'Certainly,' said Professor Wirth. 'Gareth woke me up in the middle of the night saying that someone from Asia had been trying to get a hold of some CAS employee. The reason being that he had been made aware that someone in CAS had given some advice to Australian air carriers relating to a flight route which the company he worked for was also using at the same time. My understanding was that someone in CAS had advised the Australian air carriers to make changes to their flight path to avoid part of it. I didn't know any more of the detail than that.'

'So, it was rather a difficult position that you were put into then, being asked to give an opinion with only very vague information,' commented Brian trying to make an empathetic connection with the woman.

'Yes, indeed,' replied Professor Wirth.

'So, did you give any advice or opinion yourself?'

'I don't believe I have done anything illegal here.' Professor Wirth sounded slightly defensive, this being the most expressive she had been since he began speaking with her, 'I merely expressed my own opinion on the situation, which was, if a CAS employee had advised avoiding an area, then I would do it. I didn't make any decisions for anyone. So, was that Asian man calling on behalf of the now missing plane then?'

'As it turned out, yes he was,' said Josh eagerly.

'Oh,' said the professor looking down at her feet and biting her lip with an expression that suggested Josh had just confirmed something that she had suspected already.

'Do you recall the name of the employee or employees of CAS whom were believed to have originally given the advice to the Australian carriers to change flight paths?'

'I don't recall. I'm sorry, but I really can't help any further.'

Brian noticed immediately how she seemed sure at that point that there was nothing more useful she could add. 'I wouldn't say that quite so fast, even seemingly small details can mean so much. Does the name Dr John McFay sound familiar?'

Professor Wirth paused for a moment. 'Oh yes, it does. Did Gareth tell you that? He would remember better than I would, being much younger.'

Another attempt to avoid giving information, thought Brian. 'Do you know Dr John McFay well?' asked Brian.

'Only a little. I've met his wife a few times in passing, too, Dr Karen McFay is her name. She works within the academic environment, just as I do, but I really don't have anything useful to add in relation to either of them to be quite frank with you.'

'Were you informed that a pilot from Germany was involved in discussions about the plane routes that night, and could anyone matching that description be someone known to you, or who you have heard about before?'

'No, I was not informed about that at all, who else specifically might have been involved in discussions I mean, or any details about them, and I definitely am not acquainted with any German pilots. I was just asked about my opinion on a situation in vague general terms.'

'What about the name Mr Li Wu? Is that known to you at all?'

'Why yes, it is,' Professor Wirth replied quickly. 'He studied here in Australia. In fact, he was in the same department studying for a master's degree as that in which John's wife Karen works.'

'It's a small world, isn't it?' commented Brian surprised by the coincidences.

'When people work in such areas of speciality as we do, it is a very small community around the world indeed.

'If I am permitted to ask you then, Superintendent, was Mr Li Wu the man who was on the phone to Gareth from Asia?'

'At this stage we prefer not to release the names of those negotiating on behalf of the airlines involved in the recent tragedy.'

'Oh, I see,' replied Professor Wirth. 'It's just that, if it were him, you might have wanted to know that there was some unpleasantness in the university here whilst he was a student. Some bullying, and incidences of fraud among some of the staff, that he had revealed. Some of them might have blamed Mr Li Wu for uncovering it, is all, being an ex-police worker as he was. I don't know the details beyond that, because I wasn't accused of, or embroiled in any of it, but I am sure some here in the department who were involved, either in investigating and trying to mediate the situation, or by having been named as taking part in the bullying, would know some more. The head of department would be the person to ask about all of that, and the administrative staff should be able to point you in the right direction there too.'

'Well, in fact, it seems you did have quite a lot of information after all, Professor Wirth, there's rather a lot here.'

'Yes, yes indeed when I think on it.' The professor turned her face away as she said that. 'Well, there's really nothing more I know on that topic so unless there's another query you had, I think that would be all I can tell you.'

'That's all I had to ask about, Professor. Again, thank you very much for giving me this time, and I'll be in touch should anything else come up.'

'Did you have anything further you wished to add here?' said Brian to Josh, almost as an afterthought. Josh merely shook his head to signal that he did not.

Brian stood from his chair and gave an empathetic sort of nod in the professor's direction. Josh rose too, following his lead.

'Oh yes, do feel free to get back in touch if needed, Superintendent, I'm happy to help in any way I could. Goodbye,' said the professor in her most helpful tone.

'Goodbye, have a pleasant afternoon.' And with that, Brian and Josh left her room with much to mull over. They made their way outside into the sunshine, and in the courtyard found themselves among the throng of young students they had seen through the window. The professor had been exceedingly accommodating, a woman who must have been approaching her eighties, she'd made her way to the university that day and agreed to speak with them. Yet for all her accommodations and outward pleasantries, she was very intense. Brian wondered if all physicists were like that, just like the stereotype often associated with mathematicians or astronomers. Perhaps that was just her usual manner, he thought, but there definitely was something that made him feel slightly uncomfortable during their meeting.

'Did you get the impression that the professor was hoping to avoid telling us about that conversation altogether?' Brian asked Josh when they were back inside their car.

'Definitely. I think that if it weren't for us already having knowledge of it from Gareth, we would be none the wiser just now.'

'Why do you think she would be so secretive, when as she says, she didn't do anything illegal?' Brian asked Josh.

'You just have to look at the state that Gareth's in now,' said Josh. 'No-one wants to be the person associated, even indirectly, with an incident that cost the lives of hundreds of people, no matter how innocently or how understandable any mistakes made were. Their own guilt is probably hard enough to bear without judgement from others added to it.'

'That was my line of thinking, too,' agreed Brian. 'Interesting what she told us about the unpleasantness in the university department that Li Wu studied at, and which Dr McFay's wife Karen worked at. That could be the very grudge against Li Wu that we've been looking for in terms of potential motives.'

CHAPTER SIX

'What was your impression of Professor Wirth then?' was the first question that Elsie asked Brian when they met up early in the morning, in her always impeccably neat little office, to compare investigatory notes.

'She was very much the stereo-typical female professor,' was Brian's immediate response, *and not very feminine in her features or manner*, he thought, but did not add. 'She didn't say anything suspicious, but she mentioned something potentially enlightening.'

'What was that then?' asked Elsie.

'She told me that the wife of Dr John McFay from CAS, works in the same university department that Mr Li Wu had studied at here in Australia, and that there was some unpleasantness whilst he was there.'

'That is interesting,' agreed Elsie, but with a slight look of concern in her eyes. 'Worth checking out at least.'

'Yes, I think so, I'll get on to that now,' said Brian wondering if Elsie was concerned about stepping on the toes of those covered by secrecy provisions. 'Dr McFay and his wife will be next on my list to interview.'

'You should be aware Brian, that at this stage, Dr John McFay is under no obligation to speak with us about anything which transpired that night,' clarified Elsie.

'Oh, I see,' said Brian.

'I'm sorry,' said Elsie feeling the need to apologise, and looking almost a little flustered about that.

'No, don't be, it's not your fault that this is all a little unusual and awkward. Anyway, I better get on with this investigation. Catch you later,' said Brian leaving the room.

'Sure, bye.'

The focus on Superintendent Brian Andersen's mind, as he made his way back to his own desk where he began getting on with another day in the office, was in sticking to old fashioned police methods: hunt down scandals, get the real stories, and follow the trails of money. After all, in the lead up to the plane disappearance, quite a few damaging incidents and allegations had come to light. Professor Wirth mentioned she was aware that there had been bullying and fraud in her department, which most likely did lead to scandals and missing or purloined money. On top of that, further files had been released to Brian regarding Mr Li Wu's former police team colleagues in Asia in their international paedophile sting operation. They implicated lots of Australian citizens, some Brits, some Canadians and some Americans even. Many people around the world were referenced in one way or another throughout the files and transcripts that had been collected. However, so far there was no indication that this would have impacted anyone in CAS, and with all the secrecy surrounding certain people, there was no easy way for Brian to dig deeper. That meant the university spat that unfolded in Dr Karen McFay's department seemed to have far more potential as an avenue for searching for answers in the case at hand at this point.

Finding information on a fraud or theft scandal at a major Australian tertiary institution via official channels wasn't going to be easy either though. And no doubt it would take a fair amount of time to obtain any information, even if the university did agree to release it to Brian. Brian decided to take an alternative route, that of tracing and questioning some of the staff members who were working there at the same time as the fraud occurred, and while Mr Li Wu was studying there. Elsie had helpfully given Brian all of the details of Li Wu's study in Australia, such as who he worked with whilst there, and finding them online was very easy. Mr Li Wu had received joint supervision from two staff members who had both left the university in the wake of the scandal. And he had also done some collaborative work with another higher research degree student whilst there; she was now a postdoctoral researcher in the same department. Brian decided that these three people were who he would try to contact first.

Brian contacted the first person on his list via telephone, it was a male former staff member who had co-supervised Li Wu's thesis, a Dr James Crawford. Luckily, he was available and he was at home to take the call the first time Brian tried phoning him. Brian figured that was since he wasn't in full-time employment these days. He seemed very eager to open up to Brian over the phone, and hadn't required much prompting at all, in stark contrast to the last interview he had done of a Sydney academic. He explained that the stress of the bullying he suffered at the university had taken its toll on him. He had had a complete nervous breakdown when it happened, and eventually he just took an early retirement package and left the workforce as he was unable to cope with the stress of going in there every day and having to face those involved. He claimed that he had lost all confidence in his working abilities and felt unable to find another faculty position. He recalled supervising Mr Li Wu, describing him as a polite man, and a very conscientious student. He didn't know anything about the fraud that had taken place while he was working there though, and he said he knew next to nothing about the private lives or work lives and contacts of the two staff members whom he later discovered had orchestrated the bullying he experienced. One of them, he claimed, was Dr Karen McFay. *Dr John McFay's wife.*

'Then who was the other staff member involved in orchestrating things?' was the natural question Brian was left with in this mind.

'Oh, the other was another female staff member who just so happened to be a Professor. Professor Hart is her name; so she had a lot of influence and was able to cause a lot of trouble for me, if you know what I mean.'

'If you could elaborate some more on what you mean, that would be helpful to me.'

'Well, it began with all the small things. Such as, if say, I asked for a rescheduling of classes I had been allocated to teach, she would find a way to create an objection and obstacle there, even if it in no way involved her classes or students, and didn't affect her in any way at all. But even so, that would then mean others on the organising committee would have to debate and consider that. There were lots of similar type incidents; sometimes they would delay things for me, then find that my request was reasonable and let me do as was planned, albeit after some unnecessary stress and hassle for me, but on a couple of things they just went along with totally blocking something for absolutely no real reason, other than not to disagree with her, the female Professor. She and Karen didn't work together on research or course design, but they were thick as thieves. They had actually known each other from their school days long before they both came to work in the same department. Then coupled with that was the clout or 'respect' that Karen just naturally had due to the simple fact that she was the wife of someone in the department who himself was very much one of the boy's club. So, as you can imagine, I was really up against it there. They might sound like little insignificant things I've described they were doing, but you know, these things build up over the years, and eventually you can reach a point where just one more frustrating thing is like the straw that broke the camel's back. That, and also because it did escalate over time. The things they did gradually started to become slightly more serious, in that they had the real potential to harm my career, or even end it entirely, as well as to cause me serious reputational damage.'

'Do you know what it was that made them start on you?'

'I really don't officer,' said Crawford breathing out a sigh. 'It was like I just got on their nerves for some reason, and from that point onwards, I could do nothing right.'

'Was there anything else that you think it is worth me being aware of, anything else about it all that particularly sticks in your mind?'

'Not really, no, there's nothing more I can think of to add on all of this.'

Brian sympathised with the man. 'I'm no expert in science, Dr Crawford, and by all accounts astrophysics is a very difficult study area. I was told that was your specialty and that you had done some important work during the decade that you were employed at the university. I'm sorry to hear that you felt your career was cut short.'

'Yes, yes, it's very sad indeed,' came the voice on the other end of the line. Dr Crawford had a rather quiet voice and spoke slowly and carefully. 'I've reached a place of acceptance now. I put in years of hard work as a student, then as staff I worked hard and didn't get into any trouble, or cause anyone else any trouble, but nonetheless, nothing I did was ever good enough. They just didn't seem able to stop the bullying, they were so organised, so subtle, it was so hard to prove.'

Then there was a heavy pause on the phone line: 'Oh, I'm becoming overwhelmed due to remembering it and talking about my rather wasted career. Well, I'm glad I was able to contribute some useful things while I was still there. That's something.'

'Yes, Dr Crawford, that's very true. Well, thank you again for speaking with me.'

'No problem, my pleasure, I hope it was helpful. Goodbye.'

Some useful information from him, thought Brian as he hung up the phone. The stress and remorse in the man's voice had been palpable though, even over the phone, so much so that Brian felt a tinge of guilt for having put him through the ordeal of having to answer his questions. But Brian felt somewhat satisfied and had a better understanding of the dynamics in their part of the university world. The conversation had also independently confirmed what Professor Wirth had said about something having gone very wrong in relation to staff culture during the period that Li Wu studied there. What transpired had clearly had an impact on more people than just those actively involved in the alleged fraud, a serious and insidious crime that was just very much brushed under the carpet by the sound of things.

*****

The next contact on the list was a male professor who had moved to another faculty within the same institution. He was also quite accommodating to Brian over the phone. He was the other co-supervisor of Mr Li Wu during his master thesis studies. His name was Professor Warwick Miles, and he answered the phone with a bright and almost sing song tone of voice. Brian didn't waste much time getting to the point of his call, and began making some enquiries of the Professor about how he found his time working at the department, and in particular during that same period of the alleged fraud that other staff members had also brought up when interviewed.

'Well Superintendent, yes, I was shocked, shocked indeed by the bullying in that group. I had been working as faculty for twenty years and had never experienced anything like it. I felt like I was losing my mind at some points. I had to take leave for several months due to the stress they put me under. There were bizarre student complaints and issues, although eventually some confessed that another staff member was behind all of that, they had actually put the young ones up to it, can you believe that?

'Well, yes,' replied Brian, 'I would believe it, but it is still rather shocking, like you say, given the status of those involved, university professors and lecturers at well-regarded institutions no less. What I was wondering though, was if you had any knowledge of fraud, or even theft allegations, that took place just before you were appointed there. It was just before they gave you a professorship, in fact, that there was some sort of scandal going on, wasn't it?'

'As a matter of fact, I have heard some things about theft allegations in that department. Yes, they did give me my professorship there, but it was based on work I did while I was employed at another university.'

'What do you know about the fraud?'

'At least two professors, some mid-level staff and a junior staff member were involved in the rather blatant theft ring which saw them steal money from research grant accounts, government top up accounts earmarked for specific staff members, or work-related travel funds. The theft was so blatant that it was almost comical to hear about: money would simply be transferred from the various targeted accounts and put into an account that was opened in the name of the junior staff member. The junior staff member seemed to be a bit of a patsy in the scheme. The two senior staff members, both at professorial level and earning well above the average wage, had set up a role for her that involved co-ordinating the re-imbursement of various expenses that they claimed arose from their research. They told her it would be good for her CV to show she had dealt with academic administration and disbursements. Once the cash was in the centralised account, which was held at another Australian tertiary institution, and managed by an office manager there whose child aimed to be the first in their family to get a place to study medicine, the two professors would then invoice various expenses against that account. The other institution was based on the other side of the country, and perhaps that minimised the risk of staff members chatting and noticing that they were invoicing for more research visits or expenses than they actually performed, allowing the theft to carry on for longer than expected.'

'Do you know the names of any of the staff suspected of being involved in this?' asked Brian.

'Yes, one of them was a Dr Karen McFay, and I'm not sure of the others, but I think there certainly were others, more than one other.'

Dr John McFay's wife's name coming up in relation to suspicious goings on once again; Brian weighed up in his mind just how potentially significant that was in terms of getting a better understanding of the range of the impacts that this one woman Karen might have been having through what she got involved in at her workplace.

'They hadn't gotten away with it for very long though,' continued the Professor. 'It had begun around 2005 when coincidentally a new staff member, a young female scientist, took up a postdoctoral position in the university. She was a young woman from Nova Scotia, Canada, just qualified. She seemed to be one of the targets of the theft scheme, but far from the only target. She was one of so very many as eventually seemed to be becoming apparent when it all started coming out. Unbeknownst to her, she had qualified for government top up funding that should have been added to her regular fortnightly pay. This was just some government incentive programme she should have benefitted from due to doing highly specialised work of value and particular interest to the Australian government at that time. That top-up funding, to the tune of around an additional pay add on amount of $20 thousand dollars per annum, per qualifying staff member, was not disclosed to the young scientist. Instead, it was just absorbed into the professors' personal university accounts. They were caught after around two years of doing things like that, but despite the police involvement which we all heard about, they only answered to an internal investigation in the end. They received orders to pay back the money taken, but they still remained employees of the same university they stole from, and the professors involved in all of that even kept their professorships, which as I am sure you know are positions that command respect and esteem, not to mention trust. Astonishing really, as was just why exactly people nearing the end of their careers, who were earning high wages and had good reputations they took years to develop, risked it all over what was in fact just a relatively small extra amount of income in comparison to their take home pays.

Was the extra money floating around with naive young researchers who didn't really know what they were entitled to just too much temptation for them to resist or something? Had they gotten themselves into some extreme financial strife maybe? Or was there some other reason, like a matter of principle to them. Perhaps some sort of cause they believed in that led to them imagining themselves like they were the robin hoods of the Australian academic funding system. It is very intriguing.'

'Yes, it certainly is intriguing,' agreed Brian. Although, given his years of experience in fraud investigations, Brian had seen and heard it all in terms of motivations people have for getting involved in these things. Motives he had come across ranged from people being faced with temptations they couldn't resist, peer pressure to conform to others in the group established and embedded in the fraud activities already, notions that other people were being handed on a plate things which they were more deserving of, to the outright bizarre and whacky, such as beliefs that God or some higher power had intended for them to have some pot of money that just wasn't actually their own or even connected to them or their own work or family in any way.

'It seemed as though the people who suffered most after the ring was caught, were actually those who were the victims of the theft, along with some other innocent bystanders,' continued Professor Miles. 'In the couple of years that followed, given no-one involved in the incident was fired or even at the very least demoted over it, I was well aware that several non-implicated staff members became the target of vicious bullying, and two or three left the institution to escape the toxic culture that had emerged in their workplace following the scandal. Those who took part in the bullying may have been influenced by the fraudsters, perhaps because they weren't aware of the full extent and severity of the crimes the ring members carried out. The fraudsters weren't even sacked, so from the outside of investigations maybe it all seemed fairly minor to a lot of people. Maybe some of them saw the investigation that was done as like a big over-reaction even. It could be too, that to many it appeared to have been caused by some trouble making young know-it-alls who had just come into the department, and who might have been the ones they would judge guilty in some sense, of over entitlement common enough among those of their youthful age, rather than judging the actual fully exposed fraudsters guilty.'

Misidentification of victims, which is just what Dr Crawford was describing in this, was of course a pretty common occurrence, and well-known of to those in law-enforcement or working in psychology, even if not at all well-known to the general public.

'Were any of the students at the time affected by the bullying. What about your masters' student Mr Li Wu for instance?'

'It's possible some might have pinned the blame on the uncovering of the fraud on him since he had a background in law enforcement. He was only there for one year though studying, so there wasn't too much they could do to him. I think someone who suffered more was the young girl from Nova Scotia. She just happened to start postgraduate studies in the department just before the fraud came out, unfortunately for her, so I think she perhaps did bear the brunt of that.'

'I have her name and details,' said Brian. It was one of the select few details that Elsie had deemed he could be permitted see.

'Oh good. Well, I should suggest speaking to her as well then, to get a better picture of how it was for the students.'

'Then what about your colleagues who were involved in the bullying of you in particular, is there anything you know of them that you think might have motivated them to attack you as they did?'

'Nothing that I am aware of that's for sure. I knew nothing of their other troubles, and if it took place before I started working with them, well I couldn't have been the one to complain about them, could I?'

'It's unlikely, even although it's definitely possible, that they were trying to discover who had found out about their scheme, including newcomers to their faculty,' suggested Brian. Brian was well aware how vengeful criminals could be towards anyone who gets in their way. 'What about Dr Karen McFay, she's a little younger than your two former professorial colleagues, but you say they were collaborating with her.'

'Hmm, well I don't like to spread gossip, but I do believe she was a big driver behind the bullying that I received. Might've been her, but could have been one of the others. They were all thick as thieves, ignore the pun. Anyway, I was never closely associated with any of them, I just knew them superficially as I'm around the same age. We all work in physics, although our specialties are quite different. The general public tend to see it as all more of the same thing, but to us it's actually quite varied, so our research is worlds apart really. I've never had any reason to work closely with them or any of their students. That's about all I know of them officer,' said Professor Miles. 'I hope it's been of some use to you, and in case you are interested, all of my problems have disappeared since I left that faculty and moved over here. All going wonderfully again, no worries. '

'Well, that's good to hear,' said Brian. It sounded like it was a bullying recovery success story. *The world needs more of those,* 'I hope it stays that way, thank you very much for your time. Goodbye.'

'Certainly, goodbye Superintendent.'

Well now, that had been most useful, thought Brian as their conversation ended.

A much bigger question still remained though: *was any of this information at all linked to the communication issues with flights registered to Asian nations during the flight disaster at the start of the week? Or was this just a bog standard and well-contained fraud a case that had grown into something much larger than it should ever have done?* Brian was determined to find the answers to these questions.

*****

The next probable bullying victim on Brian's list was the young female postdoctoral researcher from Nova Scotia. She was still there working in the same department. Apparently, she was on the same pay level and position after more than a decade. *Was that usual though?* Brian wondered. *It was possible that she just wasn't all that good at her job of course, but then that would seem odd for a person scouted out to be hired and brought to this country, and who was even supposed to have been given government top up funding due to showing special talent and abilities in science. Well, perhaps further investigations would shed some light on things, one thing was certain, something wasn't quite right here either.*

Since the postdoctoral researcher had been a personal victim of the theft as well as a potential victim of the bullying that allegedly followed, Brian had decided to visit the department in person to interview her, and arranged a suitable appointment with her. He brought Josh along with him again. This time when they arrived at the university for the meeting, they were shown to a shared room with several young scientists inside. A young woman with light brown hair leapt up.

'Oh, you must be Superintendent Andersen?'

'Yes, indeed, the uniform gives it away.' Brian felt himself joking, almost flirting. *My goodness* he thought, *I'm with a woman a few years younger, and I'm acting so silly.* None of the younger women in here fitted the physics stereotype as much as the older woman he'd met. Professor Wirth truly did embody it in so many ways. Times were changing though it seemed, judging by the looks of this younger generation. The traditionally male dominated areas of study seemed to have finally opened up and gotten with the modern times.

'Thank you for taking some time to speak to us both today, Dr MacGregor,' said Brian using her formal form of address. Angela was the young woman's first name, *angelic name for an angelic face*, noted Brian to himself.

'I'm sorry I don't have a private office to meet you in, maybe we could go to one of the faculty meeting rooms out of everyone's way?' she offered.

'That would be fine.'

'Follow me then,' she said, and without any introductions to the others in her room, while appearing slightly flustered with a bit of noticeable reddening appearing about her cheeks, led him upstairs to a little meeting room with some mathematics and astronomy themed jokes and posters stuck around the wall. They didn't make a whole lot of sense to an outsider like Brian, but it gave the impression they all enjoyed what they were there to research. 'Please ask away officer, what would you like to know about, just that past bullying episode ages ago that you mentioned to me over the phone, or something about the day-to-day work here nowadays as well?'

Brian hadn't been fully truthful about the reason for his interview when he'd made the appointment. Now he launched into the real reason, 'Well, I had some questions about what you might know, or have heard, in relation to some theft of university funds by staff members working here that came to light around 2007. I would like to know if you were questioned or interviewed in relation to that at the time, whether you had any knowledge of it, or any idea of what might have motivated those who were involved?'

Apprehension became readable on her face, it was pretty standard for people to clam up when put on the spot like this by serving police officers, as Brian knew all too well. She began answering his question: 'I heard some vague gossip and rumours that a couple of senior staff, and maybe some others I didn't know, were investigated over missing sums of money, but I probably wasn't even meant to have been told that. I'm not sure if it was just internal action within the university, or if it went further and was heard by any criminal court. I was only curious to hear of it because it involved a woman who seemed, from my perspective at least, to be leading some bullying that I experienced here. It started not long after I moved here; I'm from Nova Scotia in Canada as you might've guessed from my accent. In hindsight, I really wish I'd moved away fast from here around that time to be perfectly honest, but it's a bit late now and it's really not so easy for me to do so any longer.'

'Why is that?'

'Well, family commitments for one thing,' she sighed and paused for a brief moment, 'and falling behind a little bit in my level of competitiveness after so many years here. You see, I've been somewhat excluded and didn't ever seem to get the same opportunities as many others working here on a similar career trajectory did. But I wasn't sure of that being the reality of what was going on back at the time when it all started. I was young, new to all of this world of work, and filled with a lot of self-doubt. I realise now that I'm not imagining that bias that was shown against me, nor was I expecting too much at the early stages of my career. In the past, I honestly was facing too much criticism, not being supported the way others were, and being overlooked for things I had done good enough work to attain. I really should have moved on from here pretty quickly in hindsight, but we live and learn, as they say, and I wasn't terribly experienced when I started here as I said. I was a bit on the naive side maybe too, but perhaps that's just the result of spending so many blissfully sheltered years as a student as I had done prior to moving here.'

They continued to talk for the better part of an hour before Brian wound up the interview, but truth be told, it hadn't really taken long for Brian to gather that the postdoctoral researcher from Canada didn't have much more useful detail to provide him above what was already clear to him, and perhaps it was mainly the fact that he was finding it rather pleasant to gaze upon that sweet face of hers that he listened so long to her at times, rather long-winded, descriptions of things. One important thing was achieved however, which was that she too did independently confirm once again that Dr Karen McFay was one of those implicated in both the fraud and the bullying that followed. The evidence was now stacked up against her to support the picture Brian was forming of her: that she was most certainly an irresponsible meddler who was lacking in ethics and judgement, or any sense of care for those whose careers she was impacting. He had heard her mentioned so much that he was beginning to wonder what she looked like so he could put a face to the impression.

Could ill-feeling over that incident really have been reason enough for Dr John McFay not to notify Mr Wu directly about the concerns on the night the plane he was responsible for vanished? Could he have deliberately withheld that knowledge from him, even when it was such a potentially crucial piece of information? He might possibly have known lives could have depended on him sharing that as well. Or, was it all just nothing more than a coincidence?

Another open question mark still lingered over whether it was in any way connected to the more serious incident of the suspected paedophile rings with connections to Australia that an Asian police task force had investigated, both in the past and in inquiries continuing to this day. That was very much an ongoing case. In any case, it did seem logical that Asian police task forces having access to files on adoption and child safety records that even he couldn't access from within Australia, could have thrown the cat among the pigeons. Relations between science groups in Asia and those in Australia must be interesting, if not challenging at the best of times Brian surmised. But whether that had any connection to the missing Hong Kong plane, and whether any of that could ever be proven, was another issue entirely.

CHAPTER SEVEN

The heat in Sydney had steadily been on the rise in recent days, but for Brian, the morning at least would be spent in the air conditioning as he was scheduled to meet with Elsie. She invited him to come to her office, looking much more rested than she had been and greeting him with her usual warm smile.

'Good morning,' said Brian. 'How are things?'

'All good,' Elsie responded almost without thinking, 'So tell me, has anything interesting come up in what you've been looking into for the past week?'

'I interviewed some people to check out some details of the fraud offences and bullying that occurred in Australian universities in the department where Mr Li Wu studied. What I found slightly intriguing was that Dr John McFay's wife Karen, was one of the alleged fraudsters and bullies caught around the time when Li Wu was there. It's not solid proof of anything untoward, but it could be related to simmering tensions between the individuals affected by it.'

Elsie paused for a moment before saying, 'It sounds so petty, but it's true that people have been killed over much less.'

'Exactly,' said Brian.

'Another piece of information I found out,' said Elsie. 'Was that Mark Wilson, the Canadian aviation security consultant who was alerted to re-route by Dr John McFay had been socially connected to the McFays for about the last decade, mixing in the same circles ever since Mark Wilson married a close friend of their daughter.'

'So McFay's friend was told about whatever the issue was on the flight path then,' said Brian, 'even when they weren't contacting absolutely everyone who could potentially have been affected as standard or anything'.

'It seems like it, not very fair sounding when you say it out aloud, but I guess that's how the world works, isn't it?' pondered Elsie.

'Yes, and they've most likely not done anything illegal either,' added Brian.

'It seems that there was another aspect of Dr Karen McFay that wasn't so well known about, and which you wouldn't know about either,' said Elsie who now grinned like a cat who'd caught a mouse. 'She had an older son by someone other than her husband.'

With that announcement, Elsie paused for a moment, as if for effect.

Brain said nothing, but felt conscious of himself blinking strongly as he stared at her intently, wondering what the significance of it all might be.

'She was happy not to be too closely associated with her son it would seem,' she continued, 'but she did know the nurse and her husband who had adopted him and raised him.'

'Do you know who the father was?'

'It seemed she was once likely involved with an older married Chinese surgeon in her youth, and when their fling was over, he didn't want any damage to his marriage or professional reputation. Maybe it felt like an embarrassment to them to have an unwanted pregnancy at the end, so they found an adoptive home for him thinking it would be the easiest thing for all concerned.'

'Hmmm,' was all Brian said. *It was always worth being aware of things like this, but the truth was, it wasn't really that unusual for people to have or give up for adoption their unwanted babies back in those days if they were an unwed mother. So most likely, it wouldn't bring anything of significance into the investigation. Elsie's research skills were certainly pretty thorough and impressive though.*

He changed the subject. 'Dr John McFay seems to have strong links to the private aviation security sector, do you know of any reason why that might be the case?' Brian studied Elsie closely wondering if this was something she would share with him even if she knew the truth.

'At this point, no, I do not. It is rather unusual and perhaps could be worth investigating further, but that will be rather difficult at this stage given that he's under no onus to co-operate with us. There are secrecy provisions in place.'

That was Brian's feeling as well. 'I think I will try to contact Dr John and Dr Karen McFay next if you give me their details. I have left the most important interview to last, and even though they aren't obligated to cooperate, we might still get something useful out of them.'

'Sounds sensible to me,' said Elsie handing him a file with all of the information he wanted. Then Elsie stared beyond Brian for a moment, 'Would you like to join me for morning tea break?' she asked with her eyes fleeting back to him.

'Yes, of course,' Brian blurted out before he could digest the sentence. He tried to justify his instant response with the fact that it was nice that she had reached out in a more sociable way. However, part of him also warned, *keep focusing on the job Brian.* But sometimes, when he looked at Elsie's very classically featured face and bright eyes, it was hard to do that.

*****

Morning coffee break with Elsie had been a lovely way to spend fifteen minutes of that morning. Brian learned that

Elsie was single, like him, although he wondered from what she said if she had been divorced. He didn't feel it appropriate to enquire though. She lived near the ocean, renting a place in Sydney's Manly beach suburb. They found too that they did also have something else in common: a love of sailing. Sydney was the perfect place for it, and it was something that Brian wanted to make more time for again. In fact, he needed to make more time for his private and recreational life in general. He loved his work, and felt such a sense of achievement when he got promoted, but he had begun to realise how lonely it can become when work-life balance gets mostly forgotten. With that thought in mind, he switched his thinking back to the case at hand.

Brian tried unsuccessfully to get a hold of either Dr John McFay or his wife Dr Karen McFay over the phone for a couple days. Eventually he decided to head out with Josh to try to catch up with the McFays at their home. The McFays lived in a standard sort of western Sydney suburban home with a perfectly manicured front yard, all just as you would expect for a professional couple of their age. When Dr McFay saw police entering the yard as he was gardening, he stopped and gave a serious glance in their direction, looking slightly nervous.

'Hello officers,' he called over, 'are you looking for us here?'

Brian briefly explained to him who he was, and introduced his colleague Josh. Mr McFay started to look a little less tense than when he had first laid eyes upon them, but little beads of sweat were starting to form around his mouth none the less. Brian further explained that he had come to make some enquiries about a couple of matters, and that the first related to the university corruption troubles in Dr Karen McFay's department.

'Oh, I thought that was all over now,' was the exasperated reply from the round faced and balding Dr John McFay who was now sweating quite profusely. It was far more than anyone would expect over some rose bush trimming on a pleasant day such as this one was in Sydney's lovely temperate climate.

'Well, it is over as far as I am aware, but I wondered if your wife in particular would be willing to speak to me as it might help with some other enquiries?'

Brian had hoped that Dr McFay might have taken a break and invited him inside at that point, but he just carried on with his pruning.

'I do not think that's a wise idea at the moment officer, nothing personal, but my wife has been under great strain recently and she was hospitalised briefly after receiving a great shock. She is not well enough to speak to anyone at this time if it involves stressful events, and in any case, she is not here just now. The fraud and corruption probe was terribly difficult for us both, we worried she would lose her career completely, and her pension rights. We were both glad when it was finally over, and we do not want to see it re-opened again.'

'Might I enquire as to the nature of the recent shock?'

Dr McFay paused and stared at the ground intensely for a moment then he answered, 'I don't see why it would concern the police frankly. It was a personal matter: her eldest son's suspected suicide. Karen's eldest son was my step-son, and he doesn't live here with us. I think it was just too much for her to cope with.'

'How did your wife find this news out Dr McFay?'

'The hospital he was initially admitted to informed her as his next of kin.'

Suicide is one of any parent's worst nightmares thought Brian, *and all too often the news of it is delivered by people with no skill in how to best cushion the shock of it.*

'Do they know why then? Why he committed suicide, I mean.' It was not only tragic, but fascinating to Brian's enquiring mind because he didn't believe in coincidences, and this suicide happening right after the other suspicious incidents linked to this same family made Brian wary.

'No, they do not,' Dr John McFay replied to him sharply. 'It might even have been accidental because it was an overdose of prescription medications, they've ruled it as suicide because he was suffering from persistent depression. My wife looked out for that boy for years, receiving photo updates from their friend who raised him to save my wife embarrassment back then. It was part of an arrangement that worked out well for all concerned. People were so judgmental in the 80s you know.'

Dr McFay did already know all about his wife's past love affairs then.

'So, you were fully aware of all of this when you met or married your wife?' asked Brian so that he could have absolute confirmation of what he suspected.

'Yes, I was.' replied Dr McFay in a matter-of-fact way, stepping back from the bush he was pruning to look Brian in the eye. 'The boy was like a son to me, although we didn't discuss it often. I knew my wife had been involved with an older married man, but I didn't blame her for it in any way. It happened years before I married her. He was respected in his field and in a position of authority, while she was a young student when they encountered one another. So personally, I believe he is more to blame for the indiscretions. Their affair ended with my wife holding the baby, and she did what many people did in those days, she tried to find a better home for the child.

We told our three other grown up children the awful news already, so they also are mourning the death of their elder half-brother; they knew him a little. I just wanted to focus on my wife being well again and getting out of hospital, which she did yesterday, before we even think about discussing it with anyone else outside the family.'

'I can understand why your wife must be devastated.' Brian offered while he wondered if the investigation into the missing Hong Kong flight, and his step-father's involvement, had anything to do with the young man's shock death.

'My wife's in turmoil at the moment, she's going through a grieving process.'

'Might I ask, was your wife ever disciplined over corruption in the university department that she works in?'

'There is insufficient evidence officer, and that is an episode we wish to put behind us, so if there are no warrants or charges, then that is all I have to say at this time on any of this shocking business.'

It was a rather curt reaction, but then again people do like to put episodes of being investigated for fraud behind them and move on.

'There are a couple of issues I wanted to talk about today though as I said.'

'Oh?' said Dr John McFay becoming increasingly impatient.

'Yes, it involves the now missing Hong Kong flight that I'm sure you're well aware of.'

'Everyone who owns a tv or radio is now well aware of it,' replied Dr McFay with a tinge of sarcasm.

Josh was jotting all of this down in his notebook.

'That would be the case,' said Brian with a calm tone. 'But not everyone was involved in moving nearby planes around on the night when the Hong Kong flight went missing.'

Dr John McFay looked Brian dead in the eyes. There was a look of slight surprise on Dr McFay's face.

'I think it might be more comfortable if we went inside to discuss this further Dr McFay,' suggested Brian hoping that the man might have grown more amenable to the idea of letting them inside by now. But he had not.

'I think you will find that there is no onus on me to discuss anything about that evening Superintendent. Therefore, with all due respect, as I said already, if there are no warrants or charges then I have said all that I wish to at this time.'

Brian decided not to press the matter any further and so he and his colleague took their leave of Dr McFay.

Already mulling over the events of the day as he walked away, Brian realised how many people in all walks of life had hurtful or shameful incidents in their past that they kept rather hidden. Without realising it, or perhaps realising it all too well, the task force in Asia would potentially have stirred up a lot of painful memories and family dramas for people in the West. *But had that led to any of the disruptions that might've impacted on or even have caused the missing flight?*

It was hard to tell from the sky's edge.

CHAPTER EIGHT

For Brian Andersen, the past week of work had been filled with catching up on paperwork and fruitless hours spent poring through files on Australian fraud, but his weekend had been calm and deliberately he made sure it was void of any thoughts of work. Blocking out work-related stress was a particular artform that Brian had grown to understand after many years as a successful member of the law enforcement workforce. His weekend was made up of time slots that he pre-allocated for relaxing and healthy activities, because otherwise he just would never have gotten around to doing them; these ranged from using his treadmill, to walking along a scenic path, or to completing a cross-word to keep his mind active. He'd read somewhere once that some brain experts believed it to be the best type of puzzle for warding off Alzheimer's disease, and from then on, he was a cross-word fan. It became more addictive over time he found. The wonderful thing about Sydney, literally a city that had just sprawled out from the site of the original landing spot of a sea harbour, was that a stroll along the inner-city streets always meant both breathing in and feeling wonderfully embraced by that fresh sea air. Yet all the while, there was a sensation of also being enveloped within a modern buzzing metropolis; nothing could beat that combination of sensations in Brian's mind.

The restful weekend time he had just passed, had been well needed because Monday morning brought with it another great shock for Brian.

Brian was awakened 30 minutes before his alarm was due to sound by a call from his direct boss Murphy.

'Sorry if I have woken you Brian,' came the calm voice on the other end of the phone line, 'but we've had a rather serious crime overnight involving someone you called on last week: Dr John McFay, the husband of an academic Dr Karen McFay, was stabbed to death last night. As you are aware, he had some involvement in incidents surrounding other flights in the vicinity of the Hong Kong flight on the night of its disappearance. That may or may not be relevant to the stabbing overnight.'

'Is there any indication of who stabbed him?' Brian enquired somewhat stunned.

'At this stage, the main and in fact only suspect, is his wife. She had been suffering some emotional problems in recent months and was found alone with his body and acting unusually. She is under psychiatric examination and observation just now.'

'That is truly unexpected news Sir, but it seems then there is perhaps much more to investigate in relation to the fraud business and any connections to those involved in making flight path changes at the time of the missing plane incident.'

'It would now certainly seem that way. I had held off from jumping to conclusions at the outset, but we have moved beyond that uncertainty.'

'And this has come just after the man's step-son committed suicide as well,' Brian added.

'I have spoken to Elsie and she will attend the interviews with Dr McFay and her family today, she can also guide you in obtaining further information possibly. You didn't meet Dr Karen McFay at all, did you?'

'No, I did not Sir. I only spoke to Dr John McFay himself, but overall, he wasn't very keen on it to be honest and it was a fairly short conversation as a result. He wouldn't even have us inside his house.'

'Indeed, as I thought then' said Brian's superior officer.

'Well thank you for informing me of this immediately Sir,' said Brian climbing out of bed, 'I am on my way in to the office now.'

Brian set about making a filtered coffee to start the day. He glanced sideways at the fruit smoothie maker he bought recently with a view to being healthier through the week, especially when on shift work, but when once again facing yet another earlier than planned and unexpected call out, it all fell by the wayside and hot coffee it was.

*****

Upon arriving in to the office, Brian was given the up-to-the-hour briefing on the McFay stabbing matter. Police had been called around 6:30am by neighbours who saw a blood-soaked Dr Karen McFay wandering around her front yard. She was described as seemingly oblivious to her state of disarray, or in fact how she resembled something out of a horror film. She was just collecting her mail and petting a neighbour's cat. When police arrived, Dr Karen McFay didn't speak at all they told him. She seemed confused, and it was inside that they found Dr John McFay's body in a hall way, dressed in his pyjamas.

Since being taken into custody, Dr Karen McFay was being held in a secure psychiatric unit attached to a private hospital in the northern suburbs, and according to police briefings she had spoken a little about some shock with her son, and how her husband had always known something. She hadn't confessed to anything whatsoever though, and was largely incoherent. In any case, no-one would be having any sort of meaningful access to Dr Karen McFay any time soon; she was under sedation at the hospital and still sleeping deeply.

After being given a briefing on the statements taken so far, he was directed to head over to the interview area. For the time being only the McFay couple's three adult children sat in the police station interview rooms after providing their information and patiently waiting to be released from the looks of them. They were two daughters in their mid-twenties, and a son in his late twenties. All had eyes reddened from crying, and the elder brother's hands trembled as he held a tea cup.

Elsie was already there by the time Brian arrived, and talking with some other plain clothed gentlemen who were most likely on her side of policework; Brian had never seen any of them before. The plane disaster had really brought a new dimension to his role in recent weeks: an influx of new people with a very different work culture from Brian's team, and with access to very different information sources at their fingertips.

'Can I speak to you alone for a little while Brian?' asked Elsie moving close to approach him.

'Of course.'

She beckoned him towards a small meeting room along the corridor and he followed her there. There was something about the way that Elsie would almost set the scene for any new little piece of information she was about to share, that reminded him of how a professional actor would do so before delivering their lines to their greatest effect. And he realised that indeed it did increase the weight of the things she said. He would feel the anticipation growing inside him before she would come out with her revelation, whatever it was.

'I just wanted to fill you in on where we are at with investigating things on our end in relation to this, because as I am sure you've already figured out, it's more suspicious to us given that Dr John McFay was, albeit loosely, connected with the plane that has oddly disappeared, and because of his secret work.'

'That did occur to me, yes,' said Brian. 'I understand completely. Well, I certainly hadn't discussed him with anyone before our conversation just now. Only Josh and I know about his involvement on our side,' confirmed Brian.

You see how the anticipation was building now?

'Dr John McFay's involvement in re-routing Australian air carrier's planes on the night the Hong Kong flight disappeared could be a possible murder motive, but I don't want to jump to conclusions at this stage.'

'That would seem sensible given the circumstances,' agreed Brian.

'Unfortunately, there's no obvious way to get an answer on it right now,' said Elsie sounding somewhat downcast.

Brian reflected on the summary of statements from the McFays' three adult children that he had read. They all expressed disbelief that their mother could have been responsible for the killing.

There was nothing to answer anyone's major questions in the interview notes, and Brian feared that key information that could help solve the aviation mystery was information that Dr John McFay had taken to his grave. He cast his mind back to the meeting with him in his garden, when he was so keen to wrap up the conversation. Now Brian was left wondering, *did this murder have anything to do with a missing plane?* Although that question was arguably more of Elsie's team's concern than Brian's, in their respective investigations. The puzzle of it all intrigued Brian.

Brian experienced moments where he had wondered if he should have tried harder to get Dr John McFay to speak to him for longer when he had called at his house. In hindsight he felt that perhaps he should have pushed more to get a chance to speak to Karen herself, but he had been keenly aware at the time that he had no legal grounds to stand upon. On top of that, there was the added trouble of Dr John McFay having made it abundantly clear that he was finished speaking with police. He was also conscious of the fact that sometimes, pushing people too much on those types of things could lead to a complete shut down and push back from them; that was something which he had wanted to avoid thinking there would have been more time later on to try again with them anyway. *Well, it's all too late now anyhow.* Brian wouldn't have been human though if he didn't ask the question of himself and feel a slight guilt: *would things have turned out differently if more had been done by him and his team at that time to get to the bottom of some secrets? Could Dr John McFay even be alive today if they'd gotten to the bottom of it that afternoon?*

Brian was still really not convinced, despite the circumstantial evidence, that it was Karen who had stabbed her husband. There was no denying that it seemed the most obvious conclusion, yet her being the perpetrator on this just didn't sit right with him at all. *But who did kill him then?* That was one troublesome question left lingering on his mind.

Mark Wilson who was working in aviation security in Canada also played on Brian's mind a lot too. He wondered if he had heard anything yet about the death of his friend and colleague Dr John McFay. For Brian, investigating private security contractors was like embarking on a journey into a parallel world.

CHAPTER NINE

Brian had stayed up late in his apartment on the evening following Dr McFay's murder, reading until well past eleven. He was quite rattled by it, truth be told. The seemingly randomness of it all, while the murder victim was so close to a major mystery and tragedy, perplexed him. He was quite glad he did stay up late that night though, because when he decided to flick the television on to catch the late-night news, he learned right away that the wreckage of the missing Hong Kong flight had finally been found just as the news was coming out. Even though he was so far removed by physical distance from that incident, what he overheard the night it happened had brought it all in and close to his soul. It did feel like some of the weight of that had been lifted with this resolution. The newsreaders spoke in incredibly sombre voices as they confirmed what most had feared: parts of the wreckage had been found floating in a remote part of the Indian Ocean with no chance of any survivors.

The camera panned to images of large sections of the wrecked plane floating in the darkness, eerily illuminated only by spotlights from dive boats, as diving teams worked into the night to recover what they could of it. First and foremost, they were searching for the all-important black box. Another expert was next up to be interviewed:

'Joining me now in the studio is Professor David Kearn who has worked in aviation technology for over three decades,' announced the newsreader, and the screen split to show a man with a thin face who appeared to be in his late fifties.

'Good evening.' began the expert.

'What do we now know about the fate of the doomed Hong Kong flight given today's incredible discovery?' asked the news reader.

'What we do know is that the early investigations of the plane wreckage do seem consistent with it having come down and broken apart on impact with the ocean. So far there is no evidence that there has been any explosion, but divers continue to search for the black box which would give us far more information.'

'The airline has informed passengers' relatives, and there have been many tense and distressing scenes in Hong Kong in front of the airline's offices with people demanding answers,' the news reader added.

'Yes, understandably so, although we hope now that at least they might have some closure in knowing the final fate and resting place of their loved ones. We understand that each and every day since the plane was lost has felt like an eternity to those anxiously awaiting some further news.'

'There have been some reports,' began the newsreader very directly, 'that there were several other large passenger aircraft fairly near to the doomed flight around the time it lost contact with control towers. There has even been some suggestion that the other planes might have had some warning from Australia of an issue in the region that caused some of them to go so far as to change their flight path. Can you offer any insight as to why they might have done that?'

My God, they know thought Brian. *It makes a link between the Hong Kong plane crash and the stabbing murder more likely again.*

'Well, first of all,' began the Professor, 'I cannot confirm or deny whether any other aircraft changed their flight paths that evening. No other company has released any statements in response to those suggestions or allegations. I can only offer some speculation as to what might have led them to do so if they had. The most likely reason would have been either a routing error bringing some planes too close to one another and requiring a revision, or a weather system becoming visible on radars that was considered dangerous to fly into. In the latter case though, we would have expected all of the airlines to have had access to the same levels of information. It is entirely possible though that different airlines could assess the same weather information, but come to different conclusions about the risks that it posed. However, one might also question whether there was additional information that was available to some of the airlines, but not to others, and if so, why was that the case? These are questions that we hope a full inquiry into the incident would help to answer.'

CHAPTER TEN

Dr Karen McFay had been cleared by the medical staff caring for her to be interviewed by the police. Her husband's body remained lying cold in the morgue following an autopsy. While Brian was pleased he was about to finally get to lay eyes on the woman, it didn't seem likely that interviews would be very enlightening at this stage. Karen was being held under custody in a secure psychiatric unit. She had been heavily sedated, and had already been interviewed as much as was possible by the court appointed psychiatrist and also by the psychologists in the mental health unit. Brian wondered what more, if anything, would really be gained by them trying to interview her again.

It seemed the event of her husband's death, however it had transpired, had set her into a nervous breakdown state, and it was hard to tell whether she had capacity to comprehend what she was being asked, or the answers she might have given.

Reports he was given by the psychiatric team were very detailed given the circumstances, but Brian was also offered the opportunity to meet Karen in person for the first time. He chose to do so, partly because he wanted to be able to put a face to the woman he had heard rather a lot about before this unfortunate and tragic incident.

Brian and Josh travelled together to the mental health hospital. It was a private hospital set in beautiful well-watered grounds, nothing yellowing or dried out in sight. They had obviously tried to make the mental health unit as palatable as possible, but still nothing can shake that uncomfortable feeling when approaching the locked doors, having to buzz to gain admission, and seeing overly large security men everywhere ready to pounce when ordered by the nurses in charge which perhaps happened more frequently when the doctors weren't around.

The office staff were very friendly. They offered Brian and his younger colleague a cup of tea instantly. Brian declined, but thanked the nurse well.

'We should just like to pop in to visit her as soon as we can,' said Brian.

'Well, you can do that right now if you'd like,' said one of the nurses, 'because there is no-one with her at the moment. Her daughters were in earlier and she has seen a doctor and the psychologist. I'll just come with you and we'll take some security with us given the suspected background we have for her just now.'

Eventually they arrived at Karen's locked room. Karen was in her late 50s, with the face of a middle-aged woman who protected herself well from the harsh sunshine of Sydney. She looked unremarkable with a pale complexion, but she sat extremely still, and appeared to be staring ahead blankly. She didn't even turn around when Brian entered her room.

'Good morning Dr McFay,' said Brian approaching her. 'May I sit here beside you?'

Karen gave no reply. She simply continued to stare straight ahead.

In his training he had been taught to always just go through the motions in all situations, even when dealing with someone who wasn't being responsive or didn't appear capable of responding.

'Please take a seat.' said the nurse who was accompanying him.

Karen was a slim built woman with wispy and wavy greyish hair. Her face was thin, and her eyes a pale blue. Karen continued with just staring at a spot in front of her. After going through the motions of introducing himself to Karen, and trying for about ten minutes to engage her in some sort of conversation, it became clear that there was no point in attempting to pursue it any further. Brian always did see people as innocent until absolutely proven otherwise, but how could they get the truth when the only potential witness and suspect was almost catatonic?

Brian excused himself and his colleague, and was taken by the nurse to meet the psychologist in the mental health unit next. He was a very upbeat looking young man, with slick combed brown hair, fashionable eye glasses and well-dressed in a suit. Brian wondered if he dressed so well every day, or just when he knew there was a big case under discussion.

'Pleased to meet you officers,' he said, 'I am the psychologist assigned to Dr Karen McFay's case. As you are aware, she has completely broken down and it was not possible to conduct a meaningful interview with her. We did make attempts to talk to her about her late husband and if she remembered anything etc, but aside from a few murmurings, her saying something like 'didn't do', at one point, we didn't get very far I'm afraid. Our understanding is your forensics team are gathering the physical evidence to try to ascertain what happened, although it seemed that Karen was the only person with her husband.'

'Have you treated Karen in the past?'

'Yes, we have officer, she has had stress induced mental breakdowns in the past, although they have never been as severe as we are currently witnessing.'

'Was she ever assessed as being at risk of being violent to herself or others?'

'No, she was not, she would have remained in hospital if she had been.'

'So, it was a big shock to the staff here too then when you were informed of what happened to Dr John McFay, and that Karen is the main and only suspect so far?'

'Yes, I was deeply shocked. Unless there had been major changes in their family dynamic that we were not aware of, it was the view of professionals here that Karen was safe and supported at home with a caring husband and some grown up children around too. She had a mental health care plan with her GP and follow up with a psychiatrist in her community, but there was never any concern about violence at all.'

'Were you told that Karen had fairly recently had a great shock regarding her eldest son's suicide?'

'Yes, we were.' the psychologist looked visibly concerned, 'That is a very big shock for anyone, and we had factored it into her care plan.'

'The court appointed psychiatrist will be given access to police notes on that matter. No doubt the way she responded to the suicide of her son will factor into their conclusions.'

'I should expect so,' came the reply from the psychologist. 'I'm afraid the psychiatrists on duty are too busy to speak to you at this time, and they did speak to your colleagues already. I hope you understand. I also hope I've summarised for you all that they assessed and got from her during interviews, little as it was, in our psychiatric assessment notes that you may have.'

'Yes, indeed. Thank you for your time,' said Brian taking his leave of the man.

He stood for a brief moment looking upon the sad empty broken shell of a woman that Dr McFay had become. He tried to imagine how she used to be when she was younger, a woman in science, someone who would be leading students, leading research, and look at her now.

Why is life so horribly cruel?

By the time he was walking out of the exterior secure door, he just felt hugely relieved to be outside again and leaving behind the rather unpleasant feeling place.

*****

Brian had the young officer take the car around to the parking lot, that way he was able to hop out as soon as they arrived back at the station. It was nicer in many ways after having been promoted; these little luxuries were worth enjoying. On the other hand though, having more freedom to choose what was worthwhile to investigate, and when, had its own burdens too. Or maybe only for those who took their duties very seriously.

It seemed most people on earth would believe Dr Karen McFay had indeed stabbed her husband to death given the circumstances. It was the most logical deduction, and there were no reports of anyone else on the scene. Yet, it just didn't sit quite right with Brian. Maybe it was because it wasn't so long ago a jumbo plane full of people had vanished before being found crashed, while other planes in the vicinity had been diverted and all of this was connected to the deceased. Brian found it hard to tell if that were his own superior judgement and experience and therefore a concern that should be listened to, or if it were just that it was too hard to accept that Karen would do that to her husband after so many years together. Then again, sometimes people just snap, and she had been under so much pressure.

Just like Brian, Elsie also wasn't immediately convinced of Dr Karen McFay's guilt either. She had left a message for Brian asking him to come to her office when he had the chance so that they could discuss what had happened. Brian headed around to Elsie's office to see if he could speak to her right away. He found her in her office when he got there.

'Oh hello,' said Elsie pleasantly. 'Thank you for coming by, did you see the message I left for you then?'

'Yes, I did,' confirmed Brian. 'And I assume you've seen all the news about the missing plane having been found?'

'Yes, that's a relief in a way for many I'm sure, because they know now what has happened, they're not left wondering whether their loved ones and friends were hijacked and in the hands of terrorists somewhere.'

'True. The not knowing must have been horrendous,' agreed Brian. 'Personally, I never believed it had been hijacked, so I was expecting it had crashed. I was surprised that it took so long to find a wreckage though.'

'I think lots of people were surprised by that. We assume when flying on such large aircraft, that the companies who run them have perfect tracking and recovery capabilities, but not quite so, there's always some element of risk. It doesn't bear thinking about really.'

'No, it doesn't,' said Brian. *That would be one way for a passenger to ruin their enjoyment of the inflight entertainment with a drinks trolley on hand.* 'On the news last night, they were discussing suggestions that other airlines had avoided the area in question while the Hong Kong flight crew had not, and it had been unaware of any issues. It brought back that night of phone intercepts into my mind.'

'But I think it's best for us just to focus on doing the job of investigating those loosely connected to this situation among those who have been working within Australia, or have recently worked here, just as we have been. Those other bigger global corporate issues are things for an inquiry to deal with, and I doubt it would be considered appropriate for those intercepted phone calls ever to be publicly aired.'

'I'm sure you're right,' said Brian taking the hint that Elsie wanted to change the subject.

'Well, when I asked you here to discuss recent events, what I really wanted to say to you is, that I'm not convinced that Dr Karen McFay was her husband's killer. I realise how strange that sounds given all the circumstantial evidence, but we got rushed autopsy and forensics results through, and they were inconclusive. Yes, he was stabbed to death, but it was not certain that it was by Karen.'

'The difficulty is,' said Brian 'that if Karen did not kill him, then that suggests another person entered their home that evening, or through the night, but if they did, then why didn't they stab or assault Karen as well? It's not unheard of for a killer to only attack certain people in the home they enter, but it is definitely unusual, especially if their motive for attacking was not to leave behind any witnesses who might be able to describe them to the police.'

'We are actually working on the suspicion that Karen was not at home because she had left the house late at night to go driving and wandering,' replied Elsie. 'It's common in people who are experiencing either emotional problems, psychiatric breakdowns, or dementia to 'wander' even at strange hours, and it seems she had done that previously. Dr John McFay had also told you she was unwell when you spoke to him shortly before this happened, therefore it's entirely possible,' explained Elsie. 'At the moment we have had nothing useful from her in terms of testimony, so I think we need to launch an appeal for witnesses. I don't want to get this wrong, if Karen is innocent, then a very dangerous person remains at large.'

'Do you have any other suspects?' asked Brian. 'We haven't had any other recent break and enters in their area, or any killings like that by strangers.'

'No, we don't, but an obvious motive would lie with others linked to the corruption probe, or even relatives of passengers on the crashed Hong Kong flight that they only just recovered. That's a possibility because it's coming out now that some other air carriers had changed their flight paths on the night in question, so perhaps suggestion of Dr John McFay's connection to the re-routing has also gotten out.' Elsie said.

'It seems far-fetched that it would be a relative of a plane crash victim though, doesn't it?'

'Well, it seemed far-fetched when some feared for the safety of some European air traffic controllers following a crash there many years ago, until one of them was killed at his own home by the father of a passenger in the crash. Therefore, it would not be the first time someone was killed in a revenge attack over something like that.'

'You're right,' said Brian looking impressed at Elsie's knowledge. 'It is possible, but I don't think it's that likely because the relationship between Dr John McFay and the private security contractors wasn't well known to the public. So, is this something your team have begun investigating already then?'

'Well yes, we have a list of all of the passengers and have started going through who they are, and whether any of them were in the Sydney area at the time.'

'Or indeed if someone might have hired a contract killer.' added Brian. 'There was no obvious evidence of a break in at the McFay home, or any other evidence left behind, suggesting a professional job.'

'Exactly, although that sometimes makes tracking those responsible easier, but sometimes it makes it so much harder, depending on just how professional the contractor they hire really is.'

'Of course, there's the loose end of Mark Wilson who was a friend of the McFay family and his involvement with, or connection to, planes on the night that the Hong Kong plane vanished and crashed. Could the information have been released by him?'

'It's possible, but it would have been a foolish thing for him to do since he's a potential target for revenge too. And, interestingly, it's not so much his connection to the plane that crashed that would spark interest, but his connection to another one in the area that didn't get lost or crash. You see, as you are aware, because of the phone calls your team intercepted on that day, there truly were some unusual movements on that evening; some other planes seemed to change their flight path at the last minute. That could have been for any number of reasons though, such as concerns over storm cells, worry about a control tower in the original route, or some other terror activity related concern. Mark Wilson was clearly listed as a manager on the team responsible for one of those airlines that did have a plane that changed flight paths. So then, what we are suggesting is a natural question is: why was the Hong Kong flight not changed? If there was credible information suggesting a change was prudent, then why wasn't it shared with the Hong Kong flight security personnel? And there could be others asking that same question, others with a more personal connection to the tragedy.'

'Do you mean you think someone could want to harm him and his family, ironically because he was possibly part of a group that saved some other lives?'

'Yes. Exactly,' said Elsie with a very serious expression.

CHAPTER ELEVEN

Mark Wilson stepped off of the flight from Canada into the warm Sydney air with his younger wife Keana. Mark Wilson was in his thirties, tall and broad, with jet black hair and golden tanned skin. He had a southeast Asian appearance and a striking smoothness to his skin. When he and his wife had received the horrific news about their friends' father Dr John McFay having been stabbed to death, they had decided to make the long journey to attend his funeral and to offer some moral support to their children whom they had known for many years.

Keana had known the McFays since her childhood; her parents were good friends of theirs too. She had met Mark whilst on a ski resort working holiday in Canada after being given his name as a friend who could show her around over there, and she eventually emigrated to Canada to marry him after a two-year long-distance relationship. The McFays had even gone over to Canada as a family group to attend their wedding. The reality of what had just happened to their family in Sydney hadn't quite sunk in yet.

Mark had felt slightly nervous since arriving in Sydney airport. Noticing this, Keana had been going out of her way to soothe him, stroking his back, sweeping his hair, and taking his hand while they waited at the baggage carousel. He knew she was wondering why he was so tense, so he told Keana he just didn't like funerals terribly much, and that seemed to satisfy her as to the reason. But the truth was, that he wasn't entirely comfortable even being in Australia right now given his involvement in some investigations concerning aviation security on the night the Hong Kong flight had completely vanished. It had been gone for so much longer than anyone had anticipated before it had finally been found. No-one had expected to wait for weeks for news of the plane, and they were still asking why. He reassured himself he was just being paranoid, but random violent murders of people known to him who were also involved that night weren't doing much to calm his overall nervousness.

Mark was so distracted that Keana ended up having a go at hauling one of their mammoth sized suitcases off of the conveyor belt alone before he made any move to assist her.

'Well, aren't you going to help me?' she prompted.

'Sure, yeah I just didn't notice it was ours,' said Mark, and he quickly rectified the awkward situation of his slightly built wife trying to twist it off the belt beside the over eager crowd of other passengers.

Keana always did attract more than a few passing glances from those around her anyway though. She was incredibly slim, with legs of a supermodel, and auburn hair that was always impeccably styled. Together they were a very stylish and eye-catching couple.

The couple didn't have to wait long to jump into a cab outside the airport; it took them directly to their friend Willa McFay's house. Willa was the youngest of the three McFay children, born after her brother Henry and older sister Brianna. Willa answered the door looking completely shattered. She was a very thin young woman, with sharp features and dyed black hair. She had shadows under her eyes telling that she hadn't slept properly since her father's murder.

'Oh Willa, I am just so sorry about all of this, so sad about what happened,' said Keana embracing her immediately across the doorway as soon as she opened the door.

'Me too,' chimed in Mark putting on a sombre expression. It was never easy to do or say the right thing in a situation like this one. 'Thank you for letting us stay here, we will try not to get in your way too much, but if there's anything we can help with, know that we are more than happy to.'

'Oh, don't feel awkward, just make yourself at home, and you should be here after all Mark,' said Willa so emphatically that it perplexed Mark a little, 'and come in, come in off the porch.'

Willa moved aside to show the beautiful expansive and welcoming hallway of the colonial style townhouse she shared with her older sister Brianna.

'Brianna is at work still; she won't be back until later. Just make yourselves at home and follow me,' she said showing them to the guest bedroom that she had set up for their arrival. It was at the very front of the house, shaped like an old-fashioned parlour with a bay window looking out onto the tree-lined street outside.

'Thank you so much Willa,' said Keana, 'It's very nice of you to have us here and we don't want to be any trouble. We might rest just a little and try to shake off some jet lag then have some girl time.'

'Sure,' said Willa mustering a weak smile. With that she left them alone to have a quiet nap before beginning their visit to Sydney properly.

*****

After getting some sleep, Mark and Keana joined their hosts Willa and Brianna at a local Indian restaurant for a dinner. It was as if somehow everything might feel more normal over some poppadums, and at least no-one would have to muster the energy to cook or to wash up afterwards.

'So, how is your mother doing?' Keana had managed to hold off for hours already without bringing the topic up.

'Well, she's been hospitalised, and she doesn't really speak at the moment. She seems to be in some kind of shock,' answered Willa.

'Like we all are,' consoled Mark.

'We don't believe that mum was responsible for killing Dad. I know you probably wonder about that, and in case you had wanted to ask, I thought I'd just say.'

'Oh, of course not, of course not,' said Keana empathetically. 'I've known your mum for so many years and she's never been violent towards anyone.'

'The police say she's really the only suspect,' said Brianna somewhat angrily. 'But isn't that just because they haven't tried hard enough to find any? It could have been anyone come into the house late at night, just because there's no obvious break and entry signs. Maybe it was someone Mum or Dad knew, or they left the door unlocked and were unlucky that someone came into the house, like a burglar or something.'

'I think they often just look for the easiest answer to crimes honestly,' offered Keana trying to be diplomatic. If she really were being completely honest though, she would have to admit that she did believe Dr Karen McFay was guilty. Statistically speaking, it was close relatives who were to blame most of the time. Frankly, if it weren't for Karen being a suspect, the police might be considering Willa and Brianna themselves.

'Did the police try to find out if there was some sort of motive, or anyone else who might want to harm your family?' asked Mark.

'Well, they did ask and we knew of nothing, but there was one thing that the police were aware of that we found out about from them, and well, it involves you actually,' Willa turned towards her sister Brianna as if looking for reassurance. Brianna nodded back at her as if to say, go on.

'What do you mean, why would it involve me?' asked Mark.

'Well,' began Willa. 'You see, a couple of weeks back, when Dad was in contact with you discussing something to do with plane route changes, well, he didn't do the same for the plane that eventually went missing. That might have upset some people apparently.'

'I'm sorry, but this is all a bit out of the blue and confusing, the plane disappearance is a mystery to us all,' said Mark looking stunned that there was knowledge of the conversation he had had with John.

'Yes, we know that news story, Mark, and I'm sorry if this is upsetting for you,' Brianna added.

Mark and his wife Keana looked at each other in astonishment.

'Well, this is awkward, not something that has ever happened to me over curry before,' said Mark trying to make light of his complete shock as the waitress put down the dishes in front of them. 'Why should I even believe that the police brought that up anyway when your mum has just been charged with stabbing your Dad.'

'Wow,' said Keana, 'OK, I think this is something to talk about later on when we get back home. So much has happened recently and we are not trying to throw blame or hurt on anyone, just trying to digest it all really.'

'I think that's right,' said Willa, 'let's try to focus on dinner and whatever else has been happening. I'm sorry we didn't know an easy or nicer way to tell you that.'

'Is your mother going to be attending the funeral?' asked Keana changing the subject swiftly.

'I don't think so,' answered Willa, 'Our brother Henry and his boyfriend had thought about trying to go to court to get permission for that as she is under custody, but since she is in an almost catatonic state at the moment, we decided it wasn't worth trying to fight it if she's not seeming terribly aware of her surroundings just now. This will be something we will have to come back and explain to her a few months down the track once she's recovered somewhat, but for now, we want to focus on remembering Dad, celebrating his life and the good times we had as a family. I know you must remember so much of that Keana, from when we were kids and you used to come over to play at mine a lot of the time.'

'Yes, I do,' said Keana, 'I have so many beautiful memories of time spent with you and your family.'

The conversation of shared memories of good times continued, and Mark smiled and nodded, but all the while he pondered if the police would be thinking about questioning him now, given he had actually been mentioned by name in an Australian police station, and, if so, what he should say to them.

CHAPTER TWELVE

Brian was informed by his superior officer that the McFay children had invited the police force to send a representative to the funeral of their father. It was rather unusual, but nice of them to reach out. Brian volunteered to be the person to go to the service. He hadn't attended very many funerals in his life, and never one of people he had first met in the days and hours before they became a homicide victim; there was a first for everything. The invitation was particularly welcomed by their department because Mark Wilson would also be there. He was a man whom they were very interested in, but whom it was particularly hard to gain information on since he was based in Canada, and there was no evidence of any wrong doing on his part to justify a warrant. It was certain that Mark Wilson was one of the private aviation security contractors who had been liaising with Australia registered flights on the night of the vanishing plane, but unclear who knew about it.

The funeral was being held in a local Anglican church, and it seemed to be a mostly work colleagues affair. They comprised the majority of attendees, and otherwise the crowd was made up of the McFay's three grown up children and their partners and/or close friends who lined the front rows at the service. The church porch was absolutely stuffed with masses of expensive floral arrangements. Brian paused to read some of the touching cards on his way in, all of them very tactful in how they approached mentioning the family, given what was suspected to have transpired at the hands of his wife at the end of the man's life.

Brian made his way to sit towards the back of the church; he didn't want to attract too much attention by sitting down near the family. There were enough reminders of the shocking circumstances of the death as it was with Karen's noticeable absence, without having a prominently situated police officer in people's view.

The vicar was very diplomatic in how he welcomed everyone to the church; he steered clear of the topic of how the death had occurred and merely alluded to Karen by grouping her in with loved ones and family members who were not able to be present to celebrate Dr John McFay's life.

The couples' eldest child, their son Henry, who looked like a younger version of his late father, read a touching eulogy which fondly recalled his parents' marriage and made no mention of any disharmony between them, after which he was visibly comforted by his boyfriend back in his pew. Brian glanced around the church and saw mostly middle aged looking academic types, all wearing sombre expressions. It certainly wasn't easy to know what to say at the funeral of a person widely believed to have been killed by a loved one. He spotted Professor Wirth among the crowd. She appeared to be there alone, looking every bit the woman of the type of profession she was in, sitting serenely, neatly and conservatively dressed in a way that didn't draw much attention upon herself.

*****

The funeral service and burial in a close by cemetery, was followed by a reception at a local bowling club to which Brian had also been invited in a generous gesture by the family. He waited patiently in the crowd to personally offer his condolences to the immediate family and noticed what he assumed, judging by the Canadian accent, to be the man Mark Wilson that he was so interested in knowing more about, and his wife; he was correct in his assumption. He hovered as near to them as he could as people were being shown to their seats, but they were seated by the side of the immediate family which Brian was not.

The meal was a typical Australian style cheerful alternate drop comprising the option of either a grilled barramundi, or steak with truffle sauce, depending upon where a person was seated. Brian enjoyed the grilled fish with some seasonal greens. He passed on the pavlova desert, and was sipping on his coffee when he observed that conversation over at the family table seemed to get a little more heated. It wasn't long until Mark Wilson rose and left the table, seemingly going outside to take some fresh air.

This seemed as good an opportunity as any to speak to Mark, so Brian followed him out through the doors leading to a nice little carefully manicured grassy spot and introduced himself to him with his usual introductory spiel about his position within the police force.

'Nice to meet you Superintendent,' said Mark in his Canadian accent, but Brian noticed he seemed a little nervous or even agitated. The first thing that came into Brian's head was that his unease might've been because of the recent plane incident. Then Brian quickly reminded himself that Mark most likely wasn't even aware he knew of his involvement around the recent plane incident.

'Are you a friend of the family?' asked Brian.

'I have been a friend of the family for many years,' replied Mark. 'Do you really think that Karen is guilty?'

His quick launch into such a controversial topic was jarring.

'It is possible to visit Karen,' offered Brian thoughtfully, 'perhaps you might want to seek permission to do so? Details of the police investigation will be released in due course. It is recommended that all those closely related in any way at all to those involved in this unfortunate death should see a counsellor. We can provide you with helpline numbers if needed.'

'Oh no, there's really no need,' said Mark, 'I'm quite alright. I just need some more time to process everything.'

'Will you be staying in the Sydney area for long?' asked Brian.

'We arranged to be here for the next two weeks.'

'That is a long visit,' said Brian, 'with you requiring time off work at such short notice as well.'

'Yes, that's correct,' replied Mark 'We decided that if we were going to make the trip, we should stay long enough to make it worthwhile. Besides, I could do with having a break just now. We are staying with Willa and Brianna McFay. Sydney is where my wife Keana's family are from too, so we actually have lots of people to catch up with, and besides, she really just wanted to be here for her friend going through this real rough patch.'

'That is very kind of you both,' said Brian meaning it fully sincerely. The questions still playing on Brian's mind hadn't escaped his thoughts though; it was strange when someone was close to two tragedies within a fortnight of each other. Strange enough to take notice and try to figure out possible reasons why. 'If you don't mind my asking, what do you work as back in Canada?'

'I'm an aviation security consultant working for a Hong Kong centric airline route,' replied Mark.

'It was shocking news about the vanished plane, wasn't it? It was so long before it showed up, given the number of the passengers and the size of the airline and things I mean, you would have expected them to track it down within a day or two at most,' said Brian to gauge Mark's reaction. Mark's reaction was a strained one.

'Yes, it has had the whole world stunned, and that includes us too.'

'I heard on a radio programme,' said Brian. 'That some other flights that were on the same flight path as the disappeared plane were re-routed shortly before the incident. Did you hear anything about that, with your line of work I mean?'

'My friends here have already made me aware that police here know I spoke to Dr John McFay the night the plane vanished, and that I decided to re-route one of our planes based on his advice,' said Mark looking rather smug that he was one step ahead of Brian on this.

Brian of course in all seriousness was very disappointed to hear that Mark already knew what information he had about him, although he had known it was possible the McFay's would have told them police were investigating this by now, and that they had a report on his last communications with the deceased. He had just hoped that they hadn't said anything to him about it, because the art of surprise and a chance to observe a genuine reaction is always such a useful tool in an investigator's repertoire.

'If you don't mind me asking Mr Wilson, why did you rely upon Dr John McFay's opinion regarding the route? He wasn't one of your colleagues. He didn't even work in airline security.'

'John has always given me good advice in all the years I've known him. So, I had no reason to believe anything else of the advice he gave me in relation to that plane route.'

'Was he in the habit of advising you in your role regularly then?' asked Brian rather confused by the whole situation.

'Not at all,' replied Mark Wilson. 'I just meant that in general he seemed to be on the ball and gave good advice.'

Brian felt that there was some detail he was missing in this scenario, but didn't expect that pushing the issue further would lead to anything useful so he changed the focus of his questioning:

'Did Dr John McFay ever lead you to believe that he worked for the security services either here in Australia or otherwise? Perhaps in the past or something?' Brian risked just coming out and asking him that bluntly, realising it might be his one and only chance to put such a question to Mark Wilson.

'I know nothing of such things,' said Mark Wilson with a straight face that was hard for Brian to read. 'As I said, I just found him to be a smart and reliable sort of guy.'

Even if it was a lie, there was no way to prove it thought Brian who was feeling more frustrated now than he did before asking the question.

'Well, it has been nice to meet you Superintendent,' said Mark winding up the conversation.

'Likewise.'

With that, the two went back to the melancholy business of being a funeral attendee.

*****

To ensure all angles were covered, the next few days saw Mark's team investigate whether there was enough evidence to make any of the McFay children suspects in either the murder of Dr John McFay, or the framing of Dr Karen McFay; there was only weak circumstantial evidence.

One common motive for such crimes as murder within a family is inheritance. In his will, Dr John McFay had left his share of all marital assets to his wife, although the court would likely have to appoint someone to have power of attorney over her estate given her mental state. In any case, Dr Karen McFay and her husband, after a series of bad risky investment attempts, still had a hefty mortgage on their property and it was in need of costly repairs, so no real strong motive there. *The amount owned by the couple would hardly cover a hitman's travel expenses to be frank* thought Brian in conclusion.

Brian feared that Dr John McFay's murder would be remaining a mystery for the foreseeable future.

CHAPTER THIRTEEN

Brian had been a little surprised when he was given permission to take a day off to go up to Airlie Beach for his mother's birthday by his superior officer, given how busy things had been of late. Murphy seemed to appreciate that the annual trip was by now a tradition to Brian. It was always an exhausting day, going there and back, even although it was only a relatively short flight from Sydney. He arrived by lunchtime landing in the little regional airport of Proserpine, the closest one to Airlie Beach. He was among a throng of holiday makers who were just ready to jump into snorkels and head out to the Great Barrier Reef. No such fun was in store for Brian though, the heat was intense and humid, and felt to him rather like a steam bath. He'd lived in Sydney long enough that he was no longer acclimatised to the weather here. He quickly changed into some cooler linens in the male toilets before catching his minibus transfer to the town of Proserpine. It took around half an hour to get there, and the scenery along the way was beautiful: short little hardy pieces of bush that could survive the high heat tropical climate, stretching off into the sparse landscape for miles, as far as the eye could see.

This was crocodile country and the driver helpfully reminded the passengers of that fact; it was something that visitors from places like Sydney often forgot about. A wander too close to a river bank up here could mean death. It was hard to imagine because it didn't look all that different to a really quiet suburb near Sydney at times, especially when passing the same supermarket chains. Proserpine wasn't terribly large for a town, and the minibus driver dropped Brian directly outside the nursing home. The place had just recently been painted; it looked very bright and cheery.

The receptionist showed Brian to the private rooms of his mother, known to them working there as Mrs Sylvia Andersen, just as it read on her door.

The staff member helpfully knocked the door and called out to his mother inside. 'Brian has come to visit you today Syliva, can we come in?'

'Yes, come in,' came the reply from within.

The door swinging open, in towards the corridor as it did, revealed an old lady pulling herself up from her chair. The deep indentation in the seat beneath her became visible and was a testament to how often she would be found seated there, day in, and day out, as the seasons and years rolled by.

'Oh, Brian you say your name is? Do come in,' said his mother showing him to one of a neat little set of matching chairs with a coffee table in between. 'Would you like a cup of tea?'

'Oh, I don't wish to be any trouble to you, and yes, I am Brian, pleased to meet you,' said Brian shaking her hand as if it were the first time they had met. Sylvia didn't recognise Brian as being her son any longer. Brian recalled how painful it had felt the first time that had happened, but by now, he was used to it. Or so he liked to think.

Brian's mother always did have a homely look. These days her hair wasn't at all dyed, it was silver grey cut short into her head, easy for staff to care for. *Mum would have hated that previously* thought Brian. Sylvia had spread out a little around the middle, but her face and arms remained slender. She had the most unusual green eyes. She looked in fairly good condition for her age, and of course the Alzheimer's was an invisible disease.

When he would just focus on looking her in the eyes, the rest of her image blending into the background, he could forget for a moment the realities of the present they were in, and it was like looking at Mum just as she used to be. That smart, confident woman, always making sure they were well turned out, and ready to meet the world at the start of every day. If he dwelt on that nostalgia for too long, he would start to feel something like tears forming at the edges of his eyes. It was too much; he switched his mind off. *Go through the motions.*

'You said over the telephone that you were coming to ask me about some events from Airlie beach many years ago, is that right? And do you have some photographs to show me?'

'Yes, I do, shall we take a seat,' said Brian sitting down before bringing out the photographs he had brought of the family over the years, including of his late father. 'Does this man look in any way familiar or known to you?' Brian asked her.

'His face has a slight familiarity, but I wouldn't say he's is a person I know,' came the reply.

Brain swallowed back his disappointment and simply smiled at the woman he used to know so well.

*****

Brian left the nursing home caught up in a strange feeling. He would best describe it as simultaneously experiencing a renewed sense of connection to his youth and roots that was comforting because all he grew up with was essentially still there, along with at the exact same time, a crushing sensation of utter loss in the pain that was also renewed when he found himself once again seeing and confronting what was lost in his mother. She was there, but not really.

He made it back to the airport with plenty of time to wait around the single hall for the evening flight down to Sydney. Traffic just wasn't a thing in this part of the country. It felt so quiet to him now in North Queensland compared to his new normal which was Sydney. In the small airport there was one coffee shop, and happily adequate seating for waiting passengers and those come to collect people arriving, but that was it. There were no boutiques, no international flights or duty-free shopping. When he was a younger man, he couldn't wait to move out to the big city and have all of that at his fingertips, but there was something very refreshing about how it all was up here now though, and he wished he were staying on for a little while.

Then, a new kind of thought occurred to him: he began to think about how nice it would have been if Elsie had come too, and to be doing what everyone else seated around him seemed to have done. It really seemed like everyone else who just arrived in town had either headed straight out to the reef or sailed the coral sea. But there was no time for either of them to be stopping at this stage, the investigation was really taking off, so many pieces of a puzzle coming together. *Besides, what would she think if he suggested something like that? Would it seem overly familiar to her, would she be put off by the thought of being on a trip together?*

*****

Brian got home from Airlie Beach on schedule, ready to fall into bed. His body was exhausted from the heat of the north, but his mind was racing with what felt like random thoughts associated with the various cases he worked on. Something still didn't feel right whenever Brian cast his mind back to the very cold and detached way Professor Wirth first spoke to him, and it just kept coming into the forefront of his mind. For a fleeting moment, Brian had the horrid thought that her colleague Dr John McFay could have deliberately withheld the information that could have saved a plane full of people. Perhaps Professor Wirth even suspected that herself, that might explain her attitude and seeming reluctance to provide names and information. When it did jump through his brain again for a moment, he tried to push it out again, as it made him shudder because it was so cold. *Much like the attack on Dr John McFay* Brian thought to himself. *It could be interesting to know what Dr John McFay and Professor Wirth's working relationship was.* Dr John McFay was a person who possibly might have known Professor Wirth's world more than was immediately apparent, and vice versa.

CHAPTER FOURTEEN

Brian's morning at work began with a knock on the door from Elsie.

'Oh, come in,' Brian called out to her, pleasantly surprised to see her.

'Hi, would you like to grab lunch just outside with me today? Or do you have plans?' she asked.

'No, I don't have any plans and I would love to,' answered Brian. Although he felt rather nervous because something about Elsie made him want to be always impressing her when he was interacting with her, even if just a little.

There were plenty of good eateries near their office in central Sydney, and they made their way there. After browsing some of the window mounted menus, they settled on a trendy cafe with seating outdoors near the harbour bridge. They made good small talk for a half an hour over a coffee and baguette; how continental it felt in downtown Sydney sitting outside and feeling the breeze rolling in over the harbour.

'You know,' Brian mustered up the courage to say, 'If you are keen on doing some sailing on a weekend, well I would be too.'

'Yes, I would be,' she replied without any hesitation. 'I go along with some friends occasionally, but weekend after next I have nothing planned, we could definitely see if we can get on to a boat together.'

'Sounds great,' said Brian. 'I'll look into something and let you know. Something to look forward to.' Suddenly he felt incredibly happy. It was a step in a positive direction that he and Elsie had developed a relationship that went beyond work now, but he still couldn't resist the temptation to bring up the topic.

'I've been mulling the events surrounding the Dr John McFay stabbing over in my mind for quite some time now,' began Brian. 'And it really does seem to me to be highly suspicious given the circumstances with the planes that night. I'm not saying I understand exactly what the connection is, but I have a strong hunch that they certainly are connected in some way.'

'I agree with you Brian, but just like you said, I don't know exactly what that connection is, and we haven't been able to prove anything so far. Our team have completely ruled out Karen as a suspect now which is something I was going to share with you at some point later today.'

'So, you're going with the theory that she wandered that night and came back to find the scene, then had a complete mental breakdown.'

'Precisely,' said Elsie. 'While initially forensics were inconclusive, they have come back saying that they believe blood evidence points to her not having approached his body or the close environs until after he had passed away. As far as they are concerned, she could not possibly be the killer.'

'Is she any more coherent now?' asked Brian.

'Not really, she's much the same as she was when you saw her.'

'That's sad to hear,' said Brian. 'And appeals to the public for witnesses or information haven't turned up anything as far as I'm aware, is that right?'

'Yes, that's correct unfortunately.'

'Do you think this is going to be solved then?' asked Brian.

'Honestly,' said Elsie looking a bit sad. 'I hate to say it, but I really just don't think so.'

CHAPTER FIFTEEN

This morning was Brian's sailing day with Elsie. While he was looking forward to it, truthfully, he felt a little anxious about being on a boat with Elsie for five to six hours in case they ran out of things to say to one another. Their conversations had always felt easy and natural thus far though, so he was hopeful it would all go smoothly. He even wondered if he should pack some Champagne, *but would that be too weird and make it seem like he was implying they were on a date? Elsie could feel awkward about that then. Or was he just over-analysing things again, was it just generous and normal for him to share a gift with her?* Finally, after much agonising, Brian decided against bringing the Champagne.

By the time Elsie pulled into the harbour car park in her little hatchback city car, Brian was already at the vessel, having signed all the necessary paperwork to take the yacht out for the day. He saw Elsie in the distance walking along the shore front and made his way up to greet her. It was a real contrast to see her dressed casually, he didn't normally get a glimpse of the nice curve to her thighs and the slenderness of her upper legs in her more conservative office garb.

'Good morning Brian,' said Elsie.

'Morning, it's a perfect day for a sail; bright, blustery and no chance of rain!'

'We have been lucky, must be meant to be,' said Elsie cheerfully.

But the way she had answered left Brian reading a little more into her words to be honest. He had at times wondered who he was meant to be with eventually, and well, he was a man, she was a woman. He quickly put those thoughts to the back of his head. However today went, he didn't want to come across as that guy at work who reads something personal into everything and can't even enjoy casual pastimes in a sporty non-sexualised sort of way. The last thing he would want was for her to view him as some sad sleazy loser desperate to settle down now after messing around for far too long.

Elsie looked like a model straight from the sailing club magazine. She wore neat white shorts with a sailor style pin striped top. It suited her slim build and well-toned leg and arm muscles. Brian was in his shorts and tee as well. He had gone for a collared tee-shirt though to look a little more stylish; it was so nice to get out of the office with someone he got on well with and had hobbies in common with.

Brian decided to take charge and steer the boat out of its berth which he managed expertly.

'It's just like riding a bike,' he joked to Elsie.

'Indeed,' she said briefly raising an eyebrow expressively.

It wasn't long before they had their main sail up, and were fully catching the breeze, zig zagging their way across the bay. There was something truly calming about the ocean, maybe the fact that even one small part of it had more strength and mystery than any group of people put together.

'I guess you can't really tell me much more about what you have been investigating with the plane and everything?' said Brian almost thinking out loud realising he was opening up shop talk again, then wondering if that was a bit boring of him.

'No, you're right, I can't really,' confirmed Elsie. 'Other than in the vaguest of terms, and as you might have guessed anyway, it's really hard to prove anything when even top experts are genuinely baffled and can't agree on possible scenarios, which isn't a scenario I've encountered very often to be honest with you'

'Were you relieved when they found the plane then?' asked Brian.

'Yes, although I always did think one day it would show up, or part of it would. I wasn't one of those people who believed it could have completely vanished like some x-files style mystery.'

'It still strikes me as strange that the CAS employees had involved themselves with flight routes in the first place,' said Brian. 'It's just not their job. Then of course add that to the violent death of that same involved employee within such a short time-frame, and it's one great big perplexing mess.'

'I think so too,' said Elsie 'It's been two big mysteries happening in short succession. I think we can say that it is an outlier quite confidently, especially now that we've ruled out his wife Karen as a suspect.'

'What about your theory on an angry relative of a passenger on the crashed Hong Kong flight being to blame? Any new thoughts on that now?'

'The team has gone through the list,' said Elsie. 'And no obvious suspects have come out of it.' She looked off towards the distance somewhat whimsically.

'You know,' began Brian, 'I still feel bothered by the fact that I don't even understand how Dr McFay would have come across that type of valuable information relating to plane security in the first place.'

'It's not that it doesn't bother me on some level too Brian,' said Elsie, 'but I have come to a place of acceptance over the fact that we are just not going to find that out. It's almost like something we just have to take as a given and trust that it has come from the secretive intelligence world of our nation which we aren't a part of, with a kind of blind faith in the system.'

'But even though someone out there must know? I mean people like Mark Wilson for one, he was so sure it was worth listening to Dr McFay on such matters that he was basing his work around it. Who does that?'

'I think some things need to remain a little bit mysterious with good reason, even if people like us can't see that in the short-term.'

Brian gritted his teeth, and said nothing more. She was probably right, but injustice was just insufferable to a principled man like Brian. *Grandad used to always say, always remember that no matter how well-intentioned you or your fellow countrymen may be, the big wide world out there is a bad place, and sometimes you have to fight fire with fire.*

As the day wore on, Elsie and Brian found themselves able to drop talk of work for a while and discuss much lighter things. Brian found out that Elsie was divorced, as he had long suspected. She shared that she had married young and it had turned out disastrously. *A woman so beautiful, smart and captivating as Elsie must've had so many interested men around her keen to make a solid commitment to hold on to her that it's no wonder she agreed to marry one of them along the way already.* Elsie commented that she wasn't surprised to learn that Brian was single, and so far, had never married or had any serious relationship because he spent so much time working. Both of them agreed that what they most shared in common was their level of commitment to their work, and a slight, but never bitter, regret for not having had more of a social life along the way. *So, they had rather a lot in common in fact.*

As the day drew to a close, both Elsie and Brian felt their bodies begin to succumb to the exhaustion from hours of fresh air and sunshine as they pulled the lines and cast the sails one way and then the other. The arms were beginning to feel weak, and the odd yawn had crept in for Elsie. As the harbour came back into view, they brought down their main sail ready to cruise into the berth, and Elsie guided them in this time. It had been a fun day.

*****

Brian hadn't asked Elsie to go anywhere else after the tiring day of sailing, and she hadn't suggested anything either. Given how exhausted he was, he wouldn't be much company, *so better to put off any further socialising time until he could be a bit more entertaining for her,* he thought. Brian felt he had to keep reminding himself not to read too much into anything, it was nice to just be in a good friend zone with someone, and their joint task force was still active after all. That meant team building type activities such as today were perfectly appropriate, but going back to a bar or each other's places alone could be taken as inappropriate at this point. This should all be enough to satisfy him for now.

In any case, he, in all honesty, was just happy, and grateful, to have enjoyed such a beautiful and relaxing Saturday and with such a lovely woman for company; Sunday would be a day to catch up on chores. He couldn't help but let his mind drift on to wondering about what Elsie was up to, she might even have had a date already planned for that night, for all he knew. That rather harsh realisation pretty much ended his pleasant daydreaming, and work floated back into his mind again.

CHAPTER SIXTEEN

Monday morning at the office brought a rather unexpected event for Brian: it was a call from Professor Alice Wirth, and she wanted to come to see Brian. *It's not often that persons so secretive by nature decide to seek out the police, so this was going to be interesting.* Brian couldn't imagine what on earth she might want to speak to him about, but he made the appointment for later on that very day to find out as soon as possible.

For no reason in particular, it came into Brian's mind that he should call in on Elsie and just let her know about his impending visit from the Professor. She was a woman that they both found so perplexing, and instinctively knew had a head full of secrets most would love to get to share in. A bit like a living and somewhat more mature Mona Lisa, she seemed to share a private joke in all she said, her gaze certainly did feel like it was a cut deep into a person's soul which they typically like to hide.

'Good morning Elsie,' he began chirpily when he arrived at her desk. His tone was casual, a little more pally than it had been before in his office chats with her, but at the same time not making a big deal out of the new level their acquaintance moved up to since the weekend's outing.

'Oh, hello Brian,' said Elsie looking genuinely pleased to see him.

'Just wanted to let you know about a visitor I have later today as I think it's something you will find quite surprising.'

'Who might that be then?'

'It's Professor Alice Wirth.'

Elsie did look rather surprised. 'Whatever does she want to visit you for?'

'Well, that's what I do not know yet, but I said yes of course.'

'Of course. And you resisted any temptation to ask her what it was in relation to when she first got in touch?'

'Yes, I thought it best just to let her come out with whatever it is she has on her mind all in one go in here.'

'I am impressed by how you managed to keep your curiosity in check,' she said coyly, 'I find it's just too tempting to at least get an inkling of what things are going to be about personally.'

The ensuing hours of that morning did feel long in anticipation of the meeting with Wirth. Brian had spent so much time searching for anything that would give them some sort of evidence of there having been something more substantial behind the conversation he had overheard regarding the planes flying on that fateful night. He felt he needed some sort of closure in the absence of anything solid that would enable him to charge anyone with anything.

Eventually the meeting time arrived, and Professor Wirth appeared at five minutes to the appointment time. *All that she did was so polite and proper*, thought Brian. *All well-brought-up people knew to arrive five minutes before any appointment as standard; not so early as to be an unexpected inconvenience to your potentially unprepared host, but early enough to signal you were prepared to politely wait until the precise pre-agreed strike of the clock they said they would meet you on.* He followed a junior officer round to the meeting room he had seated her in to await him.

'Good afternoon, Professor,' he greeted her.

'Good afternoon, Superintendent,' she was just as he recalled from his last meeting with her, the same calm, polite and proper manner.

'What might I be able to help you with Professor?' began Brian once he was comfortably positioned in his chair.

'Put simply, I want to know whether you believe myself or Gareth to be in any sort of danger,' she began bluntly.

'Oh, I see,' said Brian somewhat taken aback.

'It was my understanding that you wanted to speak to some people in the wake of the plane incident. You spoke to me, to Gareth, and to the now deceased Dr John McFay, wasn't that so?'

'Yes, that is correct, and based upon that I made some further enquiries, all very routine.'

'It doesn't seem very routine Superintendent, if you don't mind me pointing that out. I doubt many others had such investigations into themselves after that incident involving a plane they were neither a passenger on, nor in any way actually connected to.'

'It was because you were, albeit through a third party, actually on the phone talking to the crew of a then missing aircraft,' retorted Brian. *As if she doesn't know that.*

'Yes, I imagine that must have seemed somewhat unusual,' said the professor in a matter-of-fact way.

'It isn't just somewhat unusual, it's *highly* unusual. Through your colleague Dr John McFay, some airlines seemed to have advance knowledge of an incident that was about to take place. And still, experts can hardly agree on what the incident was exactly, even after the fact, let alone how anyone could have had advance knowledge of it as people you knew seemed to.'

'And now Dr John McFay has taken the knowledge of how that came about to his grave with him,' said Professor

Wirth plainly, and rather coldly in Brian's view. *Was she pleased about that in some strange way?*

'It would appear so,' said Brian. 'If, as you say, you knew none of the details, and only gave an opinion based on Dr John McFay's views, then the trail that might lead to the source of the information has run cold.'

'That's correct, just as I told you. But do you think that was the reason that John was murdered? So that he couldn't tell anyone how he knew about there being a potential problem with that flight path, I mean?'

'It's really not appropriate for me to comment on ongoing investigations Professor.'

'Well, I would just like to know whether Gareth and I should be concerned too as we were also contacted by one of the airlines' security contractors that night. That's what I am really getting at here. I am naturally feeling quite ill at ease now after what has happened to a man I knew well for many years, and to another in his family. Who wouldn't be worried?'

'We do not have any specific concerns at this time,' said Brian completely honestly, but for some strange reason it felt so dishonest to say that.

'Then thank you for your time, Superintendent,' said Professor Wirth rising to leave without any further ado.

'Well, if that was all you came to enquire of us?'

'Yes, it was,' said the old lady.

'Then thank you for taking time to come by, and never hesitate to get in touch if you have any more tangible concerns or if anything else comes to your recollection that we might like to know.' Brian stood up too and showed her the way out. *That was somewhat of an anti-climax.*

No sooner had Brian finished seeing Professor Wirth out of the door, when Elsie had arrived at his office.

'So how did your visit from Professor Wirth go?' she asked full of anticipation.

Brian sighed loudly 'It was all a bit of much ado over nothing. She's just rather concerned that of the people involved in phone conversations with airline security the night the Hong Kong flight went missing, one was violently murdered so shortly after. She wanted to know whether we had any concerns for either her or Gareth's welfare. She wasn't in the mood for long chatting though, so I didn't get any new information from her.'

'And I presume you told her that we have no concerns, is that correct?'

'Yes, that's correct,' confirmed Brian. 'Interestingly though she took a different viewpoint on things than we had so far.'

'How so?'

'Well, you know how we had been taking the angle that someone, or some people, might have attacked Dr McFay because he saved some lives that night, but not others. Well, Professor Wirth was asking whether we thought someone had killed him to stop him from revealing how he had advance knowledge of the issue on the flight path that night.'

'Or perhaps because he wouldn't tell them when they asked him?' suggested Elsie.

'Why yes,' said Brian. 'That's another possibility of course.'

'But none of it changes the facts though, which are we still have absolutely no suspects.'

CHAPTER SEVENTEEN

A largely uneventful week passed since Professor Alice Wirth had come to visit. Without any solid evidence to go on, there was little more Brian or Elsie's team could do in relation to the stabbing of Dr John McFay. So finally, it just joined the sizeable archives of other unsolved murder cases in the city where the assailant was believed to be unknown to the homicide victim. Since the plane had been found, even though no-one had a really conclusive answer to explain what happened to it, the investigation into that mystery was winding up too, at least in so far as the Australian police were concerned. The black box had never been recovered with the rest of the wreckage, that was put down to chance, with no officially acknowledged suspicions that it might have deliberately been hidden. All that seemed left to be done, was for authorities to blame it all on inclement weather. Nature was known to be lacking in mercy after all, and that was ultimately what they did.

Then something happened which disturbed Brian's state of being buried, while holding a coffee cup, among the rather monotonous paper work that he was dealing with that day: Elsie came to Brian's door looking like she was almost about to cry. Brian had never seen her with such an expression, and in fact he felt a bit apprehensive at first to ask her what was the matter in case something majorly serious had happened that he hadn't heard about yet.

'Something awful has happened Brian.'

'What?' asked Brian in a concerned tone of voice.

'Professor Wirth has just passed away.'

'Come in, sit down.' *This really was starting to get worrying in light of the other deaths among the one small circle of old colleagues and friends. Hopefully she hasn't suffered badly in some way too, just like Dr McFay did in the violent end he came to.* He motioned to the chair and felt simply dreadful at seeing Elsie so distraught. 'Do you think it was of natural causes,' asked Brian, 'and just another of these people who happened to be loosely connected to the same aviation incident dying so close together?'

'It seems like it, the examining doctor has put heart attack on the death certificate. She lived alone and it would appear she passed away sometime overnight.

'I just feel uneasy about it given that she had just come to see you with concerns for her safety, and we've still got the unsolved murder of another one of her colleagues on our books. She did some government consultancy work that not many knew about you see, just like Dr John McFay. I suppose I can tell you about it now that she's no longer with us, and so the secrecy is no longer needed.'

'So that would explain why she was so certain that the Hong Kong flight crew should follow Dr McFay's advice,' said Brian excitedly as if he had just solved a massive puzzle for himself, then instantly wondering if he was seeming heartless given her recent demise. 'It seemed she worked with him in more ways than one perhaps.'

Brian noticed Elsie looking at him rather sternly, and toned down his excitement a little before asking: 'Is it possible she committed suicide given what happened lately?'

'It's possible, but I don't think so. What would make you think that then?' pressed Elsie.

'I was thinking it could be because of guilt over the lost Hong Kong flight. It's strange how some people really take these things to heart and blame themselves even though there was nothing more any other reasonable person could have thought to have done. It's impacted Gareth badly, he's left his job because of it, and he has even taken to living in a monastery.'

'But I just don't think that Professor Alice Wirth would ever have believed that her actions would have contributed towards the plane crash,' said Elsie emphatically.

'Why are you so sure?' asked Brian. 'Do you know more about this than you've told me so far?'

'I do as a matter of fact,' said Elsie suddenly becoming very open. 'I suppose it's alright to share this with you now that both persons involved are dead. On the night that the flight disappeared, Dr John McFay obtained top secret intelligence that there was a violent storm cell producing a lot of turbulence and hail on the path some commercial and military aircraft were following. It was top secret intelligence because disclosing it might have revealed technological capabilities and movements of reconnaissance aircraft belonging to certain governments, such as our own even, or those of our allies. The reconnaissance flights had detected the adverse weather pattern far in advance of the state-of-the-art radars used by the airlines themselves. However, it seemed that Dr John McFay did have ways of disseminating information discretely when he really wanted to. No-one ever truly anticipated that the storm cell could down a jumbo jet though according to the final official investigation. It seemed they thought at worst that there would be a rough patch in the flight, angry passengers, maybe some instrument damage, minor injuries and difficult questions asked following the incident. Even at that, McFay thought to avoid such problems by alerting certain aircraft. On that night though, as we now all know, the events took a tragic turn as the Hong Kong flight flew directly into the path of a fast-forming freak weather system which sadly did seem to overpower it completely.'

'So, is that all that's going to be in the final conclusions in the joint international investigation into the Hong Kong flight incident?'

'Yes, extremely bad weather basically.'

*****

For Brian at least, Sydney felt so very peaceful again in the days following the official closure of their branch's investigation into conversations and other happenings in the lead up to the Hong Kong flight crash. The main downside to it all though was that his time working with Elsie and her team was now over too, but she told him that she would like to keep in touch if he would too. He felt so elated when she confirmed that they would still be in contact when she didn't have to be. Brian planned that they should start by going out for dinner to celebrate their first official 'date', if he could call it that. Thinking back on one of their first conversations, Brian thoughtfully picked out a Danish restaurant to show her that he remembered almost every word that had passed between them since meeting her.

He would no longer be confined to the realm of work topics for conversations with Elsie from now on as they moved into this new chapter in their relationship together. However, Brian still wondered why McFay hadn't alerted the Hong Kong security contractor too about the potential storm, and figured he always would. He could only assume McFay didn't have the right connections with those staff to be sure his secret government work would be kept secret. Which made it all the more a sad, futile, and still not transparent footnote to a horribly tragic incident.

*****

Interlude

1962

Sally hurried in the predawn dark towards the harbour in the ancient Syrian port of Tartus. She was feeling the strain of what she was in the process of doing, glancing over her shoulder every few steps with the nerves, and growing uncomfortably sticky under the weight of her Syrian abaya dress which was comfortable aside from her scarf continually slipping down a little on one shoulder. She quietly cursed the fact that she could feel her heart beginning to pound within her. Anxiousness can lead to errors, as she had always been taught. If all went well in these small early hours before the people would begin to rise for the start of a new Mediterranean day, the unassuming and slightly withered faced Australian nurse would quickly be back to work, and even walking the hospital wards in Brisbane, Australia, within the next seventy-two hours. No-one would be any the wiser about where she had been. It wasn't easy though to ensure that everything went according to schedule with two emotionally distraught eleven-year-olds to manage, one taking each hand, and her gripping those little hands rather overly tightly in her tense state. On her left side was pretty little Hela, a slightly built girl with a caramel complexion and shining green eyes, and on her right, was her brown eyed, and slightly darker in complexion twin brother Haba, who happened to be the young man with the straightest and finest nose that Sally had ever seen.

In a way, the person who was the most present on this journey in spirit, even if only through her painfully felt absence which left what felt like a gaping black hole in her children's universe, was their mother Helen.

Hela and Haba's mother was a British woman who had come to Syria in 1951. Back in those days she was a stunningly attractive young bride, who was madly in love with a Syrian man named Nabil whom she had met close to home at her own university in England. They had become a couple within days of first laying eyes upon each other, even though the couple's childhoods and backgrounds had been so incredibly different.

Nabil had simply oozed wealth back in those student days of theirs- he was always impeccably presented and dressed from head to toe in designer wear while the other students would arrive at lectures in cheap grungy clothing. That was one of the things that first caught Helen's attention as they sat in classes together. When he took the hint after some lengthy periods of longing gazes in his direction and asked her out on a date, she believed she had finally met her prince charming. The whole courtship was like a fairy tale of old.

It was hard to describe just how different things had been for Helen in the beginning of her relationship with that man. When Nabil had first set out to woo and impress her, no expense was spared. The incredibly romantic gestures he would make for her had her in another world, and she wanted to hear nothing negative about him. He began calling her his yellow haired English princess, and compared her blue eyes to the finest sapphires in the East, as he gazed into them for extended moments with his deep chocolate brown ones growing like saucers and embodying the very promise of fulfilment of human desires. Those times together would leave Helen feeling like she was melting, and had found a place she never wanted to leave or grow beyond. As for their very different cultural backgrounds and religious upbringings, with him being from Syria and her from England, the simple truth was, they never even discussed it.

Of course, when Helen was home from her university lodgings and visiting her parents, shouting and screaming matches were often had over it between her and them. Her mind was made up though, and the more they protested, the more those moments where she was running straight into Nabil's arms, inside which she felt safe and strong with him wrapped around her, were catapulted higher and higher into the dizzying heights of elation and perfection inside her mind. In Helen's own head, there was nothing but an overwhelming sense of feeling that she was experiencing true love against the world. Common sense was no longer a part of her daily consciousness any more, she began living inside her dreams of love and togetherness with that one man who was becoming her world.

As the initial weeks of their relationship marched on and turned into months, her time spent totally alone with Nabil only increasingly intensified in terms of the pleasure it brought to her. It was far from the ever-growing negativity of her parents, and also from some other friends who felt that things were just moving that little bit too fast. The more it began to worry them all, the more they would make the occasional comment to try to remind her of why she should maybe slow things down a little with Nabil and take stock in her life. Then in turn, the more she cut them off, one by one. This went on until she had isolated herself into a world controlled by him in many ways, even if she wasn't really aware of that truth at that point in time.

It was only when their marriage had gone ahead in England, and Helen had arrived completely alone in Syria as a fresh-faced young bride eager to meet her new husband's family, that the differences in their backgrounds, religions and family customs began to take centre stage in their daily interactions. The whole situation became like a mockery of Helen's sphere of existence up until that point Nabil no-longer felt the need to impress his wife in anything at all by that stage; the first major setback she was confronted with was that her British passport literally disappeared overnight within days of her arrival in Nabil's own country. It was then that the family informed her that her husband had decided to cancel any plans to return to England in the near future. She learned from the older women of the family that they, meaning her husband and her, would be setting up a permanent home in Syria. They told her that she had to understand that she now wasn't allowed to leave the house unless accompanied and even then, those excursions outside the home would only happen when she was wearing clothing that would be considered appropriate by their standards, not by hers, and with a suitable chaperone from the family.

From that point onwards, there was at first a feeling of shock, and the creeping sensation that her shoulders were being dragged down sinking under the burden of some invisible weight towards the earth. Over the following days, that sensation was then replaced by a slow, cold realisation that she could almost taste like a bitterness inside her mouth, sliding down her throat and making a feeling of sickness in the pit of her stomach and the bowels. At first, when she still had some spark of life, drive and personality left in her, she repeatedly tried to escape from that fate she found herself in. Sadly though, she had been dragged back every time by the authorities and returned to the home of what was, to the mind of the local police, that of her owner, namely her husband. She fell ever more deeply into the abyss of depression, it became hard to move, and sometimes when Nabil would come to claim what to him were his regular rights to short snappy sex sessions with his wife, seeing her stare lying on her side with no inclination to even move, he would come in and do his business without even trying to roll her over. Not that her lack of energy, interest, or emotion seemed to bother him at all. In fact, if anything it was quite the opposite. He often would smirk to himself afterwards when pulling his body out from and away from his wife, then he would typically smack his hand on one thigh after finding his sense of release through her body, like a man who, if anything, enjoyed that the person he was using was so completely under his control and reliant upon him that they had become almost devoid of a sense of self.

The birth of the twins was something that happened fairly quickly towards the start of the marriage. Helen's own true self had been slowly getting buried further and further into the depths, but when she saw them for the first time, something new began to grow inside her again. It was a strange sort of hope, burning slowly and timidly at first, one with little substance to it, it being rather more like a dream of something far out of reach in the present than a tangible resolve, but in her heart, she knew it was something still part of her, and still pure and untinged by the situation she lived in then, which would eventually lead to something of a better future for them.

The birth of the twins had been long, dangerous, and painful. In Syria, it was entirely up to a woman's husband what medical care she would receive. Helen made it through the birth, which was medically unassisted, with both children born alive and then thriving, but the experience was less kind on her. She began to haemorrhage shortly after the delivery of the second twin, and her husband opted to leave her in the hands of God. Maybe part of what factored into his decision was the disgust that he felt and which even began to show on his face when her feelings of motherly love became apparent as he watched as she weakly raised a hand to reach towards her babies. It was the happiest she had felt since arriving in Syria, and that seemed to be bothering Nabil. However, as the situation continued to worsen, he began wringing his hands anxiously, pacing and revealing a changed expression that had moved from that usual smirk he typically wore when in the bedroom with her, and changed instead into an expression more of concern which suggested that he seemed now to feel something resembling guilt or fear. But then perhaps that thought afforded him rather too much humanity. Maybe it was just that he simply realised that in practical terms, he didn't wish for his mother or sisters to have the trouble of caring for the children if Helen were to die during this birthing time. He would also have had the hassle of finding a new wife, as that would likely be expected.

Whatever it was that led him to change his mind that day, he proceeded to instruct the hospital staff to do something about Helen's awful bleeding. Helen had only remembered feeling relieved through the exhaustion as she drifted in and out of wakefulness. By that point though, it was too late to do anything other than to remove her womb. Perhaps it was a kindness to Helen that she didn't seem to have any awareness of what they were doing to her in that moment to keep her alive, but had she been, she might have noticed the look in Nabil's eyes as he watched the doctors work, and he so fully enjoyed it.

Helen knew then that those twins were all she would ever have to leave behind when she left this world, and she was aware of that from the very start.

With young children in her care, Helen knew that an escape route back to her old life in the West was now going to be even harder for her to find and grasp if a chance should arise. In fact, it took twelve long years from the time of her arrival in that far away prison until an escape route apparently opened itself up to her, or so she had thought.

Tragically though, Helen had, in the end of it all, just passed away and left this world before she could go anywhere. All she had longed for in her final days on earth, was to get away from the place where she had endured such misery and abuse. The moment of Helen's own death was in fact not so very long before the chosen day on which she and the children had been planning on setting off with Sally. It had come after Helen endured a period of terrible suffering during a bout of untreated dysentery.

Helen had truly believed that she would be on this evening's trip back to the West with her two children. She held on to that belief firmly until her dying breath, at which point it is hard to know whether she had the capacity to understand it was all over for her now. She got through those final days of her ultimately tragic young life by day dreaming about how they would all be housed together, she would feel cool and comfortable in a nice slip dress with no stifling scarves close to her neck and upper arms. She tried to focus on that pleasant thought, especially when the illness began, for that was when she increasingly became afraid within her soul. It wasn't as though she hadn't had some inkling that there might have been something very wrong in the lead up to her death, it was just that she had been accused by her husband of paranoia when she made claims to him that she believed her in-laws had ordered her servants to pay less attention to the hygiene behind her meals and drinking water. 'Why would they do something like that?' That was what she had asked him. He walked away giving no answer, and then she found she was falling ill, and now she was dead.

Fate had landed upon a rather sad muted ending to Helen's life; she was leaving a woman who was a complete stranger to her, to set off with no guarantees at all on a difficult trek to make at the best of times, let alone with the two young children, and she would be all on her own. That woman was Sally, or just the nurse from Australia as Helen had known her while she lived and as she was organising her exit from a sad trap. *She knows what she is doing*, was what the organisation helping to rescue her had told her, and Helen put her trust in that.

As part of a clandestine international group that existed to help people in situations like Helen's, Sally worked in the shadows, and she had grown used to it being that way, so much so, that it was like second nature to her now. This job, which was meant to be delivering a mother along with her two children out of Syria and back home to a safe place of hiding in her home country in the West, was a particularly easy one for Sally compared to most, for she had originally been from Syria herself. Although she had lived in Brisbane, Australia, since her childhood, albeit under the acquired identity of an Australian Indigenous citizen meaning that she found most people were reticent to even so much as mention anything about her own background, let alone question it. She still spoke and understood the language and customs of Syria very well, she would blend in easily. She could relate completely to what the children were going through, and she really did feel like she was a part of their wider extended family, even if she would have to keep her distance from them after this rescue.

As the three reached the shore's edge, rows and rows of little boats that were slowly beginning to rise up into view, were bobbing ever so gently and reliably in the water. At critical times in the exit plan such as these, Sally's heart would often begin to race, but she could taste the success of reaching that end goal, and she thrived on that. Sally had been told that their vessel would be at the end of the pier with a lamp set nearby it. Sally knew that dawn would be coming upon them soon, and the light would sweep up and expose them to the prying eyes of the world, so there was no time to waste as they wanted to be sure to get away under the cover of darkness.

'Is that our boat, nurse?' asked Hela pointing at the first well-appointed boat at the shore end of the pier. It sat majestically, waiting proudly, ready to challenge the might of the sea with ease.

'I'm afraid not,' answered Sally with a slight laugh of consolation. 'Ours will be a much humbler vessel for this journey. We must watch out for a burning lamp. You are so clever to have spotted the first boat, but that's not the one. I think I can see a lamp burning up ahead, so it must be that one,' she said as she pointed to a small and unassuming craft. Hela crinkled her nose less impressed with this one than the first one she had set her eyes upon. 'Once we get out to sea, we will meet a larger fishing vessel, and it will take us to Cyprus. From there you two will go to your new homes, but never forget your Mummy. Do you both promise me that now? She loved you both so much.'

'I'll never forget my mummy, or any of this,' said Haba in a low toned voice, and almost defiantly. In Sally's mind, this signalling by Haba of his resolve to remain loyal to his departed mother, proved that she had won the good fight. She had stood up once again for the rights of downtrodden women in our world, and the rights of the children of a Western mother to be raised in the culture which she had both believed in, and inherited a place in through her own birth. She felt sure that she had made a connection with the boy, and that she understood his heart and mind. Looking at him was just like looking at a male version of how she recalled herself in similar circumstances in her own childhood, which was now so very long ago.

Sally had seen immediately upon meeting Haba that he was a boy with a lot of courage and inner strength, perhaps he will make a real impact on our world one day, she thought to herself as they carried on along the pier.

Sure enough, Sally was right about finding the lamp that pointed to the type of boat she was expecting, she had indeed spotted their rickety little boat about mid-way along the pier. It did look ready, but more to struggle its way through on the might of the sea, rather than to glide through it with ease. The children both looked slightly shell-shocked when taking it all in, in that moment seeing what they would be leaving this land on, and all was silent except for the gentle sound of the waves lapping at the sides of the boats. It was reassuring to Sally that no-one was around except for them. They had made it. Or so Sally had thought to herself at the time, but half-way there, is still half-way away.

*****

PART II

6 Months Later: August

CHAPTER ONE

Australian Federal Police Superintendent Brian Andersen was enjoying the most wonderful Saturday morning sleep in. He was spooning with his long-term girlfriend Elsie Whitman, when her phone rang. Elsie rolled over, picking up the handset from her bedside table in one fluid movement.

'Hi,' said Elsie. 'What's up? It's still pretty early you know.'

'Yes, I know,' came her friend Sarah's voice on the other end of the line, 'it's just that something rather shocking has just happened to someone that I think you used to know, or who you worked with once.'

'Who? What's happened?' said Elsie climbing out of bed. Elsie worked with the Australian Federal Police Specialist Response Unit after all. It was a sizeable group, so it could be any one of a number of people that something had happened to.

'He's a young man aged around 25 or something, his name was David McWellin, he did some specialist cryptography work for your part of the specialist response unit once or twice.'

'Oh yes,' said Elsie, 'I do recall meeting him, maybe two or three times, so what happened to him then?'

'Well, turn on the news right now and you'll see,' said Sarah.

Elsie hadn't been up yet to wash her face even, let alone put on her usual layer of make-up, and her messed blonde hair tousled around her face as she found the remote control and quickly located Channel Seven News. There it was, in all of its gory detail. The young Sydney man had been found dressed in a sadomasochist outfit, with gay porn strewn around the room, and he appeared to have hung himself from a ceiling fan.

'I just can't believe it,' said Elsie. 'What a bizarre way to die when he seemed so ordinary, or boring even. Do you think someone murdered him? Is it an act of terror?'

'Well, as you can see on the news, they're saying it's still unclear at this stage.'

At that moment Brian had come into the living room of his inner-city Sydney apartment and was catching up on what had happened from the running news banner.

'Someone you knew?' Brian asked Elsie.

'Not well Brian, but you could call him a colleague,' answered Elsie taking a brief pause from her conversation with Sarah. 'Sarah, I'm going to go now,' she said returning to it again. 'We should catch up on Monday though at coffee break, and we'll know more about it all by then too.'

'Alright then,' said Sarah. 'See you on Monday, bye.'

'OK, bye.'

'It does look rather suspicious,' commented Brian. 'Although some people do have weird sex fetishes, and as a rule, they say that most people who know them would never suspect it.'

'I know that, but given some of the work he was involved in, I feel a bit uneasy about it all,' said Elsie, a frown furrowing her brow.

'I know what you mean,' agreed Brian. 'Hopefully it's not a new form of terrorism or something.'

'Well, people in my unit will both be getting investigated, and running an investigation into this at the same time,' said Elsie.

'That will be interesting,' said Brian. 'And no doubt it will involve us too. I'm surprised no-one has called me about it yet in fact.'

'They probably want to rule people like me out as suspects first, seeing as I've definitely worked with him.'

*****

The following Monday morning brought with it interesting events at work for both Elsie and Brian. Elsie's unit superior had requested that all of his team should voluntarily give DNA samples to allow him to categorically rule out their presence in David McWellin's apartment. The human rights and privacy mob had been fighting having all of their DNA on file as a standard policy for years. So at this stage, with no evidence to get a warrant on any of them, it would have to be given willingly. After that he would be more comfortable putting them on the case to investigate whether it was a suicide or a murder, possibly one with a terrorist motive. Elsie had consented along with everyone else in their department. No-one in their group claimed to have known the victim personally, they only knew him as a casual work liaison they would occasionally bump into while dealing with his cryptography unit.

Brian's group were also invited to formally join the investigation once any suspicious connection between his girlfriend and the deceased was ruled out. Even though the DNA tests which everyone consented to in the end were fast-tracked, the wait for a clearance seemed like eternity. When eventually it came through on Tuesday afternoon, the first stop for Brian was a visit to the deceased's Sydney apartment. He had been burning with curiosity to get inside and see it for himself. It reminded Brian a lot of his own Sydney apartment: one-bedroom, small lounge, a separate, but small dining area, and conveniently located within an apartment block with a gym, swimming pool and barbeque facilities available.

The porn and call cards for sex workers that everyone had now heard about, had been gathered up and taken in for evidence. Going through those would be a task for someone more junior than Brian. The forensics team had explained to Brian where it had all been found, although no-one had thought so far to explore whether it was meant to convey some sort of message; that line of thinking was where Brian came in. Was it either from a cold-blooded murderer perhaps known to the victim, or from a professional hit man? The thought had struck him though, that it could even have been from the victim himself. Was it something he just could never voice while he was still alive, but wanted those around him to know about or even understand somewhat after he was gone? The scene could then be taken to imply that David might have taken his own life for some reason. The specific arrangement of the porn material around the room might be offering some type of clue as to what the underlying reason really was. Brian tried to allow himself to take the scene in without overthinking it at first, hoping something insightful might just come to him that way, but nothing was jumping out at him.

To Brian's mind then, it seemed that there were only three possible reasons why the porn and rent boy cards would have been dropped around the room. The first possible explanation was that the victim committed suicide, and as part of that final act the victim David had chosen to reveal the inner demons and vices that perhaps drove him to want to die. The second reason was that the killer held a personal grudge against either the murder victim or one of his relatives. Therefore, they wanted to make it clear that this sickening crime scene was a revenge for something they viewed as a sexually humiliating act that either they or one of their relatives had suffered. The third reason was that a terrorist or organised crime cell who targeted him because of his work had gone to great lengths to provide a big distraction away from their reason to want to kill a team member.

Brian favoured the latter two theories already. He just wasn't buying into the suicide story.

CHAPTER TWO

The more Brian and his team learned about the deceased David McWellin, the more perplexing and mysterious the case became. The forensics team had concluded that without a doubt, the late David McWellin had not taken his own life. Someone had entered his apartment and murdered him, even though there was no sign of forced entry, and no sign of any great struggle between the deceased and his attacker or attackers. There were no DNA samples found to be present at the scene that they could match to any likely killer. In fact, the whole place had been wiped down before the body was found, and before police arrived.

The man's body was discovered by his bi-weekly cleaning lady. She told officers who attended the scene that she had begun her work that day in the usual way by cleaning the bathroom. This was the room behind the first door that one encountered in the hallway upon entering the small unit. She had been completely unaware that anything was wrong until after she had finished the bathroom clean, because it was only then that she had first entered the part of the home where the body remained. She didn't notice it at first though, and was instead shocked initially by the explicit images she immediately was confronted with on call cards that had been unusually left lying all over the floor in the living area. One was already underfoot. Only then had she looked up and noticed the lifeless body swinging above her head, at which point she began screaming and ran directly out of the unit to seek help.

It didn't seem likely to Brian that the cleaning lady would have much more of interest to tell police.

According to his family, and to one close friend he had known since his university days, there was nothing obvious in the murder victim's personal life that would have led anyone to suspect that someone might intend to harm him. The victim had no wife, girlfriend, boyfriend, or children, as far as anyone was aware, and he was last seen the night that he died, socialising with work colleagues in a busy inner-city bar where he had a couple of spirit-based alcoholic drinks. The state coroner's report showed that he had a date rape drug in his system. He wasn't known for over-indulging in alcohol, and certainly was never known among friends, family or colleagues to have taken drugs for recreation.

According to his main employer, although his work itself was classified, and sometimes sensitive in nature, there was nothing that he was working on which they believed would have led to him becoming at risk of being attacked or killed in this heinous way. The police were at a loss to find a clue as to where to begin with the investigation.

By the end of the week, junior police officers had sifted through all of the pornographic themed evidence found in the murder victim's apartment, but could see no viable leads. It really all did appear to be totally random. That only left the more mundane searches such as of his calendar and work task lists and interviews with his colleagues to be done next. However, finding out exactly what he had been working on was close to impossible given his level of security clearance in his role. His colleagues were however willing to release a personal wall planner he owned. One thing which stood out as possibly unusual, was his intention to attend a public lecture by a woman general practitioner at a university. The doctor also worked on human rights issues and collaborated with some academics and other activists on that topic in her spare time. The woman's name was Dr Eleni Wood.

David McWellin's story was a particularly tragic one, and it resonated with Brian more deeply than other such cases he had worked. David had been something close to a boy genius when it came to codes and numbers, and at university he was recruited by a government agency that specialised in code breaking. They funded him to do special projects over his summer break and eventually he had taken up that line of employment upon graduation. Maybe

Brian was wrong and being judgemental on this, but it seemed he had worked so hard most of his life that he couldn't have spent much time enjoying himself. He seemed a man who had, after fully dedicating himself to study at university, completely thrown himself into a busy professional work life regime with very little play or relaxation time involved. No-one should have met an end like this, and especially not someone who had contributed so much by helping to solve complex mysteries, which no doubt would have prevented so much crime. Overall, the victim had enjoyed a stellar, but incredibly short career. David McWellin deserved the very best quality crime investigation into his own death in Brian's view. He began to realise that he identified with the man and the life he had led in many ways.

CHAPTER THREE

Brian decided it might be worth attending the upcoming public lecture by Dr Eleni Wood. That was the one which he had seen marked on David McWellin's wall planner. It was due to be held the following day. He decided he would attend in plain clothes, figuring it could be worthwhile just to check it out discretely and see if there was any obvious reason that he could surmise for why the murder victim would have been particularly interested in what she had to say. Was the victim an intelligence worker who had become disillusioned with torture practises and interrogation techniques worldwide? Was that why he was taking an interest in Dr Wood's causes? Or, had Dr Eleni Wood been identified as a potentially disruptive person to government operations and hence become a suspect on David's radar? Brian wondered whether David had been investigating her more broadly as part of his classified work which he of course was not privy to the details of.

The following evening, the auditorium was packed in anticipation of Dr Eleni Wood's talk about human rights, alleged secret rendition flights and torture by western security agencies. That suited Brian well as he could easily get a seat towards the back and blend into the large crowd without standing out too much. Brian found it easy to blend into the background, he had rather an ordinary sort of face, the benefit of not being too good looking he always joked. His hair was a dark colour since he recently tried to cover up some of the grey on his head, and his eyes dark brown, so he was not unlike many of the people of Middle Eastern appearance who were also present in the audience. While most attendees were students, there were some older people in the audience too. Brian wondered if some of Dr Eleni Wood's medical colleagues made the effort to attend these things to support her.

A round of applause broke out as soon as Dr Eleni Wood began to walk up towards the podium. She was a popular presenter and apparently well-known to most in the room already. She was a rather ordinary looking woman with very dark eyes that almost hid a hint of green in them. Her grey hair was dyed a sandy blonde shade which didn't really suit her tanned complexion terribly well.

The noise around the room noticeably hushed and the sense of eager anticipation in those present to hear what she would have to say was palpable.

She began her presentation in an almost cliched fashion with images from American run detention centres. The scenes did shock, no-one could deny that. They showed grown men posed in humiliating positions, and behaving in strange ways. Then Eleni drew a sarcastic snigger from the crowd when she made the comment:

'And some of their prison guards claim they did those things to themselves; they simply photographed it to record what had transpired ... '

Following that opener, she moved on to discuss MI6, and ASIO. She described the avalanche of new powers they had been given in recent years, and talked a lot about their lack of accountability. Brian noticed, however, that she had provided little in the way of evidence, and had no specific case studies. When questioned on her lack of solid proof, she seemed to always come back to the same circular argument that it was because they weren't accountable. Brian tried to keep an open mind, although he couldn't deny that he too was somewhat uneasy with the new raft of powers the Australian government had handed down to ASIO employees in recent times. After all, who polices those who police even the police themselves, and if no-one does, is that ok?

At one point, Dr Eleni Wood's talk took a deeply personal turn. She flashed up images of a group of plane passengers, then showed some images of debris strewn across fields in Northern Scotland. The images were from a 1986 incident that was so-named the Selkirk disaster. She talked for quite a long while about the crash. She described how a group of people had boarded that plane to fly from Edinburgh in Scotland to Chicago, USA. It had been a clear evening for flying, the crew were highly experienced and the aircraft was well maintained; there should have been nothing to worry about. Then she described how just as the plane was about to make a turn out towards the direction of Atlantic Ocean in anticipation for crossing it, it did so slightly prematurely; perhaps that was the first and only indication that something was wrong. But before it reached the ocean, a suicide bomber detonated a device inside the cabin, killing absolutely everyone on board. She then flicked back to the original slide of the passengers at the gate waiting to embark before the flight took off, and pointed out one young couple.

'That girl,' said Dr Eleni Wood, 'was my only daughter'.

She paused after that revelation, then waited, almost as if on cue like a stage artist, for the predictable gasps that went around the room.

'But who is to blame for all of this? Is it just the one person, the one *animal* as people like to call him, who set off that bomb, or is it the teams of people who made him that way, the ones who turned him into that? The public deserves to know them too, and they really should want to seek them out just as much as they do the ones who physically were responsible for detonating the bomb. We all know that there are the government teams who supposedly researched this incident, as well as other acts of terror. They work in secret and fail to reveal the truth when they do uncover it. So, what are the tax payers paying them for if they are not even answerable to us at the end of the day? Is this really in our best interests. I want the world to see who those people are too.'

The crowd burst into a round of applause with some rising from their seats.

She was really getting this audience, they were spell-bound.

Overall though, Brian was just left with the strong impression that here was a woman who wanted more than anything to know the names of members of ASIO and MI6 and to thereafter expose them. While the story was pretty convincing, about how her daughter was a victim too, and she was doing this for the greater good, Brian still just wasn't buying it. Clearly the crowd here tonight was though, so it would make sense then that she could have been a person of interest in cases that were part of the deceased McWellin's role of looking into potentially threatening activists who might expose any investigators, putting their lives in danger. Brian knew David had consulted with Elsie's team in the past on matters that could be linked to terrorism, so it was possible he had consulted for the likes of ASIO before too. That was a can of worms that Brian wouldn't relish opening; although, if it were necessary, liaising with ASIO would more likely be left to Elsie's department - once they were finished clearing Elsie and her team of any direct links to David's death that was.

*****

Wednesday of that same week saw a debriefing meeting held at the station about McWellin's death. The lack of co-ordination between all of the agencies was disappointing to say the least, but sadly it wasn't surprising to anyone in the business. It seemed as if some were primarily more concerned with removing any embarrassing secrets or items that had been left at the scene than they were with solving the crime. In any case, the cover up of the embarrassing finds was a point which seemed somewhat moot by this stage given that someone had already leaked most of the sordid details to the media anyway. They all had seen it on television last Saturday morning.

Elsie was attached as a liaison officer between Brian's department and some external agencies again, but this time she wasn't allowed to work directly with Brian given their personal and intimate relationship. Elsie would report to Brian's superior and he would feed any information to Brian's team as necessary. So far, they didn't seem to have thought that much was necessary to be shared.

They did at least arrange a joint meeting and brain storming session between Brian and Elsie's teams. Better than nothing. After the meeting Brian went back to sorting out some action plans for what he thought was worth investigating, then delegating to juniors to start working through it all.

The topic of the murder victim's intention to attend a lecture by Dr Eleni Wood came up in the joint meeting. The team had Brian relay what he'd learned about it to the deceased's former employer. All that came back in reply though, from the victim's former manager, was that some in the office had been concerned that since he first took an interest in Wood's lectures, the victim David was becoming decidedly paranoid. He believed someone had followed him at one point, and had told colleagues as much. Brian was stunned that no-one had mentioned this so far in joint investigatory meetings or even put it in the police briefing notes. The person or persons following him could have been the killers, maybe there was a description of them somewhere that police hadn't even seen. That was another item to add to the list of things to do: have a junior contact Elsie's department to ask their liaison about it.

They desperately needed something to go on here, because so far, the only other piece of evidence that the police had turned up was that a woman with long blonde curly hair was allegedly seen by a neighbour visiting the deceased's apartment around a fortnight before his death. No-one witnessed the woman leave, but that wasn't that unusual if it was late at night. The description possibly matched that of one of his colleagues, a woman who might also have been part of the crowd who was out with the deceased on his last night alive. That was considered by his employers and the police however, as most likely not at all suspicious, although the woman, Sheila Brown, would be sought out and interviewed.

CHAPTER FOUR

'Thank you for agreeing to speak with us Ms Brown,' said Officer Harry White. He gestured to a seat opposite him and his partner in their smaller interview room.

'Not at all,' replied Sheila Brown flicking her long blonde curly hair back over her shoulder. The youthful switchboard worker was one of the last people who spoke to David McWellin before his untimely death. Her overall attractiveness was distracting to the two youngish officers, truth be told. She worked in their own building, although not with them directly, and they were both pleased to have this chance to talk to her, even if it was official business. Sheila had a trim size ten waist, full hips, subtly tanned skin and olive-green eyes, and in to the bargain she spoke with a Scottish accent that sounded quite exotic to the two Australians.

Sheila felt nervous, sick with nerves in fact; she hadn't done anything wrong, or had anything to do with the death of the unfortunate David McWellin, but no-one likes being interrogated. *Always walk in the shadow of India's love* she reminded herself. She could get through this.

'Would you describe yourself as a close friend of the late Mr McWellin?' began Harry.

'Until quite recently I barely knew him, but then we were both invited to a mutual friend's birthday party a few months ago, we got talking, and we went a few places together after that, purely as friends. I'd been over to his house, or apartment I should say, not that long ago.'

'And you were one of the last people to see him alive?' asked Harry's partner, Officer Greg Walter.

'Me and lots of other people,' replied Sheila. 'We had all gone out for drinks one evening and last I spoke to him that night, he said he was feeling tired and was going to head home. It was still fairly early, around half past nine or so.'

'Was he acting in any way unusually?'

'Not as far as I could tell,' said Sheila. 'He did just seem very tired, but from what I knew of him, he was a very hard-working guy, so it wasn't that surprising to me that he would be tired by the end of the week to be honest.'

'Can you think of any reason why anyone would want to harm Mr McWellin or harbour a grudge against him?'

'Nothing that I knew of, but remember, I only knew him for a few months, so I only knew him superficially I would say. Although, from what I did know of him he seemed a nice enough guy.'

'Did he ever make any advances towards you, of a sexual nature that is?'

'No, not at all,' said Sheila.

'Weren't you ever a little bit surprised by that?'

All the time, thought Sheila, but 'No, why should I have been?' she said in reply.

'You are an attractive young woman, Mr McWellin was a single man, it would only have been natural for him to have been interested in you in that way.'

Not for lack of my dropping hints Sheila thought to herself, but what she said to them as a reply was: 'Perhaps, but he never asked me to date him or tried any sort of advances towards me.'

'Did you ever have reason to believe that Mr McWellin might have been homosexual?'

'No, I didn't,' answered Sheila truthfully. 'If he had any such interests or tendencies, he never made them known to me.'

Sheila had wanted more than anything for David McWellin to ask her out on a date, or to try making advances towards her from the moment she had met him. He seemed a pleasant enough young man, he didn't have any baggage such as ex-wives or kids, and he had a good job where he was trusted with access to sensitive information attached to government organisations and the police. She figured he'd be a good catch. Only he never took the bait.

*****

'She must be one of the hottest women who works around here,' Harry was saying to Greg, just as their boss Brian entered the tea room.

'Just finished doing some important interviews then boys?' said Brian rather sarcastically.

'Yes, Sir,' replied Greg. 'We just spoke to Sheila Brown, she was the woman who had been seen visiting McWellin at his apartment not so long ago, and she saw him on the night that he died.'

'I don't believe I've ever met Sheila Brown,' said Brian. 'Switchboard worker?'

'Oh, haven't you?' said Harry, sarcastically in return. Harry knew, in fact, that Brian had met Sheila Brown once before at a retirement do, it was about six months ago, but by that point, Brian only had eyes for Elsie, and that was clear to everyone. Harry recalled it well because Sheila had tried her hand at flirting with Brian, but she showed Harry zero interest. Harry would have done almost anything to get some of that attention that she wasted on his boss. He would have been sealing the deal by the end of the night had he been given the chance, and it had in fact crossed his mind at the time whether his boss was actually secretly gay when he wasn't taking her up on things.

'She's a lovely girl,' Greg chimed in to release the tension.

'For sure,' agreed Harry, 'I'm surprised she's still single.'

'Well, wasting her time hanging out with the likes of McWellin what can you expect,' commented Greg rather bluntly.

'I'm going to pretend you didn't just say that about our late and possibly much maligned murder and potential terror victim Greg,' said Brian rather crossly. And really, he was rather cross, it was not just a *I must pretend to care now that I'm your boss* sort of thing. From the minute he stepped inside David McWellin's apartment, Brian was reminded so much of himself and how he used to live until he got with Elsie, which wasn't so very long ago. For that reason, the whole thing felt like a personal afront to him.

*****

Sheila Brown also recalled her first meeting with Brian very well. She had flirted with him so obviously, but gotten nowhere. She didn't know at that time that he had just recently gotten together with Elsie Whitman; a woman whom to her always seemed so superior. Perhaps though, it was just because she made Sheila feel inferior that she was projecting that persona on to her. In any case, she was aware now that they were together, very much a couple.

People like Brian and others in the office often had no idea who a person like Sheila Brown was. But it was amazing what she knew of them given that she was the one answering and patching through calls and queries all the time, as well as taking countless messages.

She didn't get to hear so much from Elsie and her team in the role that she was in, but it was possible that might just be about to change.

CHAPTER FIVE

Brian was sifting through the interviews with David McWellin's family, and nothing whatsoever stuck out as odd. They were a very respectable seeming family from Adelaide in South Australia. His mother had been a stay-at-home parent, so typical of the Australian family dream of that era, his father was an engineer, and his only sibling, a sister, was a school teacher now also living and working in Sydney. They all vehemently denied allegations that their loved one had been a sexual fetishist, or that he was in the least bit suicidal.

The Australian Federal Police had interviewed the family, but Brian wanted to meet with them again to find out if any of them had any knowledge of Dr Eleni Wood, or knew why David McWellin might have been interested in her. Brian was able to arrange to personally interview the victim's sister, 28-year-old Carla McWellin. She was impeccably dressed and styled, her hair dyed an auburn colour and fashionably trimmed, and her make-up and nail polish all co-ordinated to match. She was a slim woman, and having come home straight from the primary school she taught at, was dressed in a matronly style.

'Thank you for coming here to speak to me Superintendent and officer,' said Carla.

'We are very sorry for your loss,' said Brian on behalf of himself and the junior officer who accompanied him.

'Thank you'.

'We wanted to ask you some more about the last time you saw your brother. When was that?'

'David took me out for a lovely dinner, oh about a couple of weeks ago now. He was a good brother, and he always made the time for us to have a catch up every so often. He just seemed his usual self.'

'Was your brother in a relationship with anyone that you knew of?' asked Brian.

'No, and I think he would have told me if he were,' said Carla seeming quite certain.

'Did you ever suspect he might be homosexual, or was there some other reason he was single and had no previous girlfriends that anyone knew of?'

'I think it was just because he was so shy, I mean cripplingly shy. I don't think he would have hidden it from us if he were gay, because our family aren't homophobic or anything.'

'Did you ever hear him speak much about human rights issues, or express any views on the use of torture?' asked Brian.

'He didn't talk about his work at all, but he certainly never mentioned any of those sorts of things. I would never imagine he'd be the sort of person who would have anything to do with something like that. He had a very gentle nature, he was never violent, or cruel, in any way at all.'

'Does the name Eleni Wood sound in any way familiar to you?' asked Brian.

'Not at all,' replied Carla.

'Thank you,' said Brian. 'You have been most helpful.'

For the sake of thoroughness, Brian re-interviewed Mr and Mrs McWellin, the victim's parents, as well. He flew out to Adelaide for the day to do so, Brian and his colleague taking an early morning flight together. The McWellins had a house in the quiet seaside suburb of Glenelg. It looked like the sort of place that would have been considered typical for a middle-class single income couple forty years ago, but today would be more of a millionaire's row. Sleepy little beachside hamlets like this one all around Australia had changed so much in recent decades, and they weren't really something for the little guy any more. David McWellin's family home, one of those middle-class homes still in the area since his parents bought it decades prior and hold on to it, was just a short taxi ride from the airport. Brian asked similar questions of the parents as he had of the sister, and he got similar sorts of responses. There was nothing to suggest that any of the immediate family were lying, and Brian did believe that David McWellin was killed by someone who wanted to make him look like a deviant, and to humiliate him as much as was possible.

*****

On that same week's Friday evening, Elsie had cooked dinner for herself and Brian in her apartment. They both had the weekend rostered as days off, and Elsie's apartment was slightly more spacious than Brian's place was since it was located further out of the city in the Sydney bayside suburb of Manly. They didn't have a view of the ocean, but it was just a very short walk away which made it a lovely spot. Brian and Elsie had bonded over a shared love of sailing in the early days of their relationship, and Manly was the perfect place for indulging in that hobby which they kept up together.

'So, has the McWellin murder been keeping you busy this week then?' asked Elsie pouring some Riesling wine to accompany the Barramundi fillets she had just grilled for dinner.

'Yes,' answered Brian, 'very much so.'

'So, forensics are now saying they're completely sure that it wasn't a suicide, but it seems they still have no good clues as to who might've been in the apartment and we have no idea who would have wanted to kill him. Not very much to go on at all.'

'Call me naive,' began Brian, 'but I would think a person in a role like that would be considered at risk of attack or murder by terrorists. I mean, I know he wasn't quite a *James Bond* type of person, but still, he must've worked around some like that, and in some ways cryptanalysis experts are fighting on the front line against modern types of terrorism.'

'That's true when you put it like that,' said Elsie, 'but so far, most terrorist attacks have been done by people like hijackers, shooters, or suicide bombers. So, I imagine that's what security services, much like ourselves, think about first and foremost as their focus when assessing who or what is at risk of becoming a target. It seems to me that dealing with situations like that was not so much the sort of code breaking work that David McWellin would have been involved in.'

'Well, not that we know of,' pointed out Brian.

'Yes, quite true, I could be wrong on that one.'

'It's usually you saying things like this Elsie, but do you know, that I wonder sometimes if there really is something bigger going on affecting our nation's core institutions, and perhaps this is happening in other places too, and we just haven't really woken up to it yet.'

CHAPTER SIX

Along with the rest of her colleagues, Sheila Brown had been cleared of having been in David McWellin's apartment when he was killed, or having had any contact with his body. This meant she was now free to start exploring her own promotion and employment prospects again. Sheila had seen and applied for an internal job vacancy advert for a position doing much the same as she always did, but for different branches of the Australian Federal Police force. Technically, that was a promotion, as it would mean dealing with groups like the specialist response units and liaisons to other government agencies on the switchboard. Most importantly to her though, it was a position where she would have the benefit of much more trust from colleagues than she had in the one she was currently in.

On the morning of her interview, Sheila sat in a bus that was trapped in a dedicated lane in the slow-moving Sydney morning rush hour traffic. When it had reached the point where there had been a full 20 minutes completely lacking in any movement, she decided just to get out and start walking towards work. She made the right decision because she reached the office quicker than she otherwise would have. She had a nice pair of shoes to wear for her interview, but sensibly she carried them in her bag, walking to work in comfortable tennis shoes instead.

When she arrived, she was informed that she was the first of the three candidates to be interviewed by the panel. It was a panel which consisted of three senior bosses; it was all rather intimidating. Still, if she were going to be expected to handle dealing with high-ranking individuals on the phones all the time if she got this job, then she'd have to be able to handle this sort of interview too. Sheila was confident that she could deal with the job, but none the less, she was soaked in a nerves linked sweat at the mere thought of it, and that became like a light moisture all over her body. She focused on her breathing, just like her therapist had told her to do, and repeated to herself her favourite mantra:

always walk in the shadow of India's love. That wasn't one she ever shared with the therapist however, of course.

The interview itself was surprisingly short; a mere twenty minutes. *Perhaps I had glowing references,* Sheila thought to herself when they told her they had gotten through to the end. Surely enough, she was offered the upgraded role by the end of that very same day. Sheila felt, and with a rising sense of pride in herself, pleased at what she had just accomplished. It was surreal almost. In addition to the extra prestige, she would also be earning an extra ten thousand dollars per annum. *Not bad for a morning's work's achievement* thought Sheila.

CHAPTER SEVEN

The view across the river to the illuminated and historic Story Bridge was stunning when viewed from the top deck area of the party venue. This reception area sat proudly and greedily, right on the banks of the Brisbane River in the city of Brisbane. Everything about it reflected the subtropical nature of South East Queensland. A young couple who had met one another while studying for their PhD degrees in the city were celebrating their engagement there that evening. The dancing had been going on for quite some time as the free-flowing sparkling wines and beers had everyone in the party spirit; although some preferred to stand around in the corners waiting on the waiters bringing out fresh trays filled with those drinks and canapes.

The young couple's families had both chipped in to pay for the bash, so they had been able to afford to invite a larger crowd. There were over one hundred people in attendance. That included many academics from the university that the young couple were studying at, and even some of their children.

'If this is the engagement bash, I wonder how big the wedding's going to be?' commented one twenty-one-year-old man among the party guests to his mother.

*****

Several hours later in the city of Brisbane, Jennifer Carson was sitting in her red Holden car singing along to the radio, just as she usually did when out driving alone. She was growing increasingly bored by the fact that she was restricted to at most crawling along in the late-night traffic queues. Those somehow had a strange way of springing up like a surprise in inner city Brisbane and in the oddest of places as well, even when the streets themselves never appeared to really be that crowded. Jennifer was watching carefully nonetheless though, since the few pedestrians that were out and about often crossed carelessly in front of her vehicle. As the light turned green, she removed her hand brake, noting a bus coming up fast and driving within the clear bus lane to her left. Then, just as she was about to press the accelerator, she reacted quickly and moved her foot across swiftly to slam back on the brakes instead. She did so just as a young man with blonde hair coming from her right-hand side had just walked, as if in a trance, directly in front of her path. *Hey stop!* her brain wanted to scream out - but it was too late, he was already under the bus to the left of her.

Jennifer switched off her engine, snapped on her hazard lights and then jumped out of her car forgetting to even check the safety of her own surroundings first. Someone behind her was sounding his horn, but the air was also filled with hysterical screaming from some others on foot who had witnessed what had happened up close and she soon ignored the horn.

It took about ten minutes for police, ambulance and the fire brigade to arrive, but nothing could be done to save the victim who looked to be in his early 20s.

He was in fact the same young man who had only a short time earlier been by the riverside at the engagement party that was being held there.

He had walked straight into the path of a fast-moving oncoming heavy vehicle though, and just like that, he was instantly gone from this earth.

*****

It wasn't standard practise for police in Queensland to notify Australian Federal Police, or indeed any other Sydney-based police, of accidents and incidents that take place in Queensland. News of this one did manage to make its way down south to Sydney-side fairly quickly however. Someone in Queensland had called a friend in the Sydney police service and mentioned it in the passing, so that was how it happened essentially, the Sydney-sider went on and told a friend in the specialist response unit, then eventually Elsie got a call from her friend Sarah about it the next morning:

'But why are they so shocked by this traffic accident in particular?' asked Elsie hearing just how excited Sarah's voice was coming down the line.

'Well, because once again, it's someone loosely connected to the world of mathematical modelling who has died so unexpectedly. This latest death in Brisbane was of a person who mapped bioterror outbreaks for the Australian government, and whose father was in the same line of work. So, he was part of the maths and science community, just like one of our recent victims down here, David, was.'

'But you said he just walked right in front of a bus, so no-one could think he was murdered, there were so many witnesses.'

'I know, it's just strange that's all,' said Sarah, 'and it's always a bit unnerving when coincidences like that happen. I'm still not sure if I even believe in coincidences or not!'

'Well, I do,' answered Elsie, 'they really do exist. It's a scientifically provable fact, as these deceased mathematician victims would tell us all.'

'I have to go now,' said Sarah then, 'I'll let you get back to whatever you and Brian had planned for your Sunday morning together.'

'What really does exist?' asked Brian, chiming in to the end of the conversation he had overheard as Elsie was hanging up her phone. 'Your friend Sarah doesn't believe in aliens or something now does she?'

'Oh no,' laughed Elsie. 'Actually, another piece of sad news got us on to the topic of coincidences. There's been another freak type death of a young mathematician, it was up in Queensland; they do say it was clearly an accident though.'

'How clearly so?' asked Brian.

'He was witnessed by several people just walking straight into the path of a bus that was going fairly fast in the bus lane, he was killed instantly.'

'So, what did he work on?'

'Modelling disastrous events like biological warfare and the effects it would have on major Australian cities if it happened here. He did government contractual work too basically, oh and so did his father who is also a mathematician.'

'I can see why it's been big news locally then, but they're probably right, and that it was just a pure accident with no foul play.'

CHAPTER EIGHT

Later on, during that Sunday evening following the morning when they got Sarah's call, Brian decided to have a look at some of the Queensland news websites to see what he could read about the other young male mathematician's tragic death. There was a great deal of information online, both about the incident, and the young man's family. The young man's name was Arthur Tolbert. It had a prim and proper sort of ring to it. Brian had to register his email and some other particulars before he could read the full article; *his story must be a popular one* he thought. The online version of the local rag up there was a surprisingly useful read though, as it turned out.

The young man was twenty-one years of age, and clearly he was his parents' pride and joy. He was an only son. They had a professional looking photograph of him in the newspaper, he was a handsome young man with a strong jaw and blonde hair. The description of his educational background was given too; he had a first-class degree in mathematics and was in the process of studying for a PhD in the subject when he died.

His parents, Professor and Doctor Tolbert, were both also mathematicians. His father's work was described in some detail too; they wrote at length of how he was a much-loved professor, and how he had won several funding grants to pursue work in biological warfare modelling. They seemed a lovely family, certainly a respectable and well-regarded one, so it was somehow all the more tragic to think of people like that losing an only child in such a way.

The article even gave the witness Jennifer's account of the incident. Very thorough indeed. Brian still always thought of Brisbane, albeit capital city of Queensland, as just some backwater over-sized country town that thinks of itself as a city, so he really was surprised that the journalism seemed to be taken fairly seriously. The article discussed how she described the young man as looking as if he was in a sort of daze as he walked first in front of her, and then into the path of the bus. There was even detail about the young man's mother having collapsed after feeling faint just around, or just after the time of the accident, but before having been informed of any of it. Odd.

'It was like she just knew something was wrong,' the boy's father had said of it according to the reporter.

A lengthy eulogy had also been put together and published by the victim's friends and family. That struck Brian as quite surprising under the circumstances. A man with a lot of young and eager friends springing fast to action to remember him perhaps. A google search found that. It described the young man's entire life since his birth up to the present day. He had been such a cherished child. His mother had taken a decade long break from her mathematics career to be at home to care for him until he was reasonably grown, and the parents had clearly spent years nurturing his mathematical talents. There was no mention of the victim having been in any relationship, but then again, he was still fairly young, so that wasn't terribly surprising.

Could it have been a suicide? wondered Brian. It seemed unlikely for a young man with so much to live for. He had just been out for a celebration, one that his parents also attended, so how low in mood could he have been. It was true that suicide in Australia, just like in other Western nations, was reaching epidemic levels it seemed. This was especially the case among young men who appeared to be particularly vulnerable to it.

All sorts of strange thoughts began racing through Brian's mind. *Could Arthur Tolbert have been given a date rape drug too? Was that why he was described as looking trance-like before making the mistake of walking in front of a vehicle? Or was there any other way someone could have been responsible for that? Was he hypnotised at some point before his death? Although anyone would assume someone would have mentioned it if he had been.* Of course, it was entirely possible that something in a killer's plan had gone wrong, and that Arthur Tolbert had died on his way home where he otherwise would have met a killer.

*****

Elsie really did not want to get out of bed come Monday morning.

'Oh, hit the snooze button, would you?' she asked Brian who was lying half on top of her and still in a sleep-like state.

'What?' answered Brian groggily. He had, after all, been guilty of having stayed up so late reading all he could find about the accident that happened up north. It always felt like such a good idea at the time to just push through into the night, but it was never good the following morning.

'Oh, never mind,' said Elsie. 'We'd best just get up and save ourselves from having to rush around.'

'Is everything OK?' asked Brian. 'You just seem a little bit tense is all.'

'Yes, I have been, to be perfectly honest with you,' said Elsie. 'It's to do with work; there are just some things I feel rather uneasy about.'

'Can you talk to me about it?' asked Brian.

'A little, but not in great detail,' replied Elsie. 'I just feel really concerned that another really big terrorist attack is being planned against the West, the sort of thing that we haven't seen for years. And you know that it's like nobody takes it all that seriously here because we've been so lucky for so long.'

'That's true', agreed Brian rubbing Elsie's shoulders for her to relax them a bit. 'It's been such a long time since any sizeable number of Australians have been caught up in anything awful overseas, and we just typically don't expect to get anything major happening on Australian soil.'

'You know what they say though, resting on our laurels and all that.'

'Talking of resting, I think that's over for this morning,' joked Brian. He got up and turned the coffee machine on.

*****

Essentially, Brian's reaction to Elsie voicing her concerns about the rise in the terror threat when she got up this morning was just to dismiss them, even though he was the one who asked her what was up. It really irritated Elsie when he or others did that, but she had expected as much, and it wasn't first time she'd had this type of experience either.

The ill ease and general sense of foreboding didn't leave her though, and it disturbed her all through the morning routine and her journey into work. She knew most people would encourage or expect her just to ignore this, but it was becoming increasingly tough for her to do so. Somewhere between leaving the apartment and arriving in through the front door of her work building, a resolve set in – she was going to take action today.

As soon as she got into her own office, the first thing she did was ask to have a word with her direct manager because she had a request to make of him. She knew now what needed to be done. She wanted him to open up a communication channel between herself and ASIO in relation to threats against Australia and Australians travelling overseas that she believed might be imminent. She needed him to hear this and to consider it seriously. She also wanted to know if the bereaved father of the bus accident victim in Brisbane, or his mother, were in any way involved in working in counter-intelligence in ways that weren't openly known.

She got hold of her boss's personal assistant, and she soon set up an appointment for Elsie to speak to him later on that day.

CHAPTER NINE

Sheila Brown was sitting alone on her switchboard at the moment when Elsie Whitman's boss was asking to be connected through to a call involving a senior employee of a government agency. It was the perfect opportunity for Sheila to listen in; *no-one would ever know.*

The beginning of the conversation was mundane and boring enough, and then just as Sheila thought it might be getting interesting, the switchboard lit up again and another call had to be dealt with. *Damn it* she thought as it meant that she had to divert her attention elsewhere. She dealt with the other call and then came back to the one involving Elsie's boss as soon as she could.

'Yes, Ian Grant is his name,' came the voice from the senior government agency's line. 'He is in the Royal Australian Airforce.'

Then Sheila was interrupted once again, but she was back to Elsie's boss' call as soon as possible and heard him say: 'I will think it over and decide whether or not to speak to Elsie about it, and about Ian Grant.'

What on earth was that about? Sheila was livid that she had missed the conversation. But, it was now clear to her mind that Elsie Whitman seemed to have some sort of connection with a Royal Australian Airforce man, and it had reached the ears of her boss and a senior official from an external government agency. *They must be very shocked indeed* thought Sheila to herself. By that point, she was convinced that Elsie and the man Ian Grant must have been caught having some sort of inappropriate relationship. *Poor Brian* thought Sheila, *he's such a nice guy and he doesn't know a thing about it.*

*****

In a nearby room, Marianne Chambers sat on the switchboard Sheila Brown used to work on before getting her promotion along with some other operators. It tended to receive more bizarre calls than Sheila's new one did, and some of the messages were rather strange. A young officer had asked to be put through to the operator Marianne.

'Could you please take a message for Superintendent Brian Andersen when he is next in the office?' the young officer asked her.

'I certainly can,' answered Marianne in her sing song professional voice. 'Go ahead please officer,' she said taking up pen and paper.

'Well, another officer and myself, tell him Officers Hayne and Smith, have just responded to a call-out which we believe was really just regarding a neighbourhood noise disturbance in one of the inner western suburbs. Neighbours were complaining that they thought they saw a man who lives in the vicinity, trailing around something within a sack late at night and it seemed as if he was dumping it in the bins their apartments share. The guy is described as single and living alone, he's an alcoholic in his mid-forties. What concerned them more though was that the next night, he was outside by the bins loudly shouting and swearing about how he was glad he "got rid of the bitch" and how since she couldn't even speak English, he should have sent her back to where she came from sooner, oh and something about her smelling. The neighbours thought it might have been a human trafficking case. Naturally we were concerned it could be a body or something, but the bins had been taken to the dump by the time we got around there, and as we said, no-one ever witnessed the man having a partner, they weren't sure which apartment he lives in either. Just want to make sure that the Super is happy to leave it at that is all.'

'Very well,' said Marianne, 'I'll make sure he gets it.'

*****

At lunchtime, the conversation at a cafe near to the Australian Federal Police station turned to the topic of the bizarre outing that Hayne and Smith had to investigate. The case of a mad man shouting at bins, was how they loudly described it.

'But the Super wants us to go back out there and investigate some more,' exclaimed Smith.

'Yes, he does,' called out Brian who had just happened to arrive within earshot at that very moment. 'At a very minimum, cross reference with recent missing persons reports to make sure no non-English speaking or immigrant background women have gone missing recently - ones lucky enough to be living on the grid who might actually be reported, if they go missing, that is.

'Then find out which apartment that man was from, and do some door knocking just to be sure no-one saw any females around there. The offensive racist tirade should be enough to get him on charges anyway, if there was actually anyone there that is. He certainly sounds like a bit of a loose cannon.'

*****

Officers Hayne and Smith headed back out to the scene of the neighbourhood noise disturbance once again after their lunch was over. Though it had now been upgraded by Brian to "the scene of the racist tirade" which still caused the lower ranking officers much amusement. It didn't take too much door knocking to find out the exact address of the man in question. Neighbours reported that this wasn't the first time he had been guilty of disturbing the peace whilst drunk and disorderly; past grievances included him relieving himself in the only elevator shared by the whole apartment block, and leaving smashed glass bottles around at times.

The officers knocked on the man's door, no-one was home. Secretly both Hayne and Smith were pleased he didn't answer, he didn't sound like he'd be the most interesting conversationalist to meet in a day. They were convinced that they were wasting their time, but they carried on knocking on more doors. One door was answered by a professional looking young man in his mid-twenties. He told them that he too had noticed the obnoxious neighbour lugging something large down to the bin shed. He had been closely behind him with a pile of items for recycling to take down to the communal refuse area.

'There was something that struck me as particularly odd though,' said the young man.

'Really? What was that?' asked Officer Hayne.

'It was the smell, there really was a putrid smell coming from whatever was in that sack.'

'Did it smell like a body?' asked Smith, perhaps a bit too bluntly.

'I'm not sure I'd know what that smells like, although I have smelled dead animals' bodies, and it didn't smell like that. No, it was something else, not sure what though.'

'Well, we believe that was one of the man's complaints about whatever he had bundled into that bag that night as well: *the smell.*'

*****

By four in the afternoon that day, the section of the rubbish dump most recently used for the waste from the apartment block investigated by Haynes and Smith was a crime scene. Sniffer dogs had located the offensive smelling sack pretty quickly as it turned out to have contained a sizeable volume of explosives; explosives being something the dogs are well-trained to recognise, as well as human remains.

When the bomb detonation team had arrived and opened the sack, what they first saw inside was the silicone body of an Asian mass-produced sex doll. The shape and sizing of it looked fairly realistic, enough to make some neighbours believe a body had been inside the sack carried by their disruptive neighbour late one evening. The doll even had a speech microchip, but as the drunk man who binned her had pointed out, she didn't speak any English possibly contrary to what he had been led to believe when he purchased her online. The foul and odd smell came from the explosives that were stuffed inside her. Brian wondered how on earth such an item had ended up in inner suburban Sydney in the hands of a drunk maniac.

While it was truly hard to figure out how it had come to pass that they should find a sex doll stuffed with explosives, the most logical deduction was that someone had been using such dolls to hide and transport explosives, and then had somehow mixed them up and ended up by mailing one containing the explosives out to a customer.

The next thing which had to be done was an attempt to find out who exactly mailed it out. To do this, the officers did end up having to spend a fair bit of time with the usually drunk and obnoxious man who had briefly owned the doll. He turned out to be surprisingly very helpful and co-operative with the police, mainly because he hadn't begun drinking yet that day and was hence still largely coherent. He located the emails he had pertaining to the online purchase he had made, including a credit card receipt, and forwarded all of them to the police so they could start looking into the seller.

Unfortunately though, finding the online seller wasn't as simple as it first seemed, even given all of the paperwork associated with the purchase. The advertisements and website for his online shop had been taken down, but the purchaser assured them that the vendor had proudly described himself in those as an Aussie seller, which was why he was so disgusted when the doll that arrived spoke zero English.

Even the payment system and linked bank account used in the transactions had disappeared. Brian wondered if the seller was a genuine terrorist - *what kind of moronic terrorist sells one of his exploding dolls by mistake though? Or, perhaps then, was the seller just one of many dodgy sellers of stolen goods who was moving on before police tracked down their into-the-bargain tax-avoiding sales of goods on his online store?* The latter seemed a more likely theory, the most probable turn of events was that the dolls had fallen off the back of a truck somewhere, but that in the process, somehow, one that a terrorist had stuffed with explosives got mixed up with the regular fare being peddled by some dodgy online retailers.

Very quickly, a task force was set up to try to trace the seller, hard as it would be, hoping that with some luck they would find where this explosive stuffed sex doll had actually come from. In light of this incident, Brian was reminded of his conversation with Elsie, and her feeling that something big was being planned that would affect Australia or Australian citizens. It didn't seem just so out of the question now since such big puzzles still loomed over that doll: *who hid those explosives in it, and more importantly, what on earth are they planning?*

CHAPTER TEN

'Well, Ms Whitman,' came the voice of the ASIO liaison officer on the other end of the phone line. 'What exactly are you asking us to do, or do you expect that we can do?'

'I want you to shut down some active and well-used flight paths that are over a particularly aggressive conflict zone,' answered Elsie matter-of-factly.

'And what makes you think that ASIO can even do that, Ms Whitman?

'Well, it potentially relates to an imminent terrorist attack given some information that has been intercepted this past week or so. Something could happen as soon as this week.'

'ASIO cannot dictate to the airlines where they fly overseas, we could only do that if it were here in Australia. As you are aware, airlines are very cost conscious, and they try to minimise fuel expenses. I imagine that would be the primary reason for them flying over conflict zones in some cases. If it is deemed that they are flying high enough to be safe in those regions, then really all that we can do is advise. It's up to them. But, we will investigate this possible threat that you have reported to us, thank you.'

Elsie felt incredibly dejected once she had put the phone down. Were we all really this powerless at the end of the day? Even with fancy organisations like ASIO in existence, and even when lucky enough to get the opportunity to link to one of them, it still seemed that it was all going to be left up to fate. She went to try finding Sarah in the hopes that she could speak to someone who could cheer her up a bit.

'You know how things are,' said Sarah. 'They receive so many threats and tip offs on a regular basis, they then have to try to sift through them to decide whether they're worth pursuing.'

'I know that,' said Elsie. 'But you'd think when a tip off comes from law enforcement they could be a bit more pro-active in doing something about it.'

'But didn't she say though that it's outside of their jurisdiction?' said Sarah. 'We imagine them all as being like Aussie *James Bond* type characters, but the truth is that they're bound by red tape, by Australian laws, and they have to navigate diplomatic channels into the bargain. They can't just go off and do a *Waltzing Mathilda* around the world changing things because a specialist police officer here has a hunch, even if you are an excellent police officer.'

Elsie laughed out loud, 'Yes, I guess you're right, what I really want is a phone number for the Hollywood movie version of one of these agents, and in my blockbuster version, the hot muscly man on the line would be one that takes action based on my word .... not so much the reality I suppose.'

'No, it's definitely not.'

*****

No amount of massage, or candlelit dinners with opera in the background, could take away the tenseness that Elsie was feeling later on that night. She and Brian's rotas were diverging again, and so she knew this would be the last night they would spend together until Thursday. Brian was savouring it as much as possible.

'I hate that I won't see you for a while,' said Elsie, 'I miss you so much when we aren't together.'

'I know,' said Brian. 'I feel the same. It's funny how not so long ago I was so used to living alone.'

'I was too,' said Elsie, 'but it's not really the best thing.'

'No, it's not,' agreed Brian, 'and you know, we both spend so much time together now that we should maybe think about just getting one place to share to save us both renting separately. How would you feel about that?'

'I think that's a great idea Brian, we should start looking for somewhere. Your place is too small, but it is just so convenient, with being able to walk to work even. I really love Manly too though, the suburb and the beach vibe of the place.'

'But it's so easy to just pop out there on a ferry any time we feel like it. It makes sense, given we'd be pooling resources, for us to get somewhere central. Even this very building has some larger units, like corner ones with bigger balconies and larger double bedrooms.'

'Agreed,' said Elsie, 'let's start looking as soon as possible.'

Even if the world felt as if things might be starting to unravel a little, which was how Elsie perceived it in her tense state, at least here at home, between this couple, everything was starting to come together in a truly positive way.

CHAPTER ELEVEN

The fog was thick in Germany that afternoon, and many of those booked on flights over to the Southern hemisphere were glad knowing that they would soon be getting over to some sunnier weather. One flight to the middle east was well past its boarding time. For many, getting on that flight meant they were going home, with Germany being a hub they'd flown through to connect to flights back to Australasia. For others, that flight was the beginning of an exciting adventure or holiday down under. The passengers had begun to get restless; some had taken to pacing around wondering what was going on. One man was asked if he could please take a seat and stop harassing the boarding counter staff.

The phone at the boarding counter began ringing.

'Hello, this is the check-in desk for flight GA3112, are we ready for boarding yet?' the young Nigerian air hostess answered the call in a most chirpy sounding voice.

'No, you are not ready, and you should never be,' came the voice on the other side of the line. 'This flight is subject to a terror threat and should be grounded.'

The voice on the other side of the line was cut off and an airline manager was patched through immediately:

'Please take no notice of that,' said the woman manager to the air hostess. 'There were some cranks calling and talking about threats and dangers earlier, but the plane has had a full security run down, that's what has caused the delay in boarding in fact. Rest assured that we have checked this end thoroughly and it's all good. So, you can go ahead and let the passengers board now, and you'll still be taking off dead on time.'

*****

Late on Wednesday evening, Elsie's phone rang waking her from her light sleep.

'It's me Sarah,' came the voice on the other side of the line. 'I'm working late shifts tonight and just thought you might want to know that they did step up some security on flights going through active conflict zones recently. Some airlines have chosen to avoid them altogether, but some others this evening are still laughing at the notion that anything could go wrong because they fly through these zones regularly as a matter of routine.'

'Thanks for letting me know Sarah,' said Elsie. 'I didn't think they were serious when they said they'd take my tip off onboard. Some moved is better than none at all though.'

'Oh, I didn't wake you up, did I?'

'Yes,' answered Elsie, 'but it's fine, I only just went to bed about five minutes ago, so it's still not that late.'

'Oh good, well I'll see you tomorrow most likely.'

'OK, see you later. Bye,' said Elsie putting down the phone.

*****

In that same moment, Sheila Brown was on duty late on Wednesday night, it was the usual drill, monitoring the switchboard and taking any calls that might come through. Sheila could see that a call had been placed by Sarah, Elsie Whitman's close friend. *What harm would it do to listen?* Sheila had begun to listen in:

'I didn't think they were serious ...,' she had heard Elsie say, then someone walked in the door and Sheila flicked out of the conversation immediately. *She was probably talking to her friend about her affair,* Sheila thought to herself.

'Oh, hi Gemma,' said Sheila to her colleague who just entered the room. 'How are you?'

'All good,' answered Gemma, 'I just had to come back in here to pick something up quickly because I went out for drinks with some friends after my shift ended, then I realised that I'd left my house keys here. I'm so silly sometimes.'

'Oh, of course, there they are over there,' said Sheila noticing them sitting in a corner. *I'm missing out on that conversation because you couldn't remember your own house keys* thought Sheila rather angrily, but she voiced out loud instead a much more palatable, 'Oh, it's no trouble at all. You have a good night and see you later.'

'Will do,' said Gemma. 'Bye.'

As soon as Gemma left the room, instantly Sheila tried to flick back to Sarah and Elsie's conversation, but it was already over.

The next few hours were rather quiet as was more usual for a Wednesday night, but then suddenly calls were being placed all at once. Sheila saw that a call was being made by Elsie's boss again, she listened in: 'Ian Grant, yes that's the name of the air force man, Ian Grant,' but almost as soon as she had begun listening to what he was saying about him, she had to stop to deal with other calls. They were beginning to pile up already, sitting on hold.

*****

Several hours later an Australian registered jumbo jet that departed Denmark was cruising over Afghanistan. It was passing through a high conflict zone, but flying well above the safe height and flanked by a Royal Australian Air Force state-of-the-art fighter plane. The pilot of the fighter plane was Ian Grant. Nothing was out of the ordinary about the flight, all seemed OK - until it wasn't.

'Grant, do you copy?' came the voice of an American over his radio.

'Yes, this is Grant, over.'

'We've picked up on radar what appears to certainly be a guided remotely controlled cruise missile headed towards that jumbo you're flying along with. You now have four minutes until expected impact. We are presently also instructing the pilot of the jumbo jet to turn a sharp north heading out of the region, but he won't be able to outrun the missile without some help. The trouble is, if you are that help then you likely won't be able to out run the missile yourself.'

'Count me in,' radioed back Grant.

'We have an expert from India to patch through to you. He will guide your manoeuvres, we have to get the missile to track you instead of them, but don't you worry about how that will be done, just follow. This is your choice, over.'

'As I said, count me in, and tell my family that I loved them.'

*****

The jumbo jet flight GA3112 that left Germany after some delay was cruising along in smooth skies just behind the flight from Denmark. The cabin crew were laughing about some of the crank calls earlier and how it still made them nervous at the time. Just at that point, a senior stewardess went in to the cockpit to enquire as to whether the pilot or co-pilot would like any refreshments.

'What do you need, Sirs?' she asked the pilots in her usual professional and engaging well-practised tone as she entered the small space.

'I want you to bear witness to this,' said the senior pilot tensely. 'Please take a seat.'

Somewhat perplexed, she did what he asked, quietly waiting to hear what the issue was.

A voice from the nearest local control tower soon came through on the radio:

'I repeat. You are about to be struck by a guided missile. Please try to move away from high density urban areas.'

*****

The next morning the front cover of every newspaper ran an image of the jumbo jet that had departed Germany the day before blown to pieces and spread all over the ground in Afghanistan. The whole world was in shock, there had been hundreds of passengers on board from fifteen different nations, and a large portion of them were Australian citizens. So far no-one was taking responsibility for the incident, the airline was adamant that it was flying well within recommended heights above the conflict zone, and that the route was not considered unsafe.

The media was full of unhelpful speculation that only added to the pain felt by families of the deceased victims. Some ran editorials claiming that the plane had veered wildly off course and hence the captain was to blame for the disaster, others claimed that the plane was exactly on course and that the airlines had ignored, based on economic considerations, earlier warnings to change their flight paths.

Whoever was behind it, Brian knew that there would be lots of questions being asked of Elsie back in their offices, and he felt rather anxious about that. After all, how could her inexplicable foresight that something like this was looming ahead ever be rationally explained enough to sate the inevitable interest it was going to generate?

CHAPTER TWELVE

The thought that Elsie was having an affair behind Brian's back had been playing on Sheila's mind lately. Sheila wondered sometimes why exactly it bothered her quite as much as it did. *Maybe her feelings for Brian really were something true; like love, or something extremely like it?* There was no way to get the messages about the affair through to him though, not without revealing that she had been illegally eavesdropping on conversations she was entrusted to facilitate.

But then, something very unexpected happened: a phone call came through for Elsie's boss, but he wasn't available to take it, and so they left a message for him with Sheila.

'Please let him know that a Royal Australian Air Force Pilot, surname Grant, was killed in a training incident last night, and it will be left to him to inform his reports in the office about what has happened.'

It was not only the most perfect opportunity, but likely the only opportunity she was ever going to get to let Brian know there seemed to be something going on between Elsie and that man Grant. So, she took the message, and she changed its recipient from being Elsie's boss, to being Elsie Whitman herself. *That would make them all wonder.*

She then slid a memo about it into the briefing notes on incidents that happened around the plane disaster, notes which she knew that Brian Andersen would read.

CHAPTER THIRTEEN

Elsie could barely face going into work on Thursday morning, but she fought the strong urge to pull a sickie and made herself go there anyway. The news was still dominated by stories about the shot down airliner; an airliner full of passengers, including a large proportion who were Australian citizens. There had been over one hundred Australians on board to be exact. The only thing worse than being the person who predicted and planned for a major disaster that never transpired, is being the person who predicted and planned for a major disaster that did transpire. Elsie knew that everyone would have questions for her now; questions she didn't necessarily want to answer, mainly because she didn't know how to.

An early morning call came through from Brian:

'Hi darling,' he began. 'Hope you're feeling alright, I saw the horrific news this morning, and I guess you have too. You were totally right about us all resting too much on our laurels and not being en guarde enough in this fight against terror.'

'I know,' said Elsie, 'but I just wish that I had been wrong about it all. I can't believe how many innocent lives have been wiped out just like that, whole families gone, little kids and everything. I keep thinking I should have done something more.'

'But what more could you really have done? It was a plane that was travelling overseas, and you only felt you knew that something big might happen, you didn't know exactly what and where, so none of this is your fault, please don't take it upon yourself.'

'I know that, I do really, it's all just so shocking that's all.'

'We will be together again this evening remember, looking forward to having you over to my place. Love you, bye.'

'I love you too, bye,' said Elsie.

*****

Work that morning was rather strange and strained. Everyone in the specialist response unit seemed to be aware that Elsie had predicted something major might happen to an airline, and now they looked at her as if she wasn't quite human or something. She began to understand how the Salem witches must have felt.

Elsie's friend Sarah was waiting with a friendly face and a cup of coffee to hand to her as soon as she arrived. She hadn't yet gone home after finishing her late shift.

'Hi,' said Sarah. 'Glad you made it in today, I was worried you wouldn't be feeling up to it given what happened last night.'

'Well, I wasn't exactly jumping with enthusiasm today, but I want to hear what they have to say when we get debriefed on all of this.'

Elsie didn't have to wait long for that, her entire specialist response unit group was called in for an emergency briefing session almost immediately. They had ascertained that: a plane carrying many Australian civilians was shot down when flying over Afghanistan; that it was without a doubt a terrorist attack against the West; that a staff member within the group had flagged concerns about something of this nature happening; and that a Royal Australian Airforce pilot had also died in Afghanistan during a training incident around the same time.

They were informed that in response to this extraordinary and disastrous attack, their response unit, together with other Australian Federal Police teams, would be stepping up counter-intelligence support to groups like ASIO, and expanding current investigations.

*****

Around the same time as Elsie's team was sitting through their briefing, Brian was also informed by his own superior officer that he would be responsible for a more in-depth investigation into the death of David McWellin. He was directed to specifically look for any possible connections to known, or up and coming terrorists who pose a threat to Australia.

When he returned to his desk to read through the most recent briefing materials, to his absolute amazement, they contained some information on Elsie and who she had engaged in phone conversations with recently. There were some scant notes about her having conversed with an Australian Air Force pilot based in Afghanistan, one who was now deceased. He could see that there was even another direct message from the Air Force that had been left to inform her, or the recipient of the earlier missed call as she was described, immediately and without delay about their man's death, because it was whom he had been in communication with prior to that time.

Why on earth would she be needing that? What would she have had phone conversations with him directly for anyway. That's not her job. Surely it would have been her superior he would have spoken with if it were a work thing. She never mentioned it either, you would think she might have done as it's a bit different. For the first occasion in their six-month relationship, Brian doubted Elsie, and yet he felt like a prick for doing so, all at the same time.

He wondered *was this normal in this stage of a relationship? Was Elsie maybe getting bored of him now? Maybe he could bring it up over dinner and carefully gauge her reaction to see if she gave away any hints of anything untoward?*

*****

For dinner that evening, Brian was making his own signature hot chicken burgers. He'd loosely modelled the recipe on an awesome one he ate at a chain store once in the USA, but he reckoned his was better. The chicken he used was free range and RSPCA approved because happy birds taste better; grilling up some onions was a must; the burger bun should be only *lightly* toasted; on the bottom half of the bun he would spread some mayonnaise; and on the top half, some hot sauce. Elsie loved them too. Brian glanced into the lounge room and saw that she was sitting curled up on the sofa with a glass of red wine in her hand.

'So, how are you feeling now?' asked Brian.

'Better, but still shocked,' said Elsie. She did look decidedly melancholy.

'Well, imagine how some in the air force must feel, or the women married to those guys,' said Brian awkwardly trying to fit the topic of a suspected mystery man of Elsie's into the conversation.

'Some in the air force?' asked Elsie somewhat bemused.

'You know what I mean,' stammered Brian, 'don't you?'

'No, I don't really,' replied Elsie. 'Do you mean groups like MI6 or whoever else deals with counter-espionage and counter-terrorism overseas?'

'Yes, exactly,' said Brian deciding to change the subject again, this wasn't going anywhere.

All Brian could think of was images that kept running across his mind of some hot shot Royal Australian Airforce pilot having come round behind his back, sweeping Elsie off her feet, and who knows what else. Something like that was like his worst nightmare.

CHAPTER FOURTEEN

Sheila had always been cool and calm when it came to bending the rules in her job, listening when she shouldn't, and passing on confidential information when she thought it necessary. But for the first time in her life, she had recently begun to worry that she might get caught. Even simple pleasantries people would say to her became strange in her mind, and made her suspicious. She realised that she had perhaps made a mistake by revealing the link between Ian Grant and Elsie Whitman, the link which she had only heard the scantest mention of, but which she had transformed into a mountain of evidence that the two were definitely intimately involved with one another. But weighing moreso on her mind was that she had gone even further than just revealing it to Brian; she had in fact done something even more truly awful, and risky. After she made sure Brian would see the notes linking the airman to his partner, she had then anonymously gotten in touch with the dead air force pilot's pregnant fiancé and given her the name of Ms Elsie Whitman as a potential threat to watch out for.

Whilst the worry remained for her that at any minute police could barge in and expel her from the building, another day of busy switchboards held too much intrigue to be ignored by her. She had placed a call through from an external government agency to Elsie's boss, and she had so desperately wanted to hear what was being said there. Luckily her colleague had gone out for a quick coffee and cigarette break, so she was able to. She was completely horrified by what she overheard: the man who helped save an Australian registered plane from sharing the same fate as the doomed flight that left Germany, was a rocket scientist, who was originally from India. She had no idea that a fellow Indian patriot had left his homeland and was being used in such a fashion by the Australian Government. She was utterly outraged. She felt a burning desire to get payback against the Government for it, *but how could she?*

CHAPTER FIFTEEN

The next morning Brian left for work before Elsie was even awake to start an early shift; she wasn't due in to work until the afternoon. She had been just in the middle of a nice enjoyable and well needed sleep in, when she heard a knock at the door. *Who on earth could that be at this time?* wondered Elsie somewhat annoyed. It was still only eight am, she could have done with having slept at least another hour. She slipped out of bed, and threw a dressing gown on over her light slip.

There was another rather loud knock at the door.

'I'm coming, just give me a moment please,' Elsie yelled. She stopped to check through the peep hole first, before just opening the door, because it was a door without a chain on it for security. Opening it slowly until about half-way, she saw that standing behind the door was a woman who looked to be around her mid-twenties, heavily pregnant and alone. Elsie opened the door fully, assuming the woman needed help.

'Are you Ms Elsie Whitman?' asked the pregnant woman.

'Yes, that's me,' said Elsie in response, automatically and without a thought, but no sooner had Elsie got the reply out, than she was given a massive slap in the face.

*****

'She slapped you in the face?' asked Brian incredulously over the phone a few hours later.

'Yes, that's right, she just asked my name then slapped me in the face,' said Elsie.

'Well, it sounds like you were lucky she wasn't intent on stabbing you or something.'

'Yes, I know,' said Elsie, 'but that doesn't make it ok either, I'm frightened to go out of my unit today.'

'Have you reported it to the police?'

'What, is that a joke? Apart from telling police officer you do you mean?' asked Elsie. 'I told my office already too, but I just felt that if I had made an arrest at that point when she did it, I'd end up looking like I was committing brutality against a pregnant woman. And I was in shock at the whole thing. It was hard to process it as it happened to be honest. She told me who she is though.'

'Well, who is she?'

'She is, or was rather, the fiancée of a Royal Australian Airforce Pilot who died in a training incident recently. And when I say recently, I mean as in just yesterday kind of recently.'

'Did you know him then?' Brian got to ask finally. *I have been waiting on tenterhooks to hear how she would handle this question.*

'No, I didn't know him,' answered Elsie. 'I have no idea why she targeted me or might have thought that.'

'Do you want me to come home, or are you ok?'

'No, don't come back. I'm just putting some make-up on to cover the marks now, I already had an ice-pack on my face for a while. Then I'm planning on heading in to work as usual.'

'Probably a mental health referral for her is more appropriate,' suggested Brian.

'Yes, probably,' agreed Elsie.

*****

'You just have to let it go,' suggested Sarah flicking her shoulder-length brown hair back. 'It's just not worth it to start a war with some air force or army wives, and that's what it would be you know, they stick together.'

'Don't you think you're being just a little bit extreme?' said Elsie.

'No, I don't,' replied Sarah. 'As far as they are concerned, you were having it off with her man whilst she was pregnant no less, and if anything happens to her baby, they'll likely blame you for that too.'

'Well, I've already put in an application for her to be assessed for mental health, but I haven't pressed any charges.'

'That's probably the best idea.'

'The thing I don't understand though, is who spread rumours that I was somehow involved with a dead air force pilot?'

'Well,' began Sarah looking her dead in the eye. 'Were you?'

'How could you even ask me such a thing?' said Elsie somewhat shocked.

'I'm just covering all bases, excuse the pun.'

'You know I'm in a committed relationship with Brian, I love him and I'd never cheat on him. Plus, even if I weren't with Brian, I wouldn't be involved with a man who had a pregnant fiancée in any case.'

'Fair enough,' said Sarah. 'It's just all so sexy sounding, the hot shot air force man.'

'Well, he's in fact a deceased man now anyway. Lest we forget.'

CHAPTER SIXTEEN

A week had passed since a plane full of people had been shot out of the sky. The investigation to see what Australian intelligence units could make out of it was in full swing. Elsie was at home alone again one morning, when once again, there was a knock at her door. *I'm not just opening it this time* thought Elsie, since she hadn't been expecting anyone.

They knocked again loudly. Elsie peered through the peep hole and could see what looked like two uniformed police officers and two women who looked like health professionals.

'Ms Whitman,' began one of the nurses, 'I am a community nurse, we need you to open the door. If you won't open it, the officers are allowed to use force to enter, we do know that you are in there.'

The whole thing sounded like some sort of bad joke, but the uniforms definitely looked real. *What could this all be about?* Elsie stood and wondered for the briefest of moments, but the only way to find out was to speak to them. She realised she had to open the door; there wasn't any choice.

'Hello, Ms Whitman,' said the same nurse when the four of them stepped into the room. Elsie realised at that moment just how intimidating it really was to be on the other side of these things. She was usually among the badged officers arriving to have a word with people. 'We are here because there has been a state mental health examination authority taken out on you. Do you understand what that means?'

'Yes, I do,' answered Elsie, 'but why would anyone take that out against me, I'm completely fine.'

'Are you?' asked the other nurse. And so began a series of questioning that lasted for about a quarter of an hour before the other one of the community nurses calmly announced: 'You're going to have to come with us to the hospital to be interviewed by a psychiatrist. You'll travel with the two police officers here.'

'What?' said Elsie in a state of shock. 'I don't want to go to the hospital, there is no need for any of this.'

'If you refuse to come with us, then these officers will take you there by force. It's your choice.'

*****

Half an hour later, Elsie sat waiting in a locked and sterile looking interview room at the local state hospital admissions department. Eventually another nurse flanked by a young-looking psychiatrist came in. They asked the usual list of interview questions, such as whether Elsie had ever contemplated suicide or felt depressed. Well, *mostly* they asked the usual questions. There were some things which Elsie found rather odd and strange. Such as one of them asked whether or not she'd had a new sexual encounter or relationship recently that was unusual for her. They also asked if she had applied to join the air force, or for an army job recently. None of that seemed standard at all.

If it hadn't been for Brian coming to her rescue, vouching for her and insisting that she was sane, she likely would have been locked in that place for at least that whole night. *What on earth is all of this nonsense really about?* She honestly wondered sometimes.

*****

After discussing what had happened to her with her boss, Elsie was referred to her local general practitioner who ordered her to take two days off from work to get over the horrific experience of almost being committed, which had come right after her being assaulted, when that in itself had been traumatic enough. Her relaxation time began with a warm candle lit bath followed by a massage from Brian. But inevitably, the topic of work and who could be aiming at Elsie came up.

'Who could have done that to me?' asked Elsie. In her darkest moments she'd even considered whether Brian could have done such a thing. *He would have no reason to though.* Elsie reassured herself of that much. That fleeting doubt wasn't a thought she would ever utter out loud to him though.

'I don't know,' said Brian, 'yet.'

'What do you mean, yet? How will you ever find out when they legally don't have to tell you who made the complaints about me? As you're aware, they're choosing to exercise that right to keep it from me. It's like being charged and jailed without ever seeing who was at your trial.'

'I know, but believe me, I will find out who it was,' said Brian rather ominously. 'I was actually already a bit concerned about whether someone was stalking or hassling you in fact.'

'And why is that?' asked Elsie confused.

'Because word came to my ears that you had some connection to a Royal Airforce pilot.'

'What, the one who just died and whose partner came and slapped me across the face? She's the one that should be locked up in an asylum. I can't believe that you're only just telling me this,' said Elsie increasingly growing enraged.

'I get that,' said Brian, 'but she has the sympathy vote as the one left holding the baby while her man died on her while serving our country. You're completely fine, aren't you?'

'But I was never involved with any air force man,' said Elsie beginning to recall an earlier conversation with Brian. 'Hey, wait, you brought up the topic of air force pilots not so long ago, it was kind of odd in our conversation at the time.'

'Yes, I did,' Brian began to confess, 'I admit, I was a little bit curious as to whether there was any truth to it when I first heard it. I'm sorry. But we will find out who is behind it all, trust me.'

CHAPTER SEVENTEEN

Sheila Brown turned the key she had been given to the post office box she was directed to, and thankfully everything she'd paid dearly for was all in there waiting for her. Most importantly, it contained a false passport in the name of an Australian citizen. Her photograph was on the biometrics page, except she had blue eyes in the photograph rather than her own colour which was brown. A set of blue coloured contact lenses had been provided too. There was also a ticket to Mumbai, one-way.

Always walk in the shadow of India's love Sheila reminded herself again, as she, with her suitcase already packed and by her side, hailed a taxi to take her straight to the departures area of Sydney airport. The twenty-minute ride felt like the longest time of her life; the whole way she was paranoid that some passing car would pull out police sirens and usher them over to stop by the road side at any second. But she made it to the airport without a single hassle.

Standing on the pavement by the entrance to departures as her taxi drove off, she looked for a brief moment to her left and saw a scene that took her right back to a memory of her own childhood. The child standing nearby was with a woman who looked nothing like her. She was probably a nanny to the child. The child looked around five years old, thought Sheila, or Nanda as she was otherwise known back home in India.

She remembered vividly her own arrival at the airport in Mumbai as a child. She had gone there to look for her street brother who cared for her since as long as she could remember. He had gone to the airport to beg for a job, but had never returned. He was only a young boy around fourteen years of age when she last saw him, and she had finally found a ride to take her to the airport where she aimed to find him for herself. Afterall, police in India didn't take any notice of kids like them disappearing, a harsh truth of life there that had somehow been pushed to the very back of her mind so that she didn't ever dwell on the injustice of it all very much.

As she ran into the terminal building all those years ago, that eager child that she used to be, she saw what looked like a rich child, who was not so dissimilar in appearance to herself. That had surprised her somewhat, for she was so used to being one of the invisible masses of poor people living and toiling in India. If she didn't look all that different really from a rich girl of a similar age, then why was it that she was treated as if she were invisible when that girl wasn't. They both had the same mid-brown hair, brown eyes, and lightly tanned skin. The rich child was with a woman who seemed to be her nanny, which was just as this child beside her today reminded her of. Back then, that rich child's nanny did the strangest thing though; she took the child's passport, and tossed it into a bin. Four-year-old Nanda saw the whole thing, and to help the lady, while also hoping for some coins as a reward, she fished it out of the bin and tried to run after her. She lost track of her in the crowd though, and went back to wandering around trying to figure out how to best start looking for her brother.

Eventually, an airport official stopped her and checked the passport which she held in her hand.

'Ah, there you are!' exclaimed the official after bringing her to a desk where he made some phone calls. Nanda had learned to be scared of authority, so she did what she was told and remained silent. From that point forward, Nanda was placed under the care of an air hostess who accompanied minors travelling without parents. Before long she was whisked onto a plane and spent hours wondering what was to happen to her. *Was this what happened to her street brother?* She'd wondered. *Maybe she would see him when they landed.* But when she landed, it was in Scotland where a local Scottish family awaited her. She wanted to explain that the passport wasn't hers, but they'd fed her on the plane, her first meal in some time, and the nice lady who was with her gave her a blanket to keep too. So, instead, she'd said nothing.

It wasn't hard for her to fit in to the new family in Scotland, she didn't look so very different from them. They always brought her up to love India, and her father whom they told her was a very special and revered scientist over there. Perhaps they would let her meet him one day.

The memories faded as she watched as the little girl and her Nanny went to the left of the terminal and twenty-three-year-old Nanda continued on her way to the right. She checked in for her flight to Mumbai and promised herself never to look back again.

CHAPTER EIGHTEEN

Brian and Elsie were planning on spending a relaxing night in together, and Elsie was already relaxing on the couch while he made a start on dinner preparations. Elsie felt sure now that she loved Brian, but she hadn't felt quite so happy about certain things in their relationship since his recent confession. He had basically just outright admitted to his having suspected she might have been having an affair. Even if it was only for a short time that he entertained the thought, the underhand way he tried to check out the lie of the land, by mentioning air force men casually in their conversation, was just so low. She was so hurt that he could have believed such a thing of her.

The truth was though, that for Elsie, this had all brought back memories of her previous marriage that had turned sour when her ex-husband began cheating on her with an HR person at his office. The only clue to her ex-husband's guilt had been that he began accusing Elsie of having extra-marital relationships to deflect the blame, and he became very controlling, which was so unlike how his character had been prior to that episode. She read in numerous self-help books and confirmed with her therapist afterwards though, just how common that behaviour really is when a love cheat is struggling with a guilty mind. It's like the cheaters all mostly sing from the very same hymn book.

What if this was the same scenario playing out all over again?

Brian had let her down a little with this one, there was no denying it.

But on a more positive note, and true to his word, Brian really had impressed Elsie by managing to find out who was responsible for "leaking" the slander that Elsie was involved with a Royal Australian Air Force pilot behind both Brian and the man's fiancée's back. He was sure that, whoever that person was, they were the self-same person who was responsible for almost having Elsie committed. Surprisingly to Brian and to Elsie, when her identity was revealed, it turned out that she was the same blonde curly haired woman who was the last person to have visited David McWellin at his apartment before his death, and she was also someone who was definitely among the crowd for the last night out that he attended. It was none other than Sheila Brown. In fact, Brian's superior Murphy had just been on video conference calls for the better part of a day on the topic of that woman, and so Brian had by now gotten the full run down on all that was now known about her.

Brian poured both himself and Elsie a glass of wine, handed one to her, then took a seat beside her on the sofa. Her tension was palpable, so setting his drink down for a moment, he gently squeezed both of her shoulders. When she seemed a little less uptight, he explained that Sheila Brown was in fact an Indian national who had gotten away with having worked alongside them in the police force, on the switchboard no less, while she spied on them, and she did this for years. She had even spent her time in their very own building of all places, and no-one had ever noticed what she had been doing. If that weren't shocking enough, it seemed that even now that the truth had come out, she would be getting away with it. Brian and his colleagues had been told that she had just fled the country on a false passport. So she had successfully made a run for it back to India on a one-way ticket, and likely would never look back. It was almost unbelievable.

'She's gone *back* to India?' said Elsie almost shouting; Brian had never seen her so angry. 'But she's meant to be from Scotland!'

'Well,' said Brian. 'It turns out that little detail she gave us may not have been completely true.'

'Then who is she?'

'She was spying for India.'

Elsie was literally a gasp.

'Now it gets a little bit complicated - ironically the man we thought at first was her father, a man who now lives in and works for Australia, seems not to have been related to her after all. He's a rocket scientist originally from India, some say he's considered a hero in some circles.'

'The man you *thought* was her father. So, he's definitely not her biological father then? That's what you're saying has been discovered?' Elsie was rarely this agitated, and it was a bit confronting for Brian.

'Well, yes, he is not the biological father,' said Brian. 'And it turns out she might not be so ethnically Indian as she thought either. They thought she was his light-skinned daughter he had sired by a Western colleague. He himself had a lot of English ancestry in his own family tree, and she looked quite like him, so no-one questioned it.'

'Are you serious?' asked Elsie. 'So, you think that India had someone who was not even really from there spying for them, and only on peanuts wages too, against Australia, for years potentially? She paused for a moment looking utterly perplexed. That's the craziest thing I've heard in a long time.'

'It was probably because of what happened to the girl who really was the Indian rocket scientist's daughter and the mix-up that followed.'

Brian then began recounting to Elsie the story of what had happened to that other now tragically deceased child.

'Many years ago, the Indian rocket scientist who now works here in Australia, had travelled to Poland on a special government joint project initiative. Whilst there, the married father of three had fallen madly in love with another scientist, and they had a child together. This was back in the nineteen eighties that she was born. The child's mother's husband in Poland had insisted that the child did not live with them, and an arrangement they made where she lived in India to be cared for by nannies, also proved to be unsatisfactory to him. It was decided by her parents that they would find an adoptive home for her.'

'An adoptive home for her, where?' asked Elsie suspecting that she might have guessed already.

'In Scotland as it turned out,' said Brian. 'One fateful day she had been sent with a nanny to go to catch a flight to Scotland. From there, the scientist's plan was that she would be raised as a Scottish child, but by a family in the service of India. However, it was not to be.'

'Why not?' asked Elsie becoming quite enthralled with the tale.

'Because the nanny to the rocket scientist's daughter had betrayed the family and worked for terrorists. Once they got to the airport, she dumped her own and the child's real ID, and took the child on a fake passport on to a different flight out of the country. Their flight was hijacked, and the rocket scientist's daughter and her nanny were killed in the cross-fire of a hail of bullets between the hijackers and the army in the country they were landed in. They were collateral damage as they tried to take back control of the plane basically. But, because the nanny had switched her ID documents, the authorities there didn't realise that his daughter had been killed, and that another child, the one everyone knew as Sheila, had gone to Scotland in her place after finding her passport at the airport in India.'

'Waw,' said Elsie. 'That's some story.'

'I know. The Indian rocket scientist only found out the truth about a decade after the incident when they got suspicious and did a paternity test on the child he had been paying support for living in Scotland. He effectively just washed his hands of her when he found out she wasn't his, and for many years more, he had no idea where his own daughter had ended up. He even began to doubt at times that he had ever fathered a daughter by his Polish lover, and that perhaps she had lied to him too. The information about how his daughter did end up came to him eventually though, and that was around the same time as when he made the move over to Australia. He said the truth was finally revealed to him by the child's nanny's brother when he was found to be dying of cancer. He said his sister had spoken to him of her intentions to harm their family on behalf of extremists she had become involved with, and that was the sole reason that she aimed to get a job working with his family. She just wanted to get close enough. He claimed he had been too afraid to speak out about it for many years.'

Elsie was speechless.

'It seemed that Sheila definitely was spying on us all on behalf of India though, end of the day. That is the main consideration from our own perspective, in terms of safeguarding Australian national security', continued Brian. 'But it doesn't seem likely she had anything to do with any of the acts of terrorism that have happened lately, or with any murders.'

'And she made it home to India, so there's no hope of getting her on espionage charges and finding out all that she knows now anyway.'

'No, there's not.'

Brian was filled with both suspicion and puzzlement by Sheila's motivation to gossip about Elsie in particular. Running away suggested a great deal of guilt about something. *Had she thought she was doing the right thing by Brian and the dead man's fiancée by exposing an affair she truly believed had taken place? Was she unable to help herself from spreading the rumours even though she would be fired and possibly even prosecuted for unlawfully spreading the information? If so, why? Why did she care so much? The road to hell is paved with good intentions as they say,* thought Brian. *Was it because she was spying for India that she seemed to be trying to set the cat among the pigeons? Did she think that by causing disharmony through rumour spreading she would be more likely to get more information that might be revealed in the ensuing fall out for her to take home to India. Or was there something even more sinister behind it: was she part of a group over there with a shared motivation to sow disharmony and mistrust, the kind that can bring down governments?*

It sometimes felt to Brian that they would never know now, because the Australian authorities didn't consider it worth their time or the hassle that would be involved in trying to extradite her back from India over it.

Elsie was furious still. 'You know, I do recall her, and spoke to her in the passing maybe once or twice. They say a person is supposed to know you well to have you committed! I did not know her well. I can't believe that a magistrate somewhere accepted her testimony in relation to me and believed it enough to have the examination authority served on me.'

'I'm shocked myself,' said Brian. 'Which was why I began to wonder if she had bigger connections than we realised. So, I did a little digging, and I think she does.'

'To whom? Or to what?' asked Elsie.

'Do you recall that female speaker whose talk I went to recently, Dr Eleni Wood?'

'Yes,' said Elsie, eagerly awaiting what he might have to say about her.

'Well, I believe our run-away Indian friend Nanda was linked to her and her group of loyal supporters. But that still begs the question, if you didn't have anything to do with the dead pilot, then why would her or her group of civil libertarians have it in for you? What do they think you've done?'

'I have no idea,' said Elsie emphatically. 'You know, if you want to ask me something, such as whether I have ever been involved in torture or anything like that you can, because I can answer you completely truthfully that I have not. I have never seen such a thing, or ever heard of it here.'

Brian had wanted to ask her that, but was afraid to in case she became offended. So, he was glad when she just volunteered an answer, and he believed her too. It was good to know. He decided it was a good time to share with her what he had learned about the horrific air disaster that had claimed the life of Dr Eleni Wood's only child.

'By all accounts,' began Brian, 'it had been an ordinary enough evening back in 1986 when Dr Eleni Wood's daughter died. There had been some threats made against airlines with American links or interests in the lead up to the doomed flight that she travelled on; but the authorities regularly received hundreds of those that all came to nothing. On the night in question, Dr Eleni Wood's daughter Kelly and her boyfriend Brett went through security to board a flight to the last-minute surprise romantic weekend that Brett had booked for them both.'

'What did Kelly work as?' asked Elsie.

'Kelly was a nurse by trade. While off duty, she had let her own naturally tightly curled hair grow loose and free and hang around her youthfully beautiful face as I had seen in the images from that night such as those Dr Eleni used in her presentations. Her boyfriend was a very handsome young man too: he was tall, had a strong jaw, broad shoulders and sandy blonde hair cut into a fashionable eighties style. They were both just nineteen with their whole lives ahead of them.'

'Yes, it was very sad,' agreed Elsie.

'Security was extra tight that evening, and Brett had stood out in the queue,' continued Brian. 'In fact, Brett had even been described as having looked slightly nervous due to it. For that reason, one of the security men called him aside for a search of his backpack, they seemed to be doing lots of those that night. The security guard caught hold of one item and had described in his statements how he had looked at Brett knowingly; he decided at that not to pull it right out of the bag, after all, that would ruin the surprise of what was clearly a beautifully stunning art deco diamond engagement ring. He waved them on.

It hadn't been long into their flight when the aircraft exploded into pieces in the skies over the north of Scotland. Luckily no-one on the ground had been killed, because the area was sparsely populated, but debris, body parts and personal items belonging to passengers, had been found for miles all around the main wreckage sites.'

'How gruesome,' commented Elsie looking down at the floor as if imagining the scene.

'Dr Eleni Wood has never gotten over the loss of her only child, and cruel fate would have it that she had also lost a British man described as a close friend and colleague of hers just a few months before the incident: his name was given as Dr Andrew Jones. I assume they had met when Dr Eleni Wood had spent some time studying and working in the United Kingdom.'

'Possibly,' agreed Elsie.

'Although there weren't many people around in the sparsely populated region that the plane came down in, some people had witnessed the plane crash, and even helped police and army to search for the bodies that dark night. There were pages and pages of psychiatric and psychology reports for those who were impacted, including dubious descriptions by some suggesting that certain passengers seemed alive when they first saw them, for a little while at least that was. There were chilling descriptions of some young woman who seemed to be trying to crawl or move, but no-one was listed as a survivor that night, not a single soul.'

'My,' said Eleni.

'Don't you see?' said Brian. 'It seems that Dr Eleni Wood blames the UK and other Commonwealth security agencies for what happened that night. She described in her talk how she believed that those agencies had created the monsters who killed her daughter through their policies.'

Elsie listened fascinated, 'But what does that have to do with me?'

'Because you sometimes liaise with counter-terror agencies, she possibly sees you as one of them. She likely would see you as being linked to what in her mind is "the enemy", in a sense. The trouble is, she's hugely popular, so I'm afraid that it's hard to know what to do about it if her group have targeted you.'

CHAPTER NINETEEN

Brian found that he was in fact rather intrigued even by the description of the diamond art-deco ring that the doomed passenger Brett carried in his backpack in 1986 when he boarded the Selkirk disaster flight. Brian decided to look into it some more, mainly because he simply couldn't get it out of his mind. Something just didn't seem quite right about it. It was hard to put into words precisely why it seemed so odd though. For that reason, Brian was thankful that his superiors hadn't been questioning him on this at all, so he didn't actually have to come up with anything to explain to anyone why he was spending time on this, all these years later.

Why would the male half of a hip young teen couple in the eighties chose an old-fashioned heirloom style ring for his fiancée?

Add into the bargain that decent antiques were expensive, and he wondered where on earth would the young man have gotten the money to buy something like that from? Their having the flight tickets was easily explained, because young Brett was a well-known son of an Australian aviation expert who was often given flight deals and perks through work; such things often trickle down to other relatives, *but the ring, how did he get that?* It could have been a piece handed down to him from someone in his own family of course, but without knowing that for sure, it didn't seem wise to Brian to just take this at face value.

Elsie's international contacts had proven useful again in investigating this issue. Going via each other's superior officers for the request, as they had been instructed to do for this case, Elsie was able to get in touch with the relevant British people to answer questions about the lost and found property recovered from the Selkirk disaster flight. They found out for sure that no ring matching the Edinburgh airport security guard's description was ever listed in the inventory of the collected plane debris. So, either it got lost, or it got stolen at some point along the way. It didn't seem likely that the security staff would have fabricated their account of the item, which was the only other alternative explanation.

Brian decided to try to find out if there were any other records of incidents such as thefts involving a ring of that sort of description in the UK. He spent many hours poring through record after record which he got access to via the UK team, bearing in mind that most of such items from the eighties were never properly put into electronic format. It was numerous images of badly hand written files on these things from those days that had to be searched. It seemed for a while that nothing would turn up, but then he came across a cold case from Scotland that had been translated to electronic record format.

There had been mention of the theft of an art deco ring from a woman who was killed along with her family in a barbaric home invasion a few years after the Selkirk disaster crash. Events as horrific as that were not at all standard for Scotland, let alone in the sparsely populated and quiet northern Scottish Highlands where the victims had lived. Police still sought to one day find the person or persons responsible, but nothing had been turned up at the time. Brian couldn't help but wonder if someone had perhaps found the ring in the crash debris and just decided to hold on to it. Diamonds are valuable after all. That seemed a most obvious explanation, that is, if it even was the same ring of course, which in fact couldn't be ascertained that easily.

In spite of the obvious challenges in working out if the ring involved in the home invasion was actually the same as the one Brett had boarded the crashed plane with, or not, Brian allowed his imagination to run on overdrive trying to figure it out. He just couldn't decide whether the ring could actually have been the key motivating reason for the home invasion, and the awful violence that went along with it, outlandish as it might seem. In his more grounded moments though, he would remember that he knew that most likely the ring wasn't even the same one as Brett had, and it was just a valuable small item stolen in an opportunistic fashion by the violent perpetrator. After all, the odds of it being the same ring were pretty low. Yet it still niggled on Brian's mind. In his mind's eye, he kept seeing this expensive and old-fashioned ring spinning slowly before him, the diamonds sparkling, and the gold shimmering. And then, he would repeatedly keep coming back to it being conspicuously missing from items recovered that night when he knew how thorough the ground search had been. It just didn't suit the circumstances of this young couple at all; it was just so odd from the beginning.

What played on Brian's mind even more troublingly was, if it was the same ring as the one from the police report a few years later, and if it was even the very reason for the break-in, was there anything else equally obvious that Brian and everyone who investigated this before him was missing? Maybe this fascination wasn't obvious at all though, and maybe he was just losing his mind a little. After all, no other officers ever thought so much about that ring which security described when they were investigating what might have happened that night.

Although the context wasn't pleasant, reading so much about engagement rings was somehow also making Brian's mind turn to considering the prospect of proposing to Elsie one day. He'd felt quite serious about her from the very start, and last week had been the first time he'd even had so much as a doubt about their relationship. He still felt very guilty about his fleeting doubts. In fact, he really wished that Elsie didn't know about them, because he was worried she might hold it against him on some level, and not even mention it, the way he found that women so often do in relationships. *Surely though, it would be understandable to her that anyone would be curious given that a connection, albeit described in the loosest of terms, between Elsie and the deceased pilot, had somehow ended up in police briefings when it didn't make any obvious sense?*

Brian's train of thought returned to mulling over the frustrations of the case. *Was this ring fascination never going to be anything but a dead end?*

*****

With nothing turning up either immediately, obviously or easily to provide further evidence of the ring's involvement in the Selkirk disaster theory, and nothing else new to go on, the following week it had been back to work as usual for both Brian and Elsie. Within that time though, there had been another exciting development at home: a larger and more prestigious apartment had become available in the same block that Brian was living in. It was quite a few floors higher, which meant the lift was the way to go, but once so high up there, the views from the corner wrapping windows were stunning; it was actually possible to catch glimpses of the Sydney Harbour Bridge from it.

Both Brian and Elsie were rostered on a day off the Saturday coming, and estate agents had scheduled an open home viewing for any interested potential tenants for the unit upstairs. It was an easy ride up the elevator to pop in at the scheduled viewing time to take a look. They were both quite curious to see how the upper half of their own building actually live. When they got up there, and in to see the place, they saw that they were among about ten other interested parties ready to take a look around. It wasn't surprising really, given the prestige of the place.

'I love it,' said Elsie with a kind of awestruck appreciation spread all over her face. 'I just don't want to get my hopes up too much, because I really do adore it, and it might go to someone else.'

The estate agent, Susan, as she cheerfully introduced herself to them, seemed keen to get tenants in as soon as possible, as far as Brian could tell. That was a good sign that they didn't really have too much serious competition for it in the current market. After all, they are fully aware that lots of people go to open inspections on such nice places just for the trip out, and to have a peek into the homes of the posher types, but have no real intention nor funds available to actually take the rent on.

Susan still did the thorough run down about the place for them along with everyone else, even though she knew that Brian lived on one of the lower floors already. Brian thought that was quite professional of her.

'There's a swimming pool, the gym is fabulous, and the communal barbeque area also has truly stunning views,' the agent began by explaining. 'This apartment of course has its own particular level of impressiveness thanks to the harbour glimpses. There's plenty of room to entertain out on that balcony.'

Elsie was already looking in the direction of the harbour views seeming in a daze.

'Well,' said Brian to Elsie: 'If you're happy with it, then I am too. Let's go for it.'

Elsie turned to him in amazement. 'Really? Do you mean that?'

'Of course I do,' he said, 'I can see how much you love this place, and I want to share in the rent with you so that we can get it together.' He felt just like Santa Claus gifting a little child on Christmas morn.

The estate agent was already honing in on the conversation ready to try to secure a deal.

'You know, if you are happy to put in your application for the rent as per the asking price, I can take it to the owners as soon as this afternoon, and get you approved following the usual checks by next week.'

Thought as much, no-one had been seriously offering yet, just taking a look around the place, decided Brian feeling quite pleased with himself and already imagining himself getting cozy in here along with Elsie.

'I think we'd be happy to do that,' he said looking to Elsie for a final nod of approval.

'Yes, we can, I am happy with it,' agreed Elsie.

Susan efficiently processed the necessary paperwork on the spot, and as Brian suspected they would be, they were successful in securing a lease on the rental property upstairs. It was all confirmed within the following week and a move-in date set for two weeks after that, allowing for the standard notice to the owners of their own respective current humble units. It had been a while since anything particularly fortuitous had happened for the couple, and it seemed to them like this might just have been that overdue lucky streak finally arriving to break a long spell of the mundane.

Their first night in the new place was truly special, they celebrated with a candle-lit Champagne toasted meal out on the balcony with the beautiful harbour visible as the backdrop. Brian often doubted himself in life, and he reflected for a moment on those early days when Elsie had first walked into his life, back when he was a bachelor in that little place downstairs. He remembered how nervous he was at first to even try to get to know her a little better, and now here they were, not just a couple, but something more, they were family now.

CHAPTER TWENTY

Brian came in through the door from work on a dull and dreary Monday still marvelling at their lovely new apartment that they had just moved into over the weekend prior. He found Elsie sitting staring into space, not even having made the effort to change or start making any preparations for dinner, which struck him as rather strange.

'Brian,' she said looking at him with the most serious expression. 'It's twins.'

'What?' said Brian almost stumbling with shock. 'Twins? What on earth do you mean, are you expecting?'

'No,' said Elsie. 'No, no that's not what I mean. I mean the terror attacks: they're twins, the theme of them is all about twins.'

Brian quickly took a seat. He had just been flummoxed by the momentary thought that he was going to be a Dad, and not just to one, but to two kids, so he needed a moment to recompose himself. It was a surreal feeling in that moment. The truth was though, he felt relieved in fact when it became apparent this was just another work-related discussion.

'Not many people know this Brian, and I'm telling you in confidence, but on the evening that the Selkirk disaster took place, a second British owned plane was almost blown up too. They caught that one at the airport though. A man involved was tried and sentenced in a secret closed trial. The public were never told. And now with this recent terror disaster, well, frankly it was the same thing, there were almost two planes blown out of the sky, as you would have seen in your briefing from us. British intelligence picked up on it in time, and managed to intercept the terrorist before he boarded. We have to find out who knew about that though, because they could be connected to something untoward. I say that because the general public do not know about these things at all, and that means anyone who does have knowledge of it, is a potential suspect. I think there's so much more and worse to come Brian, and I'm anxious about it.'

'The first thing that came to my mind when you mentioned twins and terrorism was of course the Twin Towers attack in 2001. Do you think that could be a part of this ongoing *Twins* theme too then?'

'Yes, it most definitely could be. And, even if it's a different terrorist group who were behind the big Twin Towers attack, they could be a related group, or even previously have been related. It's not unusual for radical groups to split off into disparate splinter cells after working together on plans originally, which could explain similarities in themes or styles of their attacks moving forward even after separation.'

'That would make sense,' agreed Brian who was increasingly feeling saddened by how much this seemed to be impacting on Elsie. She was emotionally drained. He wished he could say or do something to ease the strain, even if he really did feel out of his depth with all of this now, truth be told. Elsie's suggestions of possible connections to the Twin Towers attackers really were all making him feel rather overwhelmed.

Brian got up and walked over to the couch, sat beside her and planted a kiss firmly on her lips and said: 'You know I love you so much. You are just like a mirror of myself, and I love that about you. This is not going to happen here. We will stop them in time if it's something they're thinking about.'

'And there's something more,' said Elsie ominously.

'What?' asked Brian.

'It's something that's coming out from the intelligence community here which our department got word of, so again

I'm telling you in confidence,' Elsie cleared her throat. 'You remember that incident with the Hong Kong bound flight, the one that Professor Alice Wirth, Dr John McFay and Dr Gareth Hughes were loosely connected to?'

'Of course. Yes, I remember it well.'

'Well, it seems they've intercepted some foreign intelligence that suggests that the plane was in fact hijacked after all.'

'You mean that whole story about the weather system was a lie?' asked Brian incredulously.

'No.' Then Elsie paused for a second before explaining what she meant. 'Well, when I say no, I really mean not exactly. It was true that there was a dangerous weather cell, but it was a coincidence that happened at the same time as the incident affecting that plane.'

'So, we were told a convenient half-truth then by the higher ups, which basically still amounts to a lie?'

'I suppose so,' agreed Elsie, 'When you put it like that.'

She paused for a moment staring off into space again. It always unnerved Brian when she did that, and he wondered what she would come out with next.

'And there's more too: our intelligence community believe that the airline company did retrieve the flight recorder when they said they didn't, but kept the contents hushed. They believe the flight was hijacked after the German pilot's call to CAS, and coincidentally just before encountering the freak weather system. If it really was hijacked, then that would certainly explain why the hijacking pilots weren't experienced enough to safely pass through, or to avoid the weather system altogether, as they should have. So basically, to sum it up in a nutshell, something went very wrong with their plan, whatever that was, but the upshot of it all was the plane was destroyed anyway. Not in the way they intended, perhaps, but destroyed in another, nonetheless.'

Brian slowly sank down into the couch mulling over what he had just been told.

'I'm mind blown,' was all Brian could manage to say.

'Me too,' said Elsie. 'That's why I had to share it with you. We are not to investigate it in any way though, they've already decided that, the people higher up in the chain. That's because the information has come through top secret channels that are to remain secret. In any case, the terrorist or terrorists involved have died along with everyone else in the crash.'

'Don't investigate it?' repeated Brian incredulously. 'They have no idea what they're asking of us in that. And are you thinking what I am thinking regarding the murder of Dr John McFay? Neither of us were convinced he was killed by his wife, so could he also have been killed in a related terror attack? We know he worked for the government too, after all.'

'I don't really know what to think,' answered Elsie very honestly. 'Although given that we still have no realistic suspects with a motive, it's entirely possible that he was. And I suppose, more likely than it previously had seemed, in light of that new information confirming the plane incident was terrorism, as you say.'

'I think we have to open up the case again,' said Brian. 'I'll find some way to do it. I just have to come up with a believable reason. So long as it's something that will allow us to avoid anyone making a direct connection to this new revelation that might get anyone into trouble. Once I am able to convince management that there's something worth looking into again, I can arrange to get a small dedicated team of junior officers on to that with a new line of enquiry. By doing that we can cast the net out a bit more broadly too, just in case you are right about some bigger group out there with ongoing plans, and themes even.'

CHAPTER TWENTY-ONE

If the next day at work for Brian had achieved anything, it had made it abundantly clear that the upper brass in the force must also be rather anxious about what might be getting planned by terrorists. The biggest clue to the senior management's apparent concern, was the unprecedented levels of co-operation they were facilitating between special response units like Elsie's, and his own side of policing.

Word on the street was that they needed to find themselves a man who was known as "The General", although he was never an official member of any Middle Eastern or Western armed forces. That made it very difficult to get a handle on who exactly he was, let alone where he had been, and where he might be planning on going. Translators and surveillance officers were working hard to pick up any clues as to who he was. Some of the translated material suggested a sort of lower-level medical background for him, such as nursing. It would fit as a theory, because they had picked up some jokes about "The General" in recordings they'd made while monitoring some among minority immigrant communities. It was typical of what a male nurse might face from narrow minded types of people with fixed views on gender roles.

Brian wondered what it all really meant, because to him, something just didn't seem quite right about that particular piece of intelligence - a man who ended up leading a terrorist movement being a male nurse by trade? Could this be real? Maybe his mother or wife was a nurse? That was a possibility Elsie had already thought of when they discussed it together, one that seemed to make a little more sense.

"The General" was suspected, by some in the intelligence community, of being the mastermind who was truly behind the Selkirk disaster. Most legal and policing authorities, however, widely disputed that claim, saying that they had found and punished those to blame. Although the media reported widely that those imprisoned for it still proclaimed their innocence of the charges. It was hard to know what to believe sometimes as a member of the public, or even as a police officer like Brian who was not generally privy to security agency files.

If Elsie was correct on her other theory, and plans were all on the theme of *twins*, then this latest terror attack, the shooting down of a passenger plane and the attempt on another, could mark the start of "The General's" come back. This could be the first attack on the West by him since the eighties. And if so, then who knew what he might have planned after that? The sky was the limit, quite literally.

This whole situation posed another awkward question too though. If current intelligence that had been passed on to them was correct, then why did "The General" take such a long break between his activities in the eighties, and his re-emerging activities now? It would seem a bit strange, but then again, big plans take time to come to fruition.

Brian had instructed several junior officers on his team to investigate Dr Eleni Wood some more. It was the only really solid place to start digging again right now after all. They had heard on the grapevine, though they had not been officially informed, that she was now a person of interest to the specialist response unit, and possibly some other external agencies too. There wasn't much known about her or her family until around 1963 when they had immigrated to Australia from Chechnya. Dr Wood was the middle one of the family's three children. After their arrival in Australia, they had lived a fairly uneventful life with the exception that Dr Eleni Wood had become a rape victim in 1966. She had become pregnant through that assault, and had given the child up for adoption to a UK based family who were related to her Australian adoptive parents. That child ended up being her only child in the end though. Her only daughter Kelly was the one whom she had often spoke of publicly, the one who died in the Selkirk plane disaster.

Interestingly, many people who found themselves in the same social circle as Wood's girl Kelly, seemed to believe that Kelly was the daughter of the late Dr Andrew Jones. Dr Jones was widely described as a close friend of Dr Eleni Wood. At that time, only a handful of people knew the truth, which was that she was Eleni's child, and not Andrew's at all. After the plane disaster, it seems Dr Wood had experienced some sort of breakdown, and she began telling practically everyone she met not only that she had had a daughter Kelly, but the full details of her daughter's experience in the terror atrocity.

Brian wondered why it had been that Dr Andrew Jones was content with being widely described as related to Kelly for all that time. Why had he simply allowed people to believe he was her father for so many years, just to save Dr Eleni Wood the embarrassment of people knowing about the rape she experienced? It's quite a big thing to take responsibility for fathering a child, isn't it? Brian wondered if he was just being overly analytical about all of this, or judgemental even.

Brian couldn't help but to feel a deep sense of pity for Dr Eleni Wood over her having lost her only daughter. That was even in spite of his strong general discomfort with the woman after having heard the type of accusatory things she said while she aired her views, as she did so often in her public presentations. No reasonable person could deny that her claims and assertions did seem rather wild at times. After all, at one point she even accused the Australian government of having neglected security for her daughter's boyfriend. She gave the impression that she believed he should have had increased security given his father's line of work for the Australian Government. She seemed to insinuate that the reason there was an absence of any security detail, was because he was dating her daughter who happened to be a black woman.

Brian had checked out some of the particulars of the allegations, and it turned out that in those days, absolutely no-one in Brett's father's line of work had any sort of security detail. So there definitely had been no discrimination there. Further, by all accounts his family had no issues with his black nurse girlfriend. It seemed that Dr Eleni Wood truly was a victim of unspeakable grief, but exaggerated as her public awareness raising efforts were, there was certainly no evidence that she had ever had any direct involvement in organising or inciting terror attacks.

In following up the other active lead, Elsie had gone through her superiors to get agreement for Brian's team to re-investigate the Scottish home invasion in the eighties. In particular, they decided that they would look at the theft of an art deco ring along with Scottish police. Brian had felt sickened to his stomach reading the details of the case, because apparently to remove the ring from the woman, someone had cut off her whole finger.

Was it an act of deeply personal revenge?

It certainly sounded like it. *Just like the David McWellin case,* thought Brian.

Reading the reports, it appeared that the whole family was tortured before their violent deaths too. Scottish police had now re-opened the cold case, now taking on board the suggestion from Brian's team in Australia that the ring that was taken in the home invasion could have been the same ring missing from the Selkirk disaster plane inventory. Brian wished he had a budget that could stretch to hiring artists to make drawings of the ring from descriptions given by airport security, and also of those who knew the dead Scottish family, but sadly he most certainly did not have funding like that at his disposal. He would just have to make do with what he had to work with.

It made no sense, of course, for any terrorist to go so far as to blow up an aeroplane over a piece of jewellery. The likely chances of ever retrieving it from the wreckage would be problematic, if not impossible, for one thing. But, if it were the same ring that was later stolen in this hellish crime, it was definitely strange that it was involved in two tragedies within a short time of each other. Strange enough for him to want to know more.

Brian mulled over who Brett and Kelly's closest relatives were, wondering if any of them would have been capable of such a thing as an act of revenge, and if they had ever harboured the thought that their deceased loved one's jewellery had been stolen as they lay dead or dying in that field at Selkirk after the crash? Scottish police had never linked the two incidents in any way before. This was the first time there was any sort of investigation into that aspect of it. It certainly would have been infuriating for some people to think that their loved ones' belongings had been stolen at such a time, rather than being given assistance. Similarly so for them, if they had believed that their bodies and personal belongings weren't shown more respect, but then again, they would have to have known about it in the first place before it would be an issue. And how could they have?

One possible suspect for being a person who could have known, was Brett's aviation expert father; he might have had access to more information about the incident through his line of work. Perhaps he would have been told about his lost son boarding the plane with a ring and known that it was never recovered from the crash site. But overall, it wouldn't seem at all likely for his father to have organised something like that home invasion. He was an ordinary family man with no criminal convictions. Brian felt stupid for even considering it, even for the sake of completion. Similarly, his ex-partner, Brett's mother, had no criminal convictions or history of violence, and was unlikely to be in any way linked to a violent crime.

On the other side of this situation was Kelly's GP and human rights activist mother Dr Eleni Wood, and her unknown rapist father. The rapist father might have been violent enough to attack a family he thought had his dead daughter's ring, but given the circumstances of his fatherhood, it seemed unlikely he would even be aware of where his daughter was living, let alone the circumstances surrounding her death and the jewellery that was presumed to have been intended for her.

Of course, there was the popular doctor, Dr Eleni Wood herself, who had to be considered, and her family from Chechnya. She and her family would have had knowledge of the ring since it was missing in personal items returned to victims' family members. Police had mentioned the engagement style ring Brett was carrying on board in interviews with the bereaved family, records could be found to confirm that much. However, records also showed that both of Dr Eleni Wood's, as it turned out, adoptive parents, were now deceased, and her two siblings had never been in trouble with the law.

Dr Eleni Wood's family were described as moderate Muslims, but they were also from an area known for Muslim insurgency. While Dr Wood herself tried hard to show the world a face of peace and tolerance, the possibility that her resentments against some British and Australian people ran even deeper than it had first seemed to Brian they did, could not really be fully ruled out at this stage. She frequently openly made many inflammatory remarks about the government these days, and that is what forms the very basis of terrorist sentiment after all.

CHAPTER TWENTY-TWO

The next week brought news that received a mixed reception from some corners of society: Dr Eleni Wood was going to be awarded a peace and international relations medal for her work in trying to end torture and renditions. To many she was seen as an oracle, but to some people working within the stretched intelligence community, she was seen as more of a slanderer and trouble maker. She could stand up and accuse them of whatever she liked to the whole world, but due to secrecy rules, they couldn't defend themselves from any of it.

Her latest campaigns had involved her pushing for a Royal Commission into the work of the security services in all Commonwealth nations: nothing like that had ever been discussed seriously before, let alone been considered or looked likely to actually happen. This award was seen by many as another stepping stone on her path to success in achieving that goal, which to most was a terrifying thought.

Brian showed Elsie the article in the newspaper that mentioned it: 'What do you think of this?'

'Well, unlike you, I haven't been to see any of her talks, so it's hard for me to form any sort of opinion on the woman.'

Even though she hadn't directly told Brian, he had already gathered through his own personal deductions, that Elsie's specialist response unit had now listed Dr Eleni Wood as a possible person of interest with connections to terrorists or terrorism. He guessed that was something that he wasn't allowed to know about yet, and he wondered why that was.

'Based on what you said about her though,' continued Elsie, 'well, it's food for thought.'

'Personally, I think she stirs up racism, but I don't feel I could say that widely because she is just so popular. I'm waiting for them to start adding the halo to her photographs,' said Brian.

Elsie laughed out loud. 'Well perhaps this latest award is an intermediary step to them treating her like a saint or something. How will you cope Brian?'

'You make it sound like I'm overreacting about all of this.'

'You just seem a bit fixated on her, that's all,' said Elsie.

'I wouldn't say I'm fixated. I just feel there's something not quite right about her circuit tours is all. Maybe it's because she doesn't have proper evidence to back up some of the things she claims, particularly about our own country, and yet no-one ever comments on it. They act like it's all clearly true if she states it, and anyone who disagrees with her is accused of racism, in one way or another.'

CHAPTER TWENTY-THREE

The authorities were jittery. As the Christmas season began to reach the stores, and the heat grew more sweltering by the hour, those who spoke languages such as Arabic, Urdu, or Persian, and who worked for police or security agency surveillance teams, were having no leave approved whatsoever. Their focus was on finding any hints of terrorists either coming into the country to co-ordinate attacks, or those already in Australia activating within their cells, but so far, they had come up with nothing.

The upcoming award for Dr Eleni Wood was being discussed by many in the minority world in a very positive sense, ever since the media releases on it came out. There was no evidence showing that anyone in the public viewed her as a terror leader or terror target, but Elsie's team had a hunch that something majorly negative was also being planned to coincide with the award ceremony. They had no idea what though, or who was actually behind it.

Police were out in force when the evening of the big event arrived. Some junior officers in Brian's team were there under cover. All of them remained in contact with head office throughout the evening. The night was unusually glamourous and glitzy for an event attended and hosted mainly by academics. Rather than a university auditorium, which would have been more the conventional choice for such a night, they had chosen a stylish central Sydney hotel as their venue for the evening. Before Dr Eleni Wood was called up to receive her prize, once again there was a brief flashy intro sequence which gave a run-down of rumoured rendition flights and torture, without much solid detail, but every time the subjects came up, it was to great rounds of applause. When Dr Eleni Wood rose and approached the stage, the crowd erupted in a roar of even greater applause and whistling, with most of the room up on their feet for her. She received her award gracefully and promised to continue the fight for justice. Or her brand of justice, as Brian and some others viewed it.

Everything at the award evening went without a hitch in the end. It felt anticlimactic for that reason, but in a good way. A couple of people were stopped and searched in the area because police were so nervous that night, but they were all clean.

It wasn't until the next morning that the gruesome news came in that the bodies of two young females, in separate cities of Australia, were found dead under highly suspicious circumstances. Both young women were in their early twenties, and most notably, both of them had fathers who had worked in army intelligence roles. Brian could not believe there was any way that could all just be a coincidence.

The first of the deaths was of a young woman in Melbourne. And, much like the death of David McWellin, she had been found in her own apartment after a night out, apparently having committed suicide, but with no signs of a struggle. Once again, calling cards of local prostitutes were found in the room with the body, just as was found at the David McWellin death scene. Of course, it was even more odd seeming when the victim was a female.

The other death, and the associated crime scene was in Perth. Incredulously it followed a similar pattern right down to the calling cards for sex workers being present close to where the body lay.

The families of both young women were said to be inconsolable.

By now, the rest of the force had heard of, and were starting to agree with, the theory of these being so-called *twin attacks*. Although not related, or even known to one another, the two young women who were dead were like *twins* in the sense of how many aspects of their lives reflected one another. This was also true of the circumstances of their deaths, and the crime scenes their bodies were found in, which arguably could have been seen as deliberately staged by a perpetrator. In terms of similarities in the dead women's profiles, both were around a similar age, both of their fathers had worked in military intelligence in object tracking more specifically, and both were living away from home attending university.

While it was harder to show such a clear *twin deaths* pattern link in the recent cases involving the two young male victims, Arthur Tolbert and David McWellin, as it was for the two young women, similar parallels could still be drawn. Perhaps the perpetrator was still perfecting their kill style with them, and what they might see as the artistry behind the message sent by it all.

The bus accident involving the young man, Arthur Tolbert, in Brisbane, had to be re-examined too now. There could have been some foul play that had so far been ignored if his death was the so-called *twin* to the death of mathematician David McWellin in Sydney. The body would have to be exhumed and tests run; his parents were distraught when they were informed of that unpleasant reality. Brian did empathise of course; for the family and other loved ones left behind, resuming a body was like roughly ripping off a tenderly placed band aid on an open wound one was trying so desperately to heal.

CHAPTER TWENTY-FOUR

Elsie felt rather embarrassed and was aware of her cheeks reddening a little as her superiors personally named and thanked her in a joint task force meeting held between her own and Brian's team.

'Some of you may be aware,' began her boss, 'and others not, that because one of our own correctly anticipated the recent plane disaster, we now have active links not only with Scotland Yard in London, but also with some of the UK's top spies to help us gain more information in the coming weeks. We anticipate that there might be big planned attacks on our country, and in others in the Western world. This pro-active and international response is something we can all be very proud of.'

The joint international response team meant a huge pile of work in the lead up to Christmas, now everyone in the team's leave was cancelled. Elsie felt she had fast become rather unpopular with some of her colleagues for that reason. 'It's fine for you', was now typical of the type of thing colleagues would regularly say to her, 'You don't have kids and school holidays to work around.'

Even after a plane was shot from the sky, some still didn't seem to appreciate the severity of the terror threat that their country was potentially facing. A sobering thought.

'Don't you think this is all over exaggerated and hyped up?' Elsie had overheard some junior officers discussing over lunch. 'I expect Christmas will come and go without a problem personally, but no fun holidays for us now.'

For a moment, a sense of dread filled Elsie's mind: *What if they're right and all of this is for nothing?* Then that thought was quickly replaced by a sense of guilt: *But really, we should all want it to be nothing, for everything to be ok and no-one to get injured, and of course, that is what I want.*

One of the most exciting pieces of information that was shared by the UK with Elsie's unit, and with other security agencies in Australia, was that Dr Andrew Jones, the close friend of Dr Eleni Wood, whom she had stated was the father of her child, had in fact joined MI6, well, briefly. As part of his recruitment, a fake death had been arranged for him, but shortly after that, he completely disappeared off the radar and not a trace of him had been found since. Dr Eleni Wood certainly had experienced quite the run of back luck in 1986, and Elsie didn't like coincidences, so she decided to look into all of it some more.

There had been little to stand in the way of Dr Andrew Jones and the MI6 career that he presumably must have dreamed of. He was a white middle-class male, on paper at least, he had no prior convictions or psychological problems, and his parents were also squeaky clean. What was unusual about his application was that he was happy to leave behind his wife and two children to pursue his own interests. He had described his marriage as an unhappy one, and expressed a wish to set his wife free, and to let her and the children move on without him. While he, on the other hand, wanted now to be of service to his country. Dr Andrew Jones had the perfect background, his paternal grandfather had been an MI6 man too, so he would be carrying on in his footsteps, and he was accepted.

General files they shared the content of described how he had done training for a few months, including being sent overseas to the Middle East. But the troubling thing was, he never returned. It was not long after the Selkirk disaster occurred that he vanished, and truth be told, MI6 focused on trying to get to the bottom of that disaster, which meant that one agent's disappearance took a back seat. *Perhaps the mystery of Dr Andrew Jones hadn't gotten the attention that it deserved* thought Brian when he was informed of all of this, *but MI6 are considered among the best spies in the world, so surely they should have a good feel for what's important to get to the bottom of and what's not.*

*****

Working together with a representative from both MI6 and Scotland Yard, Elsie's team had pieced together how the murder of David McWellin was likely achieved, and also how it could have been done without there being any witnesses to it.

In the days that followed the murder, detectives had knocked on each and every door in his high-rise apartment block and spoken to all residents. No-one had seen anyone suspicious entering the block, or leaving around the time of the murder. There was CCTV at the entrance, and it had been checked, but it revealed nothing. The police were certain that the recording was genuine and hadn't been tampered with, *so how was any of it possible?*

What the joint international task force pieced together was that David's killer had been living inside the apartment block for at least a month before, and for some time after the murder. An apartment three floors up from David's was home to three men from Pakistan, with a fourth room that they also sublet to students and others. Police had questioned them, and in fact they had probably questioned and spoke with the killer himself. He had an informal subletting arrangement with the three other men who rented the apartment, but he had even given them the name and ID of his cousin who was an Australian permanent resident, instead of his own. Had he used his own name and identity, Elsie's team would have quickly discovered that he was wanted by MI5 for questioning in relation to terrorist related activities in the UK. His identity was only discovered after facial recognition technology was used to cross check CCTV footage from David's apartment block with suspects in Australia and the UK.

His cousin was supposed to be in Sydney studying, but in fact, due to a long bout of illness, he had remained at home in the Pakistani country town he lived in this term, not returning after his trip home for the holiday period. The killer had gone so far as to attend lectures, marking his name off on tutorial lists, and to do a delivery job in place of his cousin as well, all just to cultivate his cover identity. His cousin had been due to start work in Sydney as a delivery driver, but had never met any of the dispatchers in person yet, so they were none the wiser that it wasn't him who showed up to commence the job.

On the night of the murder, the killer must have received notification, likely on a disposable mobile phone, that David had had his drink spiked and would hence not be resistant to an attack that evening. Keys to the units would also have been stolen and copied in advance preparations, so after that, it was a simple case of him going downstairs, using his key to enter the victim's apartment, then carrying out the kill, all of it having been done to order. He then vanished, like a ghost.

There was a terrifying combination of both organisation and disorganisation within the cell, which made them so difficult to either anticipate or capture. The man who stalked David McWellin and then killed him, was operating as a lone wolf, but with help and assistance from a well-organised and well-informed leader. Still, at any time he was free to leave, and when he did, he simply boarded a plane back to Pakistan after the murder was carried out and disappeared. The three men he shared an apartment with were interrogated, but there was no evidence that they had any clue as to his true motives for being there. There was a similar story to be heard when it came to his cousin who lived in the country. He claimed that he had no idea that his ID cards had been stolen and were being used by his cousin from Pakistan, and that just like the rest of the family, they now had no idea where he was. The best part of it all was, no-one could prove otherwise.

CHAPTER TWENTY-FIVE

Exhumation of Arthur Tolbert's body allowed a forensic toxicology report to be done on his body. To ensure due diligence, the team examined his mother and father's hair samples also. Interestingly, what they found in both Arthur's body, and in his mother's hair, were traces of a well-known date rape drug. The amount in the mother's hair was minimal, but there was a quantity in Arthur's body that would have led to loss of consciousness within a certain amount of time. What was quite clear now was, Arthur's mother had not felt faint due to a psychic link to her son's death as had been reported in the local newspaper, but rather more likely due to having consumed some of the same substance at the gathering which they all attended that evening before the incident. Pieces of the puzzle were starting to fall into place in Brian's mind.

Police in Queensland had already set about interviewing each and every person who was at the engagement party. That was over one hundred people, no easy task. All of the wait staff who served the drinks and canapes had to be included too. Nothing threw up any useful matches though. Whoever had targeted the Tolbert family had somehow managed to get that substance into their food or drink, and it was almost certainly during that party because there was nothing to suggest any foul play within their home or family in the past. It was unclear who the intended recipient of the drug really was though, because it seemed both Arthur and his mother had ended up consuming some. His father had none of it, but that didn't necessarily rule him out as the killer's target. Perhaps Arthur had taken the drink meant for his father. It was beginning to look like they would never find out.

It was now seen as most likely an act of terror gone wrong that Arthur was killed by a bus versus at his home by a possible terrorist, but the result was still the same, he was dead.

The main question that lingered on was: had he been killed because he had found out about something big that was going to happen, or was he just unlucky to be chosen as one of a set of the now so-called *twin* terror victims.

Something else that was notable had come out in the wash in Brisbane though, and it was relayed down south to Elsie's team in Sydney via the grapevine fairly quickly. An elderly nurse named Sally had confessed on her death bed that incredibly she was not a real Australian at all. She herself was an illegal immigrant who took on the identity of a deceased Indigenous Australian woman to get into the country easily and without drawing any attention to herself. The witnesses to her last testimony reportedly sat in an incredulous silence when she began to describe how she had been involved for years in hiding and smuggling other illegal immigrants into Commonwealth nations. She admitted that she had been part of a secretive network that aimed to help parents and children who were escaping domestic violence and oppression. She could say truthfully that she had done it all with only the best of intentions, but it had played on her mind right until her final days that life hadn't turned out so well for all of them after her rescues and interventions.

Her death bed weeks had been a fairly serene experience. She was comforted by the presence of the priest, and the memories of years gone by began to flood past fast and furiously as days increasingly were filled with sleep or semi-conscious moments. Taking some laboured breaths, she began to recall the end of her journey delivering Hela and Haba from Syria in the safety and freedom of the West. As she got nearer to passing, she recalled how proud and relieved she had felt when she got the children out of their father's home safely. Her eyes lit up a little at the return of the vivid memory of how elated she was once she made it to the fishing boat meeting point where the fishermen who would provide their passage out of the hostile country were waiting. She remembered thinking that the worst of it had all seemed to be all over. It really wasn't though. Even after having arrived in Cyprus finally, where everything should have been as straightforward as anyone could imagine, Sally reflecting back on it, realised that was when it dawned on her that it seems sometimes, even the best laid plans have to change. There were meant to have been two families meeting Sally at the airport: one for the boy and one for the girl. She really was crushed when only one had turned up in the end, and often asked the question "why did they let her down like that?".

Even to this, her dying day. Sally was still racked with guilt over the fact that the escape plan had meant separating the twins from one another. It was all the worse for them because they had just recently watched their mother pass away, and she had to appease them by assuring them that they would still see one another. But that was a promise that she really couldn't keep. The problem was, it wasn't just so easy as all that to find places for people to disappear, and together, in rich first world nations like the UK. Sally had truly believed that both children would be travelling onwards from Cyprus with their respective new families on British citizen's passports. Due to how the law was back in those days, a British passport wasn't something they otherwise would have had, due to their British mother having given birth overseas and not being married to a British father. The one family which had turned up was the family who had come to claim the boy. They seemed a nice and respectable enough couple; the man was a Scottish psychiatrist, and his wife was a Welsh woman who had previously worked as a nurse. From then on, the boy would be known as Andrew Jones. *Well at least we've found a place for the boy,* thought nurse Sally as she watched him walk away with them at the time, the child fighting tears. It would have been even worse if she'd been left standing there with two children, but being left with one with nowhere to go on to next was bad enough.

It was a British army corporal and his wife who had been meant to turn up to collect the girl Hela, they were the no shows. Sally often wondered why, and what had changed their minds? Perhaps it was just that many people didn't really want the responsibility of caring for other people's children when all was said and done, even if they did feel a sense of patriotism or duty about it all.

Nurse Sally had no means by which to take the girl Hela back with her to Australia at that point, so she had gotten in touch with some contacts her organisation had near to the area she found herself in. She explained to them that unfortunately, and callous as it might seem, she really had to get back to Australia and back to work; no-one in Brisbane was even aware that she was off on adventures overseas, so she couldn't just not show up for her next rostered shift.

This meant that for that time being, the girl Hela, just had to stay behind in Cyprus with a safe family until such times as Sally could find someone in Australia who was willing to hide her and to take care of her. There had to be some sort of route into Australia for her; Sally had known those kids were counting on her, and that they had trusted her completely when they left all they knew behind them. She really wanted to manage to do what she had promised them, even if it meant paying something to a poorer family in return for the favour. There was no way Sally was going to be sending anyone back to the Syrian family that she now blamed for the murder of two children's mother. Besides, she had realised that by now they would have discovered that the twins had been taken, and they would be after her entire organisation for it. After all, they weren't a poor family or lacking in connections.

Consoling her troubled mind as she lay weak and still on the bed, Sally was grasping to reach the reassuring memory that true to her word, when she arrived back in Brisbane, Australia, she had worked tirelessly via her network of contacts to find a place for the girl Hela. So it wasn't like she had really left her behind completely. They found a home and identity for her which while unfortunately meant she would be living in a rough neighbourhood in Perth, Western Australia, was, on the plus side, with a family of moderate Islamic background. Sally hoped that would make her transition back to Western life easier. The family she had found for her had recently immigrated to Australia from Chechnya. The first thing they did when they took her in, was to have changed Hela's name to Eleni. That was the name of their deceased daughter who was surprisingly similar in age and appearance to Hela, and whose identity she would be assuming. With the Chechnyans having moved into the country just after their own daughter's sudden death, no-one in the immigration department of Australia was aware that Eleni was now a different person. That meant that Hela became an Australian citizen too, along with the rest of them. From that point on, she was known as Eleni, the new immigrant from Chechnya.

Over the years, nurse sally was updated on the children's welfare occasionally, and she always wrestled with guilt about separating the siblings. Hela's childhood didn't go quite as well as Sally had hoped, she got occasional updates via the network, and in fact, she was racked with worry many a time over it. Hela had even become a rape victim at one point which led to her having a pregnancy at a young age. She gave birth to a child who was given up for adoption in a private arrangement with people known to her own adoptive parents. The story wasn't all bad for Hela at that stage though, because she had still managed to get a place in medical school a few years later, and she went on to become a general practitioner. Sadly though, tragedy was to strike her once again: her only child whom she had given up for adoption was killed in a 1986 terrorist attack on an airline. Her child was a daughter. She had been travelling on the doomed American flight along with her boyfriend. Hela was inconsolable when that had happened.

Haba's life, or that of Andrew whom he had become, had seemed to have gone much better as far as nurse Sally could tell; albeit a short one that he had lived. He had followed in his adoptive father's footsteps and become a psychiatrist. He was called Dr Andrew Jones thereafter. However, Sally was informed that he sadly died fairly young of a heart attack in 1986. At the time of his death, the man she had rescued as a boy was married and was survived by his wife and two sons. His sons later went on to have four children between them, and Sally saw that as a sort of achievement on her part.

Sometimes Sally felt embittered that the British consulate hadn't done more to help Hela. Afterall, not only were they were the first people she tried to reach out to when she first realised that she had become trapped in Syria, but it was their responsibility to assist. Why hadn't they done something useful rather than just giving her Sally's organisation's contact details? If they had acted, then she and her organisation wouldn't have had to get involved in the first place, and she wouldn't have been left to carry the enormous guilt over the parts of the less than perfect mission that went wrong.

At least though, she knew she had done her very best. When the moment came for her to leave this earthly life, she went with a clear conscious.

As far as Brian's interest went though in Sally's emotional death bed recollections and confessions, the bombshell revelation was that she had mentioned Dr Eleni Wood by name. She had revealed and confirmed that her true identity and original name was Hela, a girl from Syria. She had also confirmed that she was the sister of a deceased man, Dr Andrew Jones, whom she helped to place in the UK. Finally, there were some names now to go along with some vague rumoured existences.

Luckily, the person that Sally confided in had felt duty-bound to report it to the police, and so the information had made its way to Brian and Elsie's ears. After that, and when police made it clear this was a potentially important line of inquiry, relatives had searched Sally's home and found some very detailed diaries providing further explanation.

This meant that not only was one of the biggest critics of the Australian security services guilty of identity theft and fraud, but that MI6 suffered a massive security breach. They had, albeit briefly, hired a man who was in no way related to the family that had raised him, and yet family connections had formed the main basis for their judgements on his character and suitability.

When Elsie heard the news, she was just relieved that finally they had some information on Dr Eleni Wood, something deeper than the superficial manicured stage image she carefully presented to the world. The illegal immigration case would have to be investigated now. Dr Eleni Wood would only have been a child when she made the move to Australia, but still have been old enough to understand at least on some level, and to recall what had happened when she joined the Chechnyan family. *Was she aware that the late Dr Andrew Jones was her brother?* That was the first question that came to Elsie's mind in light of the new information. It was likely the sort of thing that most other people would just have dismissed as being of low importance. Elsie had a particular talent for picking up on little details like that.

*****

Not so long after the truth was revealed about Dr Eleni Wood, or Hela as she was called at birth, Brian was happy to get some further clarification on matters related to his pet obsession in the case. This being of course the significance, or not, of the expensive art deco ring carried on board. Incredibly, Scotland Yard had confirmed to their satisfaction that the ring that was carried on to the Selkirk disaster flight, and the one cut off from a woman's finger in a violent home invasion in the following years, were likely one and the same piece of jewellry. They were working on the theory that a relative of either Brett or Kelly could have been involved since it was a highly personal attack.

The ring itself, according to an art-deco expert, was a very old piece that had been listed as stolen. Brian had been right in his suspicions over it, it was indeed extremely valuable. It had been reported as stolen by the family of an elderly widowed woman, Mrs Bentick-MacBen, who Kelly was hired to care for as a private nurse. The police had some very clear photos of it in their files. It was a stunning ring that the old lady had been gifted for her twenty-first birthday by her parents. Her parents had been from a well-to-do family clearly. The band of the ring was made of platinum, no expense had been spared. In the centre was a very clear square cut diamond, and on either side, a square cut emerald. The ring was a beautiful and eye-catching piece.

Mrs Bentick-MacBen had been suffering from the early stages of dementia, that was the reason why her children had hired the private nursing team that employed Kelly to help care for her at home for as long as was possible. Sometimes flurries of memories of her youth would return as her disease progressed, and Mrs Bentick-MacBen would dress up and relive her glory days, believing herself to actually be in them still. Perhaps, thought Brian, on one morning when Kelly had arrived to check on her, she might have found the old woman having something of a party with herself. Brian imagined that she would be wearing a dress from the nineteen twenties, if she was still slim enough to fit it. On her head she might have sported a matching head band, and her cheeks would have been rouged. She had most likely looked out her precious stone studded art-deco style ring recalling, through a clouded memory, her parents gifting it to her, and the excitement she had felt at the time when she first set eyes on it.

By the time Kelly arrived, she likely would have to have helped Mrs Bentick-MacBen get undressed, while hearing about all of the eligible young men she'd met that night, and been asked to put her ring back in her jewellery box. Brian surmised further, that maybe that was just the kind of moment when temptation became too much for Kelly. Brian could imagine how she might have looked at the incredibly clear diamond centre-piece as if spell bound, and promptly slipped the ring into her pocket. After all, Mrs Bentick-MacBen wouldn't have noticed at all, it would have been like taking candy from a baby.

Weighing it all up now, it seemed then that the young couple's doomed impromptu trip to the USA was less about a romantic proposal than it was about Brett helping Kelly to sell the ring to someone stateside. Fencing it out there could better ensure a buyer who wouldn't report it to UK police, or get picked up on by them by chance while they covered something else. They knew it wouldn't be important enough to be listed as lost or stolen property over there. By that point, Kelly probably felt she couldn't return it even if she wanted to. She would have been in too deep by that point already. What better place to go to offload it then than somewhere as large as the USA, and where antiques are also incredibly popular.

The new evidence linking stolen property to Eleni's deceased daughter Kelly, who also died in a tragic terrorist incident, and the information that her own Australian identity was completely fraudulent, was enough for Scotland Yard and Elsie to both want Dr Eleni Wood brought in for questioning. After all, it was also combined with the revelations that her uncle Dr. Andrew Jones, was linked to identity theft, then had managed via that channel to get himself inside MI6, and was listed now a missing person, which hadn't even been properly investigated at the time. If all of that weren't reason enough to see that there was likely something more to it all, and that seemed to have gotten missed in the past, the distressing violent deaths of those who then got hold of the ring Kelly stole, added an even deeper sinister twist.

CHAPTER TWENTY-SIX

Dr Eleni Wood was not at all happy at being brought in for questioning, and the day she came, she brought with her one of Sydney's top human rights lawyers. *Probably all provided to her as a free service*, Brian thought to himself feeling the resentment growing inside him, *I should be so lucky to afford a top-notch professional like that if I ever needed it.* For that reason, he was in some ways glad he would just be a spectator in this interview. The lawyer was a smartly dressed man who looked to be in his mid-forties. His hair was a mousey brown, and his glasses were overly large for his face. He had a firm expression that seemed to suggest that he would take no nonsense from anyone.

'My client is being targeted and harassed because she challenges authority and defends the defenceless in this country,' he began, almost like a robot running on a programme.

Truth be told, Elsie tuned out and daydreamed while he ranted on in the usual expected way. Although, she was very aware that she only had a limited time to spend with this woman to see if she could get anything useful from it.

'I put it to you, doctor, that your name was not always Eleni Wood, that you are in fact a person named Hela who moved here as an illegal immigrant as part of a Chechen family when you were around eleven years old. Is that correct?'

Dr Eleni Wood looked completely shocked. *How and why did they find out after so many years?* The alarm was written all over her face.

'My client will not answer that question,' responded her lawyer. 'What evidence do you have to disprove that my client is who she claims to be?'

Truthfully, she had no evidence whatsoever. At the moment, it was only hearsay, they didn't have any solid evidence, and her lawyer had called their bluff. Moving on, Elsie brought up the subject of her brother: 'Were you a close friend of a deceased man named Dr Andrew Jones of the United Kingdom?'

'Yes, that is no secret, he was a colleague and friend,' replied Dr Eleni Wood.

'Was he your brother Dr Wood? And did you ever know him by the name Haba?'

'Again, you cannot prove that,' interjected her counsel. 'The man, Dr Andrew Jones, is deceased and my client says he was a friend of hers, that is all.'

'Did you have a daughter named Kelly Cress who you gave up for adoption?'

'That is very widely known,' came the terse reply from Dr Eleni Wood, 'I often speak of her in my public lectures on terror and hate. She was a black woman, and I believe that she would still be alive today if she were white.'

'And why do you believe that doctor?' asked Elsie's colleague Graham.

'Because they didn't let any white couples linked to Australian security agencies get on planes of airlines that had received threats and that got blown to pieces. Did they?'

'I would suggest doctor that it was your daughter's own choice to board that plane,' said Graham sternly.

'Why would she choose to do that anyway? She never told me or anyone we knew that she was planning on going to America. Did you read in your notes that it has been reported that some people thought they saw a girl matching her description still alive on the ground after the incident. Why wasn't she saved then?'

'As you must know as a medical doctor, it wasn't possible for anyone to survive that disaster. They fell from the sky at such a great height,' said Elsie sympathetically. And her sympathy was indeed genuine. Dr Wood struck Elsie as a woman who truly believed the outlandish things she would often say.

'Then maybe someone put her on the plane's wreckage afterwards. Why would she just randomly choose to fly to the U.S. anyway? It doesn't make any sense. She never told me or anyone we knew that she was planning on going to America. It's entirely possible that her body could have been planted there and your kind in the UK wouldn't even investigate because she's black. Why don't you tell the truth?'

Not rising to the bait of her questions, Graham carried on with the line of questioning.

'Scotland Yard in the United Kingdom have reason to suspect that your daughter and her boyfriend had made the last-minute trip to the United States to find a buyer for a piece of jewellery that your daughter was suspected of stealing from the home of an elderly woman she provided nursing services for,' said Elsie's colleague Graham bluntly.

'How dare you speak about my daughter like that,' said Dr Eleni Wood, her hazel-coloured eyes flashing wildly with anger then beginning to well up with tears. 'You are now trying to discredit her and to soil her beautiful memory.'

'When you are calm enough to answer doctor,' interrupted Elsie, 'I would like to ask you if you were ever involved in any sort of work, or anything at all, that might have made you or your family a target for terrorists?'

'I am a GP, you are well aware that it was my daughter's boyfriend Brett who had family who worked for this government. So, if anyone was a target of terrorists, it would more likely be their family.'

'I would like to ask you another personal question,' said Elsie. 'Who was Kelly's father?'

'Now, now, this is getting very personal here officer,' began the lawyer, 'you don't have to answer that Dr Wood'.

'I don't know who he was,' answered Dr Eleni Wood quickly, and to Eleni's surprise. 'I was out walking home alone late one night from a friend's house, and that's all I recall of the whole thing really. I survived it, I am still alive. No-one is saying I was happy or proud over how it all came about, but I still loved my daughter; I always will, and I won't let you or anyone label her a thief.'

At that, Dr Wood's lawyer called the interview to an end. While he didn't show too much by way of emotion, he did cast a fixed gaze on the doctor for a moment accompanied by an expression that showed a side of his humanity. It was clear that he felt genuine pity for her.

It had been a short one this questioning session, but there really wasn't anything else that Elsie could think of to throw at her that might elicit some further useful response. She hadn't learned anything she didn't already know through today's interview. The little bit of prodding she had done of Dr Wood already, had released a lot of emotion from her, if nothing else.

She had no grounds to detain her any longer in any case. So she would have to just call it a day, and move on, ... well, for now.

CHAPTER TWENTY-SEVEN

Half past midnight. Ahmed was only about a third of the way into his night shift monitoring calls between those suspected of having terrorist sympathies who were on his monitoring list. The only thing that was suspicious lately, was the complete lack of inflammatory remarks or vitriol against the West from those he was listening in to. It was as if they all knew that they were being monitored. *They probably did know,* he thought to himself, *that's why they aren't openly talking about it.*

There was absolutely nothing useful coming out from any of the expensive and time-consuming monitoring stations that had been set up. Terrorists were getting smarter, and some of them had enjoyed a lot of help from some of the best lawyers in Australia in recent years. Elsie and her team had spent hours poring through translated transcripts of suspects' conversations, but she had learned nothing at all.

Elsie sat down to take her break time along with Ahmed that early morning, although she had to wait for him to finish his prayer time before he had joined her.

'When I'm on night shifts, I can't observe the usual day prayer times,' he explained to her. 'So, I just do it during the night instead.'

'Well, that makes sense,' began Elsie. So, there's really nothing coming out here that is of use to us then,' asked Elsie, hoping she might have missed something.

'Nope, nothing at all,' said Ahmed confirming her worst fears. 'They just talk about inane things such as music.'

'I don't know what else we can do,' Elsie said. 'I have such a strong feeling that something big is brewing, but if they don't discuss it, then how can we ever prove or prevent it?'

'There's always got to be someone somewhere who slips up though, don't you think so?' said Ahmed.

'But they might not be on any of our warranted suspect lists ...'

'That's true, but I think it's best to stay optimistic. What else can we do anyway?'

'Well, I've heard of some forces turning to psychics for help,' said Elsie only half joking.

'I don't believe in any of that,' said Ahmed. 'I reckon when they get something right, it's been through their contacts or through the grapevine basically.'

'You're probably right,' said Elsie.

'As you guys in the lead have requested, one of the main things we've listened so carefully for was any mention of the man they called "The General". There's been nothing about him so far.'

'They could have another code name for him by now of course,' suggested Elsie.

'True, that's possible, but it could just be that the guy's died or something.'

'I know, but I just don't think he has. I think he's very much alive.' *Just like Dr Andrew Jones,* as the sentence was finished in Elsie's mind. That was a theory she really didn't want to share with anyone though. It just sounded a bit too much like a conspiracy theory.

CHAPTER TWENTY-EIGHT

Janet Dresdale eyed her slightly uneven make-up inside the mirrored lifts of the Royal Colonial by the Park. She was on the thirtieth floor, a long way to go down still before she would be arriving at the first floor where the function rooms were. She had rushed slightly as she didn't want to be late for the young teachers' awards night. Not least of all because she was meant to be the one giving out the awards. Maybe she would have time to pop into the ladies' downstairs to fix it up before she had to go in. She hoped so anyway.

She watched as the numbers slowly counted down towards one, the first floor where the reception was being held, and then suddenly the lift came to a grinding halt. She was somewhere in between floors one and two. *Oh, maybe it'll get going again in a moment,* Janet thought to herself. When it certainly didn't, she pressed the call button to phone through for assistance.

It rang out.

That's a bit odd and worrying thought Janet, *maybe I'm not in the only lift that's stopped and stuck.*

Janet decided to try again, she held the call button for five seconds, and once again it rang out then stopped. Nothing.

Then the lights went out.

Panicking slightly, Janet fumbled around in the dark to try to find her phone inside her handbag. She could feel it, and she managed to fish it out. She searched the internet to find the hotel's number, and called their front desk. There was no answer, and she was put on hold.

She waited on hold for around five minutes, scared and trembling in the dark, before deciding to try calling a friend instead.

*****

Alison McGregor tried furtively to answer her ringing mobile phone which was just within reach inside her coat pocket, when she heard a loud voice shouting in her direction:

'You, you there, stand up and put your hands up immediately, right where we can see them.'

Alison began trembling and in her state of fear she found that she couldn't move a muscle. She wanted to obey the loud voice demanding she raise her arms up, but she couldn't make her muscles move.

The man who had been shouting at her walked towards her in fast strides and shot her at point blank range through the head. When her body fell to the ground, he reached in to her coat pocket where the ringing noise was coming from again, and pulled out her mobile phone.

'*Jay-net, Drezzzdale,*' he said as he sounded her name out in his thick foreign accent while reading it off the phone screen. 'She will have to wait,' he yelled, and then moved on tossing it onto the floor.

*****

Elsie and Brian were out in a trendy restaurant enjoying a rare date evening together.

'This is why I love checking out hidden gem restaurants that get glowing reviews in the Sydney Morning

Herald. It's amazing when you find a place as good as this,' Brian was saying.

'I know,' agreed Elsie, 'you can tell the pasta here is all freshly made, it's just delicious. And the flavours are blended in a subtle way. Because of the freshness of the ingredients they have used, they don't need to overpower them with too much seasoning or the addition of too many herbs.'

'Exactly,' said Brian, 'I need to try making something like this at home.' At which point his telephone rang.

'Hello,' said Brian while swallowing down the remainder of his mouthful of food.

'Brian, so glad I caught you. There's a rather serious emerging terror and hostage taking situation taking place at a major hotel in Melbourne, and if you're able to, then I'd like to call you into the office immediately for a briefing.'

'What's the name of the hotel?' asked Brian.

'The Royal Colonial by the Park,' answered his superior.

'Wait,' said Brian, 'Don't they have one of those here in Sydney too? It's got the same name at least.'

'Possibly,' answered his boss. 'Why?'

'I'm just thinking of the *twins* theme that seemed to come up is all. So, I'm wondering if we should get some armed police over there, you know, just in case?'

'You may just be right Brian, that's good lateral thinking. I will order a check on the Sydney *twin* hotel too, just in case.'

Just as Brian was hanging up his phone, Elsie's phone began ringing. She checked her mobile, and saw that it was her boss: 'Elsie, we need you to come in here immediately, we have just been informed that there's a hostage situation at a hotel here that overlooks the park.'

'That's happening at a hotel in Sydney too now?' said Elsie looking at Brian incredulously.

Brian had been right, but how he wished he hadn't been. The *twins* theme makes a return once again.

*****

By the time the armed police that Brian's boss had ordered reached the Sydney hotel that was also called Royal Colonial by the Park, it was far too late in many ways. All of the doors were locked, and armed terrorists patrolling the entrance had taken hotel reception staff hostage, to use them as human shields. The police could only wait and look through the locked glass doors at them. Eventually a call came through from the terrorists to Sydney police headquarters. They told police cooly that the entire high-rise hotel building had by now been rigged with explosives, that guests had been told to stay in their rooms or they would be shot, and that if police or army tried to enter, then they would just blow the whole place without any hesitation nor any further negotiation.

The entire area surrounding the explosives rigged hotel had to be evacuated now. It would have been standard procedure anyway, but the confirmation that they had explosives set up, and the threats they made, meant it was all the more urgent.

Brian was told to oversee the evacuation operation in central Sydney. At the same time a colleague of his was doing a similar thing in Melbourne.

In a way, we too are just like twins, dealing with twin attacks, he thought to himself.

CHAPTER TWENTY-NINE

By now, police negotiators had realised that they were dealing with the biggest terror situation to ever take place on Australian soil.

They realised too, that the intelligence they had intercepted about an awards night being a possible terror target, hadn't referred to the award night Dr Eleni Wood attended at all, nor to the two young women who lost their lives that same night, but to this evening that was now unfolding. Both hotels they had targeted were packed, as they knew they would be, the Melbourne one particularly so, since the teaching awards were being held there.

Police negotiators had already asked for some hostages to be released as a show of good faith. In response, the terrorists in the Melbourne hotel brought the body of the shot teacher Alison McGregor to the ground floor. He clumsily dragged her out of the elevator, limbs flailing, dropped her on the floor in good view of the glass doored front entrance, and then just left her lying there with matted hair draped in splashes of blood saying into the radio he was using: 'Take her. Here is your show of good faith.'

There was no way for swat teams to get to the hostages without being seen. Helicopters flying around the perimeter were visible from windows where guests were used as human shields to allow terrorists a view outside. The roof-top areas were also manned by the terrorists, and it was made clear that any attempt by police or army to land there would lead to the detonation of the explosives by the captors.

What was still unclear, was what exactly the hostage takers actually wanted. Ordinarily there would be a series of demands, such as release of prisoners, or demands for cash, but there was nothing of that sort forthcoming.

Negotiators and police had tried to come up with plans and schemes to find some way to engage with the terrorists, and to get some of their own people in there to help get the hostages out. If they could only find a way to get in, and to get sniffer dogs in, then even better, because then they could check if they were telling the truth about the hotels being rigged with bombs that could bring them down. One suggestion was to ask them to let Channel Seven news crews enter the building to film them and give them air time. Of course, the real plan was that it would be police and army who would actually go inside in their place masquerading as the press. Right off the bat, the terrorists said no to that anyway.

All of the terrorists that police had sighted so far were wearing suicide vests, which the police suspected were most likely fully operational. It was, therefore, assumed that the gang had planned for this siege to have a disastrous ending no matter what should transpire. Any guest trying to leave via front or rear stairs would meet a terrorist with an automatic weapon and a suicide vest. And, if the police were seen trying to make their way to the roof, the terrorists had promised to bring down both of the buildings immediately.

Brian himself had no doubt in his mind whatsoever that they had explosives like they claimed they did, and would be capable of bringing down those two huge buildings. He couldn't get the thought of the stuffed sex doll they had recently found out of his mind. *If something as innocuous and ridiculous seeming as that was in the country, and stuffed with real dangerous explosives, then what else was?*

*****

The siege went on like this for forty-eight hours. No hostages were released in all that time, and so, eventually the government gave the green light for the police to hand control over to the army to allow them to storm the building in the hope of getting as many out alive as possible. The sound of the army helicopters filled the air in both cities as the first one arrived and hovered above the Melbourne hotel. Onlookers could see a soldier line-roping his way down to the roof with his colleagues providing cover by firing on the terrorists. Within thirty seconds a series of massive explosions ripped through the entire hotel, and police and army could only watch as it imploded on itself and fell to the ground.

Within a minute of this happening, the leader of the Sydney siege must have given the order for the same fate to befall the sister hotel he had over-run. A series of explosions went off again in Sydney, but this time the building stood. That hotel had been built in a period of time in Sydney when it had become fashionable for some high rises to be constructed strong enough to withstand earthquakes. Sadly, however, it stood even after the detonation, only to be devoured by ravishing fire anyway, in the aftermath of it all.

Firefighting crews began arriving from all around the central business district, and water bombing planes made their way to the scene. A few people ran out of the front of the building, they were those who hadn't died in the terrorists' final acts, and it was clear that many guests were trapped by the fire on high floors. They didn't have long before the smoke inhalation would kill them all, let alone the fire. Army planes attempted a dangerous landing on the roof at one point, but it was deemed too risky, so they took off again after circling over the top for a while. They decided on sending in a set of search and rescue dogs though. The dogs were trained to make their way down and out through the building, alerting their handlers if they found anyone alive, and if they died, as they probably would, then so be it. It all seemed so unreal to Brian as he watched it unfold. It was like watching a movie.

The blaze burned long into the small hours of that night, by the end of it all, hundreds of innocent people had lost their lives. The terrorists were all dead by the climax of their attack, hence they obviously couldn't be questioned. Now it would be up to the nation's top investigators to piece together what had happened.

Elsie couldn't help but to feel like nothing more than a complete failure.

CHAPTER THIRTY

In the days immediately following the shocking attacks on two top end hotels in two of Australia's leading cities, ASIO was on overdrive trying to get the full backgrounds on all involved. The media were incredibly trying to play down the threat to the public to allay fears. Brian presumed someone somewhere had decided there was a risk of scaring the public too much, which could then lead to unrest, hate crimes and fuelling the rise of the far right. It was harder still to fathom how any news presenter could, with a straight face, tell the public that these terrorists had not been proven as yet, to be part of any wider network attacking the West.

Meanwhile, for Brian and Elsie's department, the focus was on re-examining old leads to search for anything that might have been overlooked before the full extent of the problems became clear to the police. Afterall, with no living suspects remaining to be interrogated following the *twin* hotel sieges, that was the best chance for finding clues relating to what was to come next.

On this particular morning, both Elsie and Brian's team sat together in a joint brain storming task force meeting where they were discussing the set of four autopsy reports from what now appeared certain to have been the terror motivated murders of four carefully selected young people. The two young girls killed on the night that Dr Eleni Wood had received her award, both had traces of date rape drugs in their system; it was the same drug found in the bodies of the other two victims, and one victim's mother's hair strands. It seemed that the method of the killings was intended to have been similar for all. They each were drugged so that they would be incapacitated when their killer came to call, but Arthur Tolbert had died by walking in front of a bus before the killer could get to him.

It was also the new working theory that the person or persons involved in those murders had also been responsible for the killing of Dr John McFay, and somehow even linked to the seemingly natural heart attack that Professor Wirth had suffered. It made a lot of sense now in hindsight, and given that all immediate family and other acquaintances had effectively been ruled out.

What the taskforce was trying to work out, was whether there was some sort of hidden message or clues in the killings that would help indicate what to expect next, and who was behind all of this. What made this terror cell so spine chilling, was that they didn't seem to feel the need to advertise who they were, or to make propaganda videos taking the credit for their attacks. This meant that there was very little by the way of clues for police to go on.

The attacks definitely seemed to have a *twin* quality about them, that was something everyone present could agree on. Dr Eleni Wood was likely a *twin* to the missing Dr Andrew Jones, and they were the only twins that Elsie could think of who had crossed their paths in this case. It made sense to focus further investigation efforts on them. Some of the staff present were still hung up on the fact that Jones had gotten through the security checks to get into MI6, and the naive belief that surely that must have counted for something, in terms of proving there wasn't much reason to have any concerns about his good character. Elsie wasn't so convinced though that it proved his good character, and she said as much in the meeting; he wouldn't have been the first one to enter a major nation's security services as a mole or terrorist intent on taking things down from the inside after passing their screening checks with flying colours.

The superior officer raised a photograph of Dr Andrew Jones on the screen as they debated it all and said: 'This man hasn't been seen or heard of for years, and he is now even believed to be the uncle of one of the Selkirk terror disaster victims, which would suggest to most that he could not have been involved in any way in planning that attack – unless, that is, he really did not expect his niece to be on the flight that evening and fate just played a hand in that.

That is entirely possible, however, given that her ticket was a last-minute purchase.'

He allowed the room a minute or so to mull things over in their heads before saying, 'So far, there have been *twinned* human victims, *twinned* targeted aircraft, and *twinned* hotels, so what should we be expecting next people?'

He scanned the room with an eager expression on his face.

Brian was the first to raise his hand.

'Yes, superintendent,' said his superior officer. 'What would you like to add?'

'*Twinned* cities and towns on an even bigger scale than what have just seen with the hotels in two cities.'

Several of the others nodded in agreement, this was clearly part of the past attacks, and logically, they must have seen it as a practise run. Sadly though, it did nothing to help them figure out what might be planned next in any level of detail that would be enough to prevent it. So far though, and in the absence of any other solid leads to follow, at least it was the best guess yet as to what might be being coming up next.

*****

The taskforce immediately began working under the assumption that there was a plan either for something to happen in the lead up to, or right at Christmas. It was likely for this to involve attacks on a set of Australian cities, if not *all* major Australian cities. It was a good starting point for them to start brainstorming. Furthermore, it was believed likely that these would be coinciding with similar terror attacks on their *twin* cities around the world. If this were true, this would be one of the largest most elaborate terrorist attacks that the Western world had seen for many years. And could the West survive something on such a scale if no-one prevented it? That was unclear.

They were already at the start of December, and a start on investigating potential leads saw them busy drawing up lists of all of the major cities in Australia and their *twins* located overseas. There were multiple *twin* towns in most cases. Each and every one of them had to be contacted and advised to be on heightened alert. The superior officers were quite clearly nervous and afraid to look like fools to people all around the world by doing this.

What if they were all wrong though, and absolutely nothing was planned?

CHAPTER THIRTY-ONE

On Sunday evening Elsie lay wide awake in bed next to a loudly snoring Brian. She had barely slept a wink. Thoughts about the cases she was working on kept swimming around her head. If Dr Andrew Jones, or Haba as he was likely really called, were still alive, and if he were the one co-ordinating everything from somewhere in the Middle East, then there had to be some way for him to communicate with his followers. Quite suddenly on that night, the thought struck her like a bolt of lightning, and she jumped out of bed:

'Brian, wake up!'

'What?' said Brian startled almost falling out of bed. 'Why aren't you asleep? It's so late, I was asleep.'

'Yes, I know,' said Elsie. 'And I know we are supposed to go through each other's bosses to even discuss this case, but I have to tell you this: I think I finally just figured something out. Besides, you are lying right here next to me, so it would seem rather ridiculous to wait until we're in the office.'

'What?' said Brian sleepily and with a yawn.

'Well, I think that "The General" uses music to communicate with those he leads. I think we need to look into their music to break the codes.'

'It's possible, but at this time of night ... really, you need to get back to sleep.'

'No, I need to call Sarah, she's on night shift just now. I need the team to start working on this right away.'

*****

Every time Elsie saw a countdown to Christmas out on the high street, it felt like a reminder of how little time was left for them to figure out what the code was that the terrorists were using, and, just as importantly, who the organisers and ground level planners all actually were. To her satisfaction, the team was by now actively following up on her hunch and looking into music from the Middle East for hidden messages or meaning. The focus was on the music coming out of Syria, since that was the original home of the only set of *twins* that were persons of interest, and that music came from their mother tongue.

Given his amazing linguistic skills and ability to hone in on what mattered, Ahmed was of course the lead on this project. Ahmed thought he possibly had actually found something already in some of the songs all produced by the same people.

'Listen to this,' he said to Elsie, playing part of a music sample for her and Brian's benefit.

'I'm sorry, but that really means nothing at all to me Ahmed, it just sounds like random noises.'

'Well, to me it sounds like regular song lyrics - mostly. But every so often there are some background vocals in a very local vernacular from the part of Syria that Hela and Haba, or Eleni and Andrew, had really come from we think. Interestingly it just translates as AJ, which as you know could stand for the initials Andrew Jones, so it could be like his musical signature for those who are in the know about it all.'

'Before I would say, well that's just genius,' said Brian increasingly intrigued, 'I wonder if you've gleaned anything other than a reference to AJ out of the lyrics?'

'Well, in a couple of songs first broadcast in the lead-up to the murders of the four young people, there were some references that you could take as being relevant. Such as, there were lines about "math should be easier," that didn't seem to fit well with the rest of the lyrics, and girls being called something that would translate as similar to "naughty girls." Again, that's something that might be seen as offensive and out of place if they were referring to local young women in Syria. For that reason, it's slightly strange and hence worthy of note.'

'We need to find out who is linked to the music production on their end', said Brian, 'and who they are connected to here. That way, I'm hoping we should find the real persons of interest in this country.'

CHAPTER THIRTY-TWO

By Tuesday of that week, Brian's team had been briefed on the thoughts and plans of Elsie that had seen him woken up from his sleep the Sunday prior. His team had been drafted in to help with the large surveillance task that lay ahead. As always, discretion was paramount, even within the wider police force.

Every clue in the musical game pointed to a group of producers with links in Syria and in Australia; they had an office in Sydney and in one in Melbourne. The police in Elsie and Brian's teams had gone from zero leads to an abundance of them. The hard part now would be trying to find solid evidence on those people listed as likely suspects. Thankfully the courts had granted them warrants to monitor the suspects, but it really felt like a race against the clock.

This was their mission: stake out the centres these music producers were running; intercept any chatter amongst the music producers about lone wolves; and search for anything that would give a hint as to what the targets would be.

For a long time, one of the biggest challenges in Western world security had been the threat of so-called lone wolf attackers; their moves were almost impossible to anticipate due to the absence of a central leader or any group gathering locations in the lead up to their planned attacks. "The General" seemed to have changed this though, in what might be thought of as a hybrid model of terrorism, or in a sense, he was trying to call on wolf packs made up of these lone wolves.

When Elsie heard Brian describe the current state of affairs in that way, it gave her an idea.

'You know what,' she began at one of the team brain storming sessions, 'the fact that "The General" might be putting out messages and instructions to his lone wolves, could be our one opportunity.'

'How do you mean exactly?' asked her superior officer.

'If we find a way to put out false messages, there's a chance to ensnare someone in the group, then use that to work out what's really going on. We would likely need to turn someone on the inside to make that happen though.'

'Brilliant,' said an eager and younger officer.

'But wait,' said a more experienced one. 'While it's a good plan in theory, if we get it wrong and approach the wrong lone wolf for the job, we've gone and forewarned them all that we are on to them. They will realise that we're doing surveillance on them.'

Why was nothing ever straightforward in this job? Elsie couldn't help wondering at times.

'Based on what we've got so far though, which is limited,' explained Elsie, 'I think we would be hard pushed to do much worse than we are already doing. It's a calculated risk, but I think a risk worth taking.'

'Fair point,' said Elsie's superior officer. 'This is what we will do, we need a list of former employees of the music producers here and then I will liaise with ASIO to see if they can advise as to who among the suspected broadcasters and music distributers could most easily be turned to work for us.'

*****

The heat had already become sweltering as Sydney was fully in summertime and well into the Christmas season. It was not at all the most fun time of the year to be hiding in vans and cars trying to gather evidence on suspects. Again, many hours of man power were being spent in difficult and expensive conditions while staff wilted like lilies, but all of this effort was so-far still getting the investigation nowhere. Brian could certainly sense whenever they gave updates that the superior officers were beginning to fear that they would soon look like fools if nothing turned up.

Then something did turn up for a surveillance van parked next to a record distribution office; it was a delivery of something quite different from the usual loads they had been watching getting carried in. A small mini-van had pulled up outside the business, then the driver got out and picked up some medium sized boxes from the back that didn't look anything like the usual CD and vintage record packages they'd been delivering before. Within fifteen minutes a call was placed from the record distribution office that the surveillance team could record, it was to a number over in Syria. Ahmed was busily recording and translating at the same time.

'I can't believe it,' said Ahmed when he called in to Elsie back at the office. 'Something useful for once, he's saying that the ID's have arrived. Sounds like they're providing or selling false IDs.'

'Finally, we've got something solid. Thank God,' Elsie responded. 'I'll start the process right now to get a warrant for that place.' She could only hope she could get the warrant in enough time to figure out what they were playing at.

'I feel like walking straight in there, pointing this gun at his head, and demanding he turn them all over right now,' said Mark, who was one of the other surveillance team members, to Ahmed.

'Well, you can't just do that,' said Ahmed. 'And we don't have any warrant to enter that place either, well not yet anyway.'

CHAPTER THIRTY-THREE

Brian and Greg sat themselves towards the rear of the city bus that a man named Abdul was driving. He was the man ASIO got him the details of. After a short time, Abdul stopped the vehicle next to a multiplex cinema where a group of about fifteen youths were waiting to board the bus. A group of three youngsters rushed ahead without taping their fare card or a credit card.

'Hey, get back here,' said Abdul. 'One at a time, come back and let me see you all come through one at a time.'

'Asshole,' said one of the youths of about twelve years.

'That's it,' said Abdul to the youth. 'Apologise to me immediately or you're not riding this bus.'

'Just apologise,' said one of his mates.

'No, I don't want to, why should I?' said the first youth sulkily.

'Say sorry,' said Abdul. 'And I'll let you on.'

'OK, sorry,' said the sulky youth begrudgingly and showed his fare card. They all boarded the bus one by one and sat around Brian and Greg.

The bus was running late when it reached a major interchange, and Abdul asked everyone to alight as he was taking a comfort break. Brian and Greg alighted and followed behind him.

'Excuse me, Abdul,' called Brian from behind him.

He flashed his badge and said, 'Superintendent Brian Andersen here, can I have a word with you?'

'I haven't done anything wrong,' was the first thing Abdul said.

'No-one is saying you have,' said Brian. 'We just want a quick word with you is all.'

'Then can you wait until I take my comfort break, I really have to go?'

'Sure, no problem,' said Brian. 'We'll be right here.'

After around five minutes had passed, Brian was concerned that Abdul had run off, but just at that point he returned. Brian pulled out a flyer for the Syrian music distributer that was of interest to them. 'Do you remember these guys?' he asked.

'Yes, I used to work for them, a couple of years back now, but I left, retrained as a bus driver and well, here I am.'

'We are concerned that some illegal activities have been going on at the record label. We're looking for a person who cares about the future of this country and who would be willing to work with us to infiltrate them for information. Do you think you might be that person?'

*****

When the chance had come along for him to do something so patriotic for Australia, Abdul had jumped at it; no-one had ever needed him like this before. It was a feeling he found that he very much liked.

It wasn't at all difficult for Abdul to convince the owners back at the Syrian record label distributors that he was disillusioned with his job as a bus driver and wanted to return to running errands for them. Driving and delivery was the job he did for them previously. Luckily for him they were happy to have him back because another driver had just suffered a stroke and would be off work for the foreseeable future.

Truth be told, Abdul had had his own concerns about the record label outfit that he used to work for, it was one of the factors that inspired him to leave and retrain as a bus driver for the city.

Abdul was in the back of the distribution centre, one day after his return, where he was searching around for boxes of CDs to drive out and deliver to their stockist stores. It felt like he'd never left. Most things looked as expected, but he did notice a couple of boxes that were a different shape from the rest. He had a quick look around to check no-one else was about, and he opened one up to take a look inside; he figured he could say he was confused about which boxes he was to take if he got caught. Inside were stacks of passports, driver's licenses and birth certificates, they were mostly in South American names. Abdul quickly brought out his phone and photographed some of them. Wonder what that's all about, he thought.

Abdul wasn't to meet with Brian and Greg again to avoid being seen with them. But even more clandestinely, he'd been assigned a post office box as a drop location for whatever he might find or photograph that looked potentially of interest or suspicious. He printed out photographs of the fake IDs at home and detailed the rest of what he'd heard or observed. For instance, it had struck him as strange that some employees discussed childcare centres their kids were at. They discussed moving some of them, and he wondered why.

CHAPTER THIRTY-FOUR

Christmas was approaching fast, and the joint task force were relieved to have found out something about the intentions for the false ID boxes. Their first thought was that perhaps terrorists from the Middle East were planning to use stolen identities of South Americans to confuse police and security agencies. Then they realised there was more likely another reason for this: it seemed the record label was running a protection business for South American drug cartel linked dealers who were establishing themselves in major Australian cities like Sydney and Melbourne. The protection and ID business was most likely a fundraiser for the Middle Eastern terror group. This meant that vice had to be involved in the investigation too.

'This thing just keeps getting bigger and bigger,' said Brian to Elsie over evening's dinner.

'I know, it's good to have the extra help from the narcotics side, but that makes it even more likely that information on what we're investigating will get leaked one way or another.'

'That's true, sadly,' agreed Brian.

'And the false arrests that happened over in Europe didn't help much either, what with some police there being so jumpy that they've arrested the wrong people. It lets the real terrorists know they're being extra vigilant this Christmas season.'

'But I think they expect that anyway Elsie,' said Brian. 'It is arguably the most popular time of the Christian calendar after all.'

'I just feel under so much pressure now though, ever since I was right about that one air disaster, it's like some people expect I must be some sort of oracle, and that anything else I so much as consider must be about to happen.'

'I know, it's pretty tough,' said Brian getting up to walk around to give her a hug. 'But you know, you have found something pretty major anyway, it's not the list of terror targets we were hoping for or anything, but because of you, there's now proof that record label is supporting drug cartels, and possibly we'll cut off a cash flow to terrorists once narcotics gets their teeth into investigating that.'

'Thanks Brian,' said Elsie. 'You always know how to make me feel better. The hardest part though with this latest development of us having to work with narcotics as well, will be convincing them to hold off going in quickly and arresting them all for drug trafficking related activities before we get the names of key players in the terrorism game.'

*****

Fourteen days until Christmas, and police Officer Darren Hale sat outside his child's daycare centre wondering who the dark-skinned man he'd never seen before walking into the centre in front of him was. He was wearing a backpack, and long heavy pants on such a hot day. Darren entered the door just as the man was conversing with the head of the centre.

'Um, Taneel, yes that's the one I'm here to pick up.'

Didn't he even know the kid's name? Officer Hale wondered to himself.

The head of the centre, Sharlene, was a plump woman. She was around fifty years old and wore her brown coloured hair in a loose perm more popular with women in their eighties.

'Oh, hello Darren,' she greeted Officer Hale as he entered.

'Hello,' he said back.

'Can I just see some ID from you please?' Sharlene asked the other man.

'*ID!* Officer Hale,' in an instant he had his gun drawn and held to the man's head.

*****

Brian's superior officer began their emergency team meeting with: 'I am currently fighting to manage what description of today's incident appears in our newspapers. As some of you may be aware, one of our officers is already on mental health leave after an over-reaction he had at his daughter's childcare centre.'

The man's partner shifted uncomfortably in his chair.

'I must remind all of you of your duty not only to take note of your own mental health and well-being, but to report if your partner or other colleagues are struggling. We all know the stress of this case is getting to some of us, here and abroad, as Christmas approaches.

There was some mumbling going on around the room, because the truth was, recent weeks had taken their toll on the mental health of just about everyone in there.

It seems too that one of the crimes we have anticipated over Christmas is a plan for the delivery of a batch of false ID documents to help illegal immigrants and drug traffickers who largely seem to have come from South America.'

At least we know we'll get some guaranteed convictions out of that one. Brian was still very anxious about how this was all going to look for the force, if by the end, and after so much overtime and man hours spent scrutinising what felt like almost every Middle East linked person in inner Sydney at least, nothing major actually happened.

Another one of the superiors stood up and started his morale boosting pep talk to the team, or that's what Brian took it to be at least. Truthfully though, he did feel a bit uplifted by listening to it. He reminded them that nothing a dedicated police officer does is ever really wasted. Even if we don't see the value in our work today, tomorrow, or even by the end of the year, we know that much more than we did yesterday. And that's something that's always worthwhile.

*****

In the end, Christmas time in that year came and went peacefully in Sydney, and in other parts of the world too. The sense of relief among Brian and Elsie's side of the force was enormous. But the question remained: was there still something major being planned in the world of terrorists in the near future, but just not over Christmastime as they had first suspected.

Just how long was their end game really anyway?

CHAPTER THIRTY-FIVE

'Do you realise Elsie Whitman,' began Ahmed, 'that - and I know people keep saying it – but that you are an absolute genius?'

'How so?' asked Elsie as they were walking through to her office.

'Because the music really is stuffed with codes and pieces of information. And we've worked something else out too now: we don't believe that the missing Dr Andrew Jones, or Haba as he was known in childhood, is dead. In fact, we are almost certain now that he is the man they call "The General". It even makes sense then about the link to nursing we couldn't understand: he was brought out of Syria and sent to England by a nurse, and perhaps some presumed she was his mother.'

'It does make complete sense,' agreed Elsie. 'Given he did undergo intensive training in Western intelligence methods, he's a formidable threat. I'm just hoping that maybe we'll somehow finally find a way to ensure nothing else is planned against the West from his group. Something that still doesn't make sense though, is why the Selkirk disaster would have killed the niece of "The General", if it really was he who co-ordinated that also.'

'Like the boss said,' replied Ahmed, 'His niece and her boyfriend bought last minute tickets for that flight, her mother didn't know she'd planned the trip either. So, it seems that by a twist of fate, she had gotten on the flight that her own relative was targeting.'

'Maybe that was why he disappeared from the radar around that time? Perhaps he even thought the UK or USA government had suspected he was involved in the plot and out of fear he went into hiding. He might even have started to believe that the government itself had killed his niece for revenge? Perhaps thinking they might even have tortured her first, or handed her over to the Americans.'

'He could have become so paranoid,' agreed Ahmed, 'such that it wouldn't surprise me if he did believe something as extreme as that. His alleged sister, Dr Eleni Wood, has some pretty extreme views too. It's clear that she sees officials in the West as monsters.'

*****

That same evening, Elsie came home to the delicious smell of roast chicken being cooked by Brian. It wasn't long before talk turned to work again in the couple's place, as it typically did.

'We got the latest briefings from your team this afternoon,' said Brian. 'Dr Andrew Jones a.k.a. Haba, a.k.a. "The General", is now topping the USA's most wanted list. Apparently, there's a massive bounty on his head, dead or alive.'

'I've felt for a long time that he was probably still alive somewhere, but now they're pretty certain of it.'

'So how do you feel?' asked Brian. 'You were the driving force behind bringing to light the fact that he was still around and likely a big leader over there.'

'Well, I'm pleased to have my suspicions validated. But we all know what it means when they get put on the American Law Enforcement Lists, it's all out of our hands now really. If they do finally catch him, and I hope they do of course, there will be no mention of us at all. It's all a little bit anti-climactic.'

'You know what,' said Brian. 'I had a bit of an epiphany myself this afternoon when reading this.'

'What was that?' asked Elsie somewhat intrigued.

'Well, you know how we were convinced they are planning something even bigger on this *twin* theme again, and we thought Christmas was the likely time? If we now believe that "The General" is the illusive Dr Andrew Jones, Dr Eleni Wood's brother, then it would make more sense that he would plan something big to commemorate the death of his niece, Eleni's daughter Kelly.'

'Maybe,' said Elsie, non-committally.

'And when did she die?' asked Brian rhetorically.

'It was in the lead up to Valentine's Day,' he then said with a very self-satisfied look.

Elsie let out a long drawn-out breath, then said: 'So not Christmas, the big Christian celebration that most people think of first if they have to ask what they associate with important Western religious feasts, but still an occasion marked by the Christian calendar. Or in other words, something that's big in the Western world, but with clearly Christian roots.'

'Precisely,' said Brian. 'I think that there might still be a plan for something to happen on a day like that.'

CHAPTER THIRTY-SIX

It was now well past Christmas, and Abdul was still working his job as a delivery driver and odd jobs man for the Syrian record label of interest to the police. He'd kept his head down and then just listened and waited since the time he had last sent a message to his recruiters. Nothing out of the ordinary had happened since that seemed particularly unusual, that was until this day, when he was asked to pick up something under circumstances that really did seem a bit odd. He was then instructed by one of the managers to collect some boxes late at night at the end of that day, from a car park where the other delivery man, as they referred to him, would be waiting. He was then told to bring the boxes in to the music distribution centre as usual.

'At that time of night?' complained Abdul. 'I'll do the collection if that's when it has to be done, but I'll drop the boxes here to work in the morning at my usual time, I don't want to be driving about all night.'

'OK, OK,' said the boss, to Abdul's surprise in fact. 'Just bring them here in the morning.'

*****

Abdul felt sick with nerves throughout the whole drive to the meeting spot in the car park. He felt rather like he was in a gangster movie where the boss had found out that he's the mole and is sending him someplace dark and quiet to be 'dealt with'. Abdul had considered trying to contact Brian that day to get them to stake out the pick-up, but it was all a bit last minute, and he had no real solid evidence that there was anything anymore illegal than usual going on. They hadn't even seemed to have done anything since he last sent them some evidence after all, not as far as he could tell.

The car park was deserted apart from one vehicle. It was a sedan family car, Abdul quickly jotted down the registration plate before he exited his own vehicle - just in case. *At least if I don't come back, they'll have a clue who did it,* he thought somewhat pessimistically.

'Hi there,' said Abdul smiling towards the other man who he now could see was a tall pale Caucasian male. He kept his focus on looking calm, but he certainly didn't feel it.

'Hi,' he said back. His face was quite wrinkled, and was expressionless giving practically nothing away about himself. 'The boxes are in the boot. I'll help you carry them around.' And he did just that, without saying a word. Within two minutes their transaction was done.

'OK then,' said Abdul. 'See you, bye.'

The other man said nothing, then just simply got into his car and drove off.

Abdul, relieved that nothing out of the expected had happened, got back into his van and started driving towards his home. Then he pulled over to the side of the road. He did that when he was almost there, and only once he was absolutely sure that no-one was following him. A moment of bravery came upon him, and he opened up one of the boxes, shining a torch inside to check the contents. It was sets of papers such as passports, driver's licences and other forms of realistic looking ID, this time in the names of Middle Eastern men. Abdul felt sick right into the pit of his stomach: he felt sure that these weren't just for illegal immigrants or drug dealers, these had to be for terrorists. He got back into the front of the van and drove straight to the Australian Federal Police office that he knew Brian worked at.

He parked out at the front of the building leaving the boxes inside his van and entered.

'How can I help you?' asked the woman on the front desk.

'I need to speak to a Superintendent Brian Andersen immediately,' said Abdul.

'I cannot say whether that's possible or not Sir,' said the woman at the desk. 'I'll have to check if he is on duty this evening or not. He told me if it was an emergency, I could contact him at any time even at his home, he told me to tell you the name Haba.'

'In that case,' said the woman. 'I'll get in touch on his emergency line and see what we can do.'

Brian raced to his workplace immediately upon receiving the call that Abdul was standing at their front desk. He knew Elsie's team would be brought in too, so for ease, he just woke her up before getting ready to go and brought her in with him at the same time.

Once Brian saw the contents of those boxes and matched the registration plate of the delivery man to a Commonwealth passport office worker; he woke up his superior boss as well. Within the hour they had a warrant to view and copy the entire contents of the boxes. Rather than arresting and questioning the record label staff right away, they decided to try to trace each and every false ID to find out who would be using them. Finally, they would have a way to monitor the untraceable lone wolves. This was a gold mine level find.

CHAPTER THIRTY-SEVEN

After so many long weeks of federal police monitoring of the ID recipients whose identities were all found by Abdul, it was indeed just in the lead up to Valentine's Day that a joint operation involving police in several countries, and spanning multiple continents, saw the arrest of over one hundred lone wolf members of the *Wolf Pack* terrorist cell.

For this Valentine's Day, Brian joked to Elsie that his gift on the theme of *love,* was making the world a safer place again for all - well, for a little while, at least.

He told Elsie that he was more than happy for her gift to him to simply be that she was now the most at peace within herself that he had seen her in the longest time.

Of course by Valentine's Day itself, all of the arrests had been made, and everything at work had slowed right down again. There were no more excessive overtime shifts and stressed-out co-workers to deal with for a while.

Brian and Elsie were having an at-home romantic meal that night. After spending so much time out of the unit working, it was nice just to stay home, settle in, feel relaxed, and get cosy. Brian took charge of the cooking that night and made some extra effort to set the meal out nicely on their outdoor dining table. He set up some simple, but mood capturing candles too and poured some wine. Then he called Elsie out onto the balcony. She walked out, brushing her hair aside in her usual way. Brian noticed just how much he found that it still charmed him so.

'Oh, real French Champagne, how lovely, this is beautiful Brian. And it's such a lovely day to sit out and just chill.'

Brian pulled the chair out for her and helped her get seated.

'Quite the gentleman today, aren't we?' she said.

He sat down opposite her, and was staring at her so intently she was finding it rather odd. 'What is it?' she said with a bemused laugh.

'Help yourself to some canapés, won't you? I covered them, just to keep the flies off.'

'Sure,' said Elsie after having a sip from her Champagne. She lightly picked up the cover on the little plate, and in shock, almost dropped her Champagne glass.

'Well, do you like it?' asked Brian.

Elsie was staring at a massive and beautiful cushion cut diamond. Almost as if in slow motion, she picked it up, and tears began to form at the side of her eyes.

'Allow me,' said Brian getting down on one knee. He took the ring from her grasp, and then asked, looking her straight in the eye, 'Elsie, will you marry me?'

'Yes!' she exclaimed and threw her arms around him kissing him.

Brian took the ring and slid it onto her finger and said, 'Now we're together forever'.

'And I'm completely sure that we really will be,' said Elsie, and she meant it. The tears of joy were beginning to come, and she felt not only blissfully happy that she was now engaged to someone she really loved, but proud of herself that she'd really put the bad experience of her first marriage behind her, and so nothing was hindering her fully enjoying and experiencing her life. She had grown so much as a person, and she was moving on to the next level of a wonderful relationship with a great man that she truly deserved.

*****

The identities of several of the lone wolves that were obtained through Abdul, had enabled something else to happen beyond the first wave of strategic arrests: the Americans claimed to have used them to intercept what they believed were communications from AJ, or "The General" himself. They determined that he was based in Syria. They were messages between his organised Australian and international so-called wolf packs that they were able to hone in on. It was the first time in over three decades that anyone had found any clues as to the man's whereabouts. It was a truly massive breakthrough.

Elsie was certainly right on another one of her other predictions too: when the case started coming together and the high-profile arrests began, it was the Americans taking all of the glory.

In some ways, it felt to Brian like their own task force that toiled over it all for such a long time, and gained some of the initial insights that made the success possible, had never existed. He reminded himself though, that it was the end result that really mattered, not his own personal work gaining recognition, nor his own pride. He saw himself as a man whose main goal in his working life was to serve the public in the way he knew best. That way, was through protecting them, from any kind of threats, and even from themselves at times.

On Valentine's Day itself, the President of the United States of America held a special press conference to release the news to the world. It was televised nationally, and simultaneously broadcast overseas too. He began by solemnly telling the listening world:

'I can relay to you all today, that United States Special Forces have killed the Syrian-based terrorist leader Dr Andrew Jones, also known as "The General".

We can now confirm that this man was indeed the one responsible for masterminding the Selkirk plane bombing disaster of 1986 which took place over the skies of Scotland in the United Kingdom. It was an incident which caused the death of his own niece, as well as claiming the lives of many Americans. He was also involved in the disappearance and ultimate crash of a passenger plane bound for Hong Kong in recent years after his group targeted that flight too.

Even more recently, he had been responsible for masterminding several other terrorist attacks which were carried out on Australian soil.

It is clear to see that the man posed an international danger to human life.

We also know that the man had been in the process of orchestrating another large-scale international terror attack at the time during which he was located and ultimately killed by the forces of the government of the United States of America.'

*****

Back in Australia, the Australian Federal Police eventually concluded that the violent murder of Dr John McFay was likely carried out by the same person who murdered David McWellin. It was hypothesised that Professor Wirth might have had a heart attack brought on by extreme fear over someone prowling around her house, and it was most likely that the same perpetrator was involved in that too. The only suspect in it all, who had since fled to Pakistan, was never ever found.

*****

Brian and Elsie, but Brian much more so, both searched their souls for months afterwards trying to find true closure. They had just gone through a time in their lives that felt dedicated almost as much to finding loose ends that would never be fully explained or understood, as it had been to saving lives and preventing terrible disaster on an unthinkable scale. What they both came to realise in the end, was that when investigating from the edge of the clandestine world of the security services, enduring mystery was to be expected, and that was no failing on their part. One should perhaps be relieved in some ways that it was not so easy to get to the bottom of it all. After all, if they could, then our country's enemies could too.

*****

In the wake of the dismantling of the terror cell, and when all of the details came to light, a posthumous medal for Royal Australian Air Force pilot Ian Grant was announced for his bravery and role in selflessly saving the lives of passengers on an Australian registered jumbo jet during a terrorist attack.

*****

One morning, several months later, and quite out of the blue, Elsie received an apology card in the mail from the deceased Australian Air Force man Ian Grant's fiancée.

The End

Even long after the evening's watch is over,
For some, the lamp will always be lit,
It stays with them long into the night, and creeps slowly, then
dwindles into a quiet death as the morning rises for with us to
meet.

Those who watch over us all, are never alone,
For just as their souls unite to guard our mortal fragility,
So does that unified energy that we as a people combine
to send back out into the universe,
Spinning like the canopy of stars above, as it weaves a magical
ethereal tapestry that binds us all together,
Forever as one.